I0831267

DISCOVERY

Also by Jerry Labriola

—Murders at Hollings General

—Murders at Brent Institute

—The Maltese Murders

—The Strange Death of Napoleon Bonaparte

—Scent of Danger

—Object of Betrayal

—Deadly Politics

—Global Shadows

—Diamonds and Pirates

—Dangerous Triangle

—The Blue Baron Mystery

—The Saga of Hodge

—Spying for Keeps

Coauthored with Dr. Henry Lee

—Famous Crimes Revisited

—Forensic Files

—The Budapest Connection

—Shocking Cases

DISCOVERY

A NOVEL

BY

JERRY LABRIOLA, M.D.

STRONG BOOKS

Strong Books
P.O. Box 1194
Middlebury, CT 06762

First Printing

ISBN 978-1-928782-98-8

Library of Congress Control Number: 2017961715

Published in the United States of America by Strong Books, an imprint of Publishing Directions, LLC

Printed in the United States of America

Dedicated to:

Kristen, Mark, Xavier.
And to Nick, Andrea, Quincy
Jaiden, Naomi and Violet.

ACKNOWLEDGMENTS

My heartfelt thanks to the entire staff at Strong Books, an imprint of Publishing Directions, LLC.

NOTE

To avoid the complexities of multiple languages versus English, nearly all dialogue is presented in English.

Descriptions of all cities and countries are accurate.

PROLOGUE

Criminal investigator and international treasure hunter, Paul D'Arneau, had grown tired of his work of twenty years. Especially circling the globe over and over again. He persists in traveling, however, but with an entirely different purpose. Before leaving, he puts on hold his part-time jobs as a karate instructor and a forensic science lecturer.

He longed to become unstrapped from a definitive purpose and to return to many sites in search of what he termed, "the progress and legitimacy of religion" and how it was somehow tied into Napoleonic lore. It would be a most vague undertaking, but such a search has always been on his mind, expressed within the mantra as stated by Jesus: *Follow me*.

But follow me where, and why and how?

His answer lay in an innocent intent to evaluate people, places and things that he hasn't paid attention to before. This is now his mission and could best be achieved by writing a book! During upcoming travels, he makes what he labels "Discovery Notes", with the idea of putting them all together when the mission is over—but not until then.

Thus, the book's content, once behind him, is currently viewed as being there before him in places like Argentina, Switzerland, Germany, France and Italy—plus England,

Hungary, and Greece. He has visited them all before, some more than once, and each one for either a treasure hunting or investigative purpose.

He begins by writing mere snippets, reviewing photographs, seeking preliminary advice from old friends, consulting notes about his favorite military figure, Napoleon Bonaparte, and ultimately decides that the book should be non-fiction. And all the while he is searching, he is **being** searched. Again key questions*: By whom? Why?*

Out of the blue, he is advised to combine this dual longing with another tour of criminal investigation.

PART ONE

Chapter 1

June 1

Guy Martin was the only one in Paul D'Arneau's circle of friends who favored the drastic decision, and Guy was the only one who knew enough about world-wide churches to influence Paul's thinking. Early on, at the *International Herald Tribune,* Guy specialized in history and political reporting but then drifted into writing a weekly column titled, *The Influence of Religion and Napoleon Bonaparte.*

They had often traded beliefs about the topic, Guy's based on his research and writings, Paul's on his discoveries while attending church services in as many countries as time had allowed. And even some synagogues. Their last conversation about it lasted nearly an hour, for the ins and outs of the decision had to be weighed thoroughly.

They were about to have lunch at Bonfiore's Restaurant near Paul's home in East Falmouth on Cape Cod. Guy had come down from the *Tribune's* Boston facility to attend an Episcopal summit in Hyannis and dropped by to visit with Paul. Their friendship was as old as the restaurant—built in the 1980s. It was Paul's favorite haunt, whether he ate there or not, for he enjoyed the atmosphere as much as the food—the soft background music, the kitchen aromas, the seating arrangements. Booths hugged paneled side walls and patrons' initials were etched into the tops of dark oak tabletops.

As was their custom whenever they met there … with notebooks open, they sat opposite one another in a booth the owner had labeled "Paul's Place". It was beneath a window that looked out onto Buzzards Bay and was cracked open during dry spells. But this day, it was closed, as lightning flashed by and wind drove rain droplets against it. The air inside and out smelled damp and dewy. Paul frowned as he glanced up at a hazy sky while entering, certain that a late morning drizzle would usher in a major thunderstorm and wondering why there was no front walkway. Rather, the main entrance opened directly onto a rich, well-manicured lawn.

All wall space, including that above entry doors, was crowded with pictures of Cape Cod landmarks, like lighthouses and recognizable beachfronts, boat harbors and the old Harwich trampoline, and the busy fishing stations of Provincetown.

Paul mentioned the cities he'd be visiting—Buenos Aires, Lucerne, Paris, Catania, Nuremberg, London, Budapest, Athens—and then asked, "Want to come along?"

"No way. I'm busy doing what I'm doing. But I must say good luck, and I admire your fortitude."

Paul then commented on the recurring coincidence that they seemed to wear the same type clothing whenever they met, whether blue jeans and a light leather jacket in the fall or winter, or pinstripe pants and sleeveless open-collar shirts in spring or summer. They always laughed about it and this day was no exception. Guy reached over to run a hand over Paul's red shirt and said, "Red. At least not blue like mine." Paul reciprocated by running his hand over Guy's briefcase—as overstuffed as his own.

At an even six feet tall, muscular and nearing fifty, Paul had blond hair streaked with gray stands above his ears, and light blue eyes. Clean-shaven, his craggy face belied a calm voice and ready smile that often overtook the margins of a square jaw. Guy, on the other hand, was decidedly shorter. A puffy face recessed his dark eyes, and a ruddy nose stood out against a pale complexion. His flint hair seemed ironed out and a grey mustache appeared to be pinned on. Specks of light reflected off the spaces between pens inserted into a plastic pocket protector. He took out one of the pens and pointed it around in the air as if he needed to in speaking.

"But what about your wife?" he asked.

"Sylvie?"

"Yes. Is she included in your new travel plans?"

"I was hoping she'd come along, but she couldn't get time off at the Oceanographic Institute over at Woods Hole.. They're funny that way, especially if you're a top administrator. I told her I'd scrap the idea then."

"So what was her reaction?"

"I remember it so well. She said, 'Don't you dare. You've been talking about it for months. Go ahead. I understand'."

"And?"

"And I said, 'But what if I bump into a charming chick in a church?' She ignored the remark."

Soon, Paul's favorite waitress came over, flashed his favorite smile and asked all the questions he had answered many times before.

The two men ordered the same thing: hot dog, mustard, relish and French Fries.

While waiting to be served, talk with Guy took an unexpected turn. He began slowly as if it were a rehearsed script. "Paul, I've been thinking … have a better idea and you can kill two birds with one stone."

"Come ahead. I'm all ears."

"Well, still focus on religion but allow for a larger undertaking, one that combines churches and pastors with crime that's run amuck. The bottom line is there's plenty of evidence that many criminals are reaching their goals with the help of clergymen and women who serve as undercover agents for them. I guess 'fronts' is an appropriate term. In many large cities, there are hierarchically organized families with groups called 'crews' and 'regimes'. So do get accustomed to different terminologies as you go along. And I know you and I share the same admiration for Napoleon, so bring him into the equation too."

Paul was flabbergasted. His face might have turned a rosacea crimson by becoming incited, but years ago, he'd finally determined it to be a liability when confronting adversaries, so he had learned how to turn it on and off. This time, however, he let it take its course. As he went to straighten a tie he wasn't wearing—a habit he'd developed during his student days—he said, "Now wait, Guy. Let's get this straight. You're saying that completely illegal activity is supported by outwardly legal and God-fearing people? But you're bringing old-fashioned criminals into the picture."

"Not old-fashioned any more. It's a digital world now … even among criminals, no matter their age. It's only the tip of the iceberg, but, as an example, there's more and more evidence that they bribe pastors they know are frequenting prostitutes. It's a significant number of pastors. They know because they—the mobsters—provide them."

While Guy spoke, Paul was drawn to a table across the room. A man was staring at them—non-blinking, lips turned downward. He wore a cherry-red rain jacket with raglan sleeves and two big patch pockets. It reminded Paul of Gene Kelly kicking up his heels in the classic *Singing in the Rain*. Paul thought he saw a wink but wasn't sure. He had never seen the man before. It bothered him to a degree for he recognized practically every individual who happened to enter there. East Falmouth was not exactly located along a main thoroughfare. But just as he had grown tired of traveling and of spotting suspicious looking men—and of even thwarting their attacks—he was willing to take on a different-faceted enterprise. And writing a book about it for good measure. He so informed Guy and indicated he valued the advice and that he would keep in touch with him.

"I've got to think about it, Guy. However, it sounds like a worthwhile undertaking, one I'm willing to consider."

So I'd be examining the progress and legitimacy of religion. And I'd now be adding criminal investigation to it. I thought I'd be getting away from that, but the combination sounds exciting.

He decided not to mention the stranger across the room at all; and he resisted an urge to approach the man and introduce himself, even though he felt reasonably certain such an introduction was not necessary.

Paul wasn't sure how or when he would begin the new approach but was anxious to get underway. One thing was certain, however: he would not launch most of it with phone calls or emails. Less impact. Instead: eye-to-eye visits. Wherever and whenever. No matter how far away. In addition, he wanted to avoid the peril of telephone and Internet hackers. The only exception this time around was securing the cooperation of an individual he'd worked for on several previous occasions. It could be done by telephone. The man was Leon Cassell, longtime chairman of *Gens de Vérité*, a French organization that had been in existence for more than two centuries. *Vérité* was a private group that worked alongside the government and was noted for solving many worldwide puzzles. It was in this connection that Leon had regularly sought Paul's assistance. Experience in traveling to most parts of the world had been necessary and, because of that, Cassell's choice person to lead various challenges was Paul, over and over again. A hefty retainer fee had always been offered, along with the assurance that air travel would be available on a moment's notice. Anywhere. Anytime. Even in the middle of the night. The chairman had a strong connection with the Royal Air Force out of London and one of its U.S. arms, the Joint Base Cape Cod … BCC … located in Hyannis, not far from Paul's home. One of JBCC's smaller planes manned by a pilot friend—Ansel Stone— would usually remain at designated locations while Paul tended to business, no matter how long it took. Airport personnel would even dispatch a limo to and from Paul's East Falmouth home whenever it was needed. A concurrent allowance was that Paul could be armed with a gun or two on any flight. He was often armed with a loaded Beretta Cougar .45 in a left shoulder holster and a Heritage Stealth 9 mm. in a right ankle rig.

By the time he and Guy had finished a quick meal, the man with the stare and probable wink had disappeared.

"When will you start?" Guy asked, "… whether you include my idea or not."

"As soon as possible. I really can't wait."

"When's possible?"

"A day or two. I've got to clear up something first."

"I won't ask what. That's too nosy."

"No, not at all. I just worked my tail off for a Connecticut client who had a box of valuable jewels stolen from under his nose. They're worth a fortune but, more than that, they have sentimental meaning for him and his wife. Well, long story, but I finally located it in Vienna last week and gave it to them. Now they want to meet with me further about it. Not sure why but apparently a telephone call won't do. Involves insurance of some kind. So I can do that tomorrow, and then I'm free. What is it they say … *free at last*?" Paul could feel a measure of elation as he uttered the words.

Their remaining conversation was as quick as their meal and as they dashed toward their cars through a pounding downpour, their shoes squishing in the saturated grass, they waved their briefcases at one another. Guy drove off but Paul lagged behind, consumed with thoughts about what he would do while sitting in his car. And straightening them out there, for he was always at his best in analyzing thoughts during loud inclement weather. He believed that such surroundings blocked out all irrelevant reflections, and this heavy storm qualified as one such occasion.

He sat quietly for a full five minutes and by the time he felt ready for some serious thinking, the bad weather had cleared except for shadows cast by leaves still dancing above his car. He rolled down the window and immediately experienced the smell of fresh grass and flowers from a nearby pasture. It all had a soothing effect.

Just as storms had disguised inconsequential things, so too had international investigative work shoved religion aside. But not forever. The mere writing of the book he had planned finally urged him to get started. His mind became flooded with ideas he had relegated to secondary status, for a time when he might finally resurrect them, and when he might first consult with four confidants. They were located in Calabria, St. Helena, Buenos Aires and Gibraltar.

One never knew it or even imagined it—including Sylvie—but Paul had accumulated considerable information about religion. And Napoleon. He'd simply filed away articles through the years, promising himself he would review them eventually. Likewise, whenever he had the opportunity, he had attended church services—for nearly any denomination and in as many countries his work had taken him. He kept it all secret, for he figured that being erroneously viewed as a religious zealot might not fare well with those hiring him for purely investigative reasons. But the time had come to hash over the many snippets he'd accumulated and judge whether or not some were appropriate to include in his book.

Furthermore, he recalled that some snippets might even be essential for the well-being of healthy churches, a consideration that might assist him if he were to become a consultant to newly formed ones. It was a thought he frequently entertained.

He dug through his briefcase and located several scraps of paper containing five characteristics of a strong church, one that he would be proud to attend on a regular basis and to assist in its everyday affairs. It was just last year that he had affixed them onto a single sheet. He read from it:

The five things it takes to make a great and healthy church:

1—**Love, acceptance and forgiveness**. People enter just the way they are, allowing the Holy Spirit to do the refining work within their hearts.

2—**Hunger for personal growth**. People show a strong desire to know God in an intimate manner.

3—**Shift from traditional to contemporary worship**. Most healthy churches offer both.

4—**Prayer**. Obviously a high priority.

5—**Service. Exhibiting active volunteerism. S**erving God with all the talent, time, giftedness, passion, temperament, and energy one can muster.

> *So what did this gain me? An organized synopsis of what I might be dealing with? And it's a starter for the book. Also, I might see if these five issues apply to each random church I select. And also, is my decision to take on Guy's advice the best one? Becoming involved again with the issue of crime? Yes, of course! My private investigations of the past might lead me to key personnel in religious circles. As for Napoleon, justification of the military commander's mindset might give the book some pizazz.*

Paul planned for the military commander to be a secondary consideration, although for years he'd appreciated that Napoleon had a keen understanding of the power of organized religion in social and political affairs and paid much attention to bending it to his purposes. Paul's favorite Napoleon quote was, "Skillful conquerors have not got entangled with priests. They can both contain them and use them."

By the time he was ready to drive away, he had covered what he'd hoped to for the day, and even what he hadn't hoped to, for Guy's suggestion had been unexpected. But welcomed. He hightailed it back to his home, although periodically slowed down to enjoy the fresh country air that filled what he always viewed as a beckoning road from Bonfiore's to East Falmouth. Happy about his upcoming mission, he couldn't wait to tell Sylvie about the changes in it.

Chapter 2

It was 1:45 when Paul arrived at their home at 88 Crest Lane. He could have waited for Sylvie to return from work. Instead, he planned on phoning her office. Yet, it wasn't unusual for him to pause between driveway and front door and admire both house and property. Such was the case once again as he plopped down on a side bench and took out a handkerchief to mop his brow on the muggy day.

He slowly looked around as if it were the first time he'd ever done so. To his right, a stone fountain was centered among ornamental grasses and purple-flowered Persian mint. Its scent hung lightly in the air.

Off to his left, a small garden featured shrubs with bright colored foliage, evergreens and bold-leafed New England flax. There were also sea holly and arching leaves that contrasted sharply with the sword-shaped leaves of the flax.

As for the house, it was a two-story Victorian mansion that was defined by a symmetrical facade, front gables, scalloped shingles, a large bay window and pre-cut embellishments on a cornice and wrap-around porch. Friends often referred to it as an estate, a term Paul found disagreeable for, to him, it implied something chilling and stiff rather than warm and comfortable.

He could have risen and gone in but, as he often did, continued to sit and imagine the inside layout. Many times, it was part of a game he played with himself, whether he was in a hurry or not. He was in a hurry, yet played the game because the success or failure of his imagination was at stake and he always found time to test it.

What he pictured was a large recessed living room containing a fireplace and coffered ceiling. Nearby was the family room that also served as Sylvie's work space. Then came the kitchen that boasted a breakfast bar and pantry.

The upstairs was Paul's ultimate challenge. He envisioned a bedroom suite that included a private vanity, a corner whirlpool tub, a separate walk-in shower, a large exercise room, and another fireplace. There were two additional bedrooms across a wide hallway, one of which he had originally used as a computer room and study. But he easily remembered morphing the larger of the two into what he labeled a "man cave" with an oversized oak desk and matching chair, several black metal stools, numerous floor lamps, a single Morris chair, a bar and wine cooler, a surround-sound system, a small N screen and his computer, printer and copying machine. All available wall space constituted his private library with floor-to-ceiling shelves stuffed with hundreds and hundreds of books, old and new. He pictured many of them, their topics ranging from astronomy to Zambia. But especially some he'd written himself, like

Napoleonic Strategy; Napoleon and Volterraio Castle; Napoleon's Final Defeat; and several of his mystery novels, including *Diamonds and Pirates* and *Spying for Keeps.*

Imagination test over. No mistakes.

Once inside, he slid open a window and inhaled the little air of the moment. He then took down *Napoleon and Volterraio Castle*, expecting to read part of it during the upcoming flight.

Next, he sat at his desk chair and dialed Sylvie's private line.

"I'm back," he said. "Got a minute?"

"For you? Definitely. How did it go?"

"Good meeting but he shocked me, I must admit."

"Oh? How?"

"He recommends I combine religion with crime."

There was a brief silence before she responded. "You got me there. What's that supposed to mean?"

Paul gave a skimpy version of Guy's revelation about criminals, pastors and prostitutes. And he included bribes and "a digital world."

He hadn't counted on her reaction. "It's right up your alley, Paul, and actually would make a more interesting book, given a possible contribution to nabbing criminals and dim-witted pastors. He's talking worldwide, I assume?"

"Worldwide."

"But," she continued, "I really can't believe the sex part."

"About prostitution?"

"Yes. Did he say how prevalent it is? I mean for pastors."

"Very. He used the word 'significant'."

"And it serves as a cover for crime?"

"Hmm, that's a good phrase. Maybe even for a chapter title in the book."

Paul said he'd elaborate further when she got home, and he would have bet that, given the nature of their conversation, she would arrive earlier than usual.

Chapter 3

Paul's feelings rose and plummeted sharply, for he didn't quite know where to begin. He told himself that his original intent was to examine the progress and legitimacy of religion around the world and, as part of that, to see how many churches qualify for the *List of Five* being included in their everyday affairs. But he wondered if the whole question of religion had taken a back seat in favor of leaving room for thoughts about his many criminal investigations. That, in turn, led to a review of all the times he had to deal with the Mafia. With a consigliere or underbosses and lieutenants. With La Cosa Nostra; the Chinese Triads and Tongs; the Italian 'Ndrangheta; even the Yakuza in Japan. His dealings were sometimes as enemies but usually as friends based on one syndicate competing with another one.

He understood the mentality of the entire underworld and much of this was due to the influence of one Fabio Calderone from Calabria in Italy. He was once a top commander of the Padrino, the second highest level within the entire 'Ndrangrata organization. They had met years ago when Fabio spent thirteen years attending various schools in the Chicago area. He was now as fluent in English as an Italian and they had grown to be close friends. Close and safe. Once, a while back, Paul had even hinted at his eventual intention of exploring international religion. He was prepared to defend the move, but Fabio merely fashioned a blank stare.

Paul had always wrapped their friendship in tight secrecy, content in believing that Fabio was trustworthy and had never double-crossed anyone. Paul kept his distance from other mobsters, relying instead on Fabio's intermediary skills whenever necessary. In particular, Fabio was once the Mob's expert on front organizations before voluntarily stepping aside. He was growing weary of such an important role and so-informed Paul when they last spoke. Paul remembered the time well … and his friend's last comment: "There are decent mobsters and dangerous ones, and the decent ones won't hurt either you or me."

Like the brightest spark in the glow of a July 4th sprinkler, the solution became clear. Once again he would turn to Fabio, placing a call to the barber shop he had taken over in Calabria. It had once belonged to fellow mobster and cousin, Rocco Stratta. Fabio assumed ownership of the business upon Rocco's murder. Before that, when he was more active with the Mob, Fabio worked in a meat factory, slicing slabs of beef that hung from ceiling hooks. Paul thought it ironic that his Italian friend had gone from cutting meat to cutting hair.

"Paul! Everything okay?"

"Okay. Same there?"

"Yeah. Good to hear from you."

"I should call sometime when I don't need a favor."

"Favor or not … good to hear your voice. What's up?"

"Well, I've retired from treasure hunting, but thought I should still travel some."

"Travel for what?"

"That religious thing."

"Good … good … and I admire you for it."

"But there's a new layer and that's where you come in. At least I hope so. I was thinking of paying you a visit rather than having a discussion over the phone. I'm afraid it'll be a case of 'in-and-out' wherever I visit. 'Quickies' because there'll be a slew of them. And if you're wondering why I can't settle for information over the phone, it's that yes I could, but it's not the same as in person. Two reasons, Fab: one, I get a lot from somebody's body language and two, phones can be tapped these days and I'm not willing to risk it. So it's in person with every one of my contacts."

"Understood, Paul. But can you give me an idea what seeing me would be all about? I mean in general terms."

"No problem. All about what you once told me regarding front organizations and how they're related to religion and criminal activity. I'd like to hear it all again. And even if someone's listening in to what I just said, I haven't given them much in the long run."

"Okay, I'd welcome your visit. Got a time in mind?"

"Is tomorrow too soon?"

"Not at all."

"Great! I'll be there around six p.m., your time. Will you still be in your shop?"

"I'll make sure I am."

There were two other people he wanted to engage before the day ended. One was Vincent Broussard, a young history professor at Harvard University, and the other was Thatcher Drinkwell, Constable of Police Service on the far-off island of St. Helena, where Napoleon was banished and died six years later. Vincent had accompanied Paul on most of his trips during the past six years, and Drinkwell was the leader of a worldwide network of researchers called "histarians" … with an "a", not an "o".

Vincent stated he'd be happy to take part again. He cited his past times with Paul, as friend, cohort and, during dangerous spells, as bodyguard. Drinkwell said he'd contribute what he could, although he apologized for the distance Paul would have to travel from Calabria to get to the remote St. Helena between South America and Africa.

"To receive the kind of support you could give, Thatch … it's one-hundred per cent worth it. And I'd rather it be in person and not over a phone. I can't tell yet when I'll get there. Maybe in a day or two."

Paul was generally overjoyed by the course of events thus far and celebrated in his usual way. He munched on some crackers while balancing a cup of tea as he paced back and forth in his "man- cave." That habit plus rubbing what he called his "decision scar"—an old linear wound on the undersurface of his chin—often took place whenever he felt elated, challenged or even concerned. He nearly spilled some tea as he rubbed the scar.

Sylvie did arrive earlier than usual and found Paul sitting at the kitchen table, stirring his second cup of tea. She walked over and gave him a hug that smacked of worry over his safety. Then when she sat opposite him, his thoughts became divided between a deep love for her and for his concern about the mission ahead. He rose, walked around the table, and ran his hands up over her back as he kissed her on the lips. His kiss was longer than her hug and torn emotions were piqued.

Above the stove, the ticking of a small clock situated between salt and pepper shakers seemed louder than usual to him, and even the smell of the tea seemed stronger. But he shook off the thoughts and the senses and informed her of the three phone calls he'd made plus his plan to leave for Calabria at six in the morning.

"Then to St. Helena from there?"

"Yeah. It's a little shorter distance from Italy than from here."

"So you'll come home before starting your visits to churches and parishes?"

Paul nodded and noticed that her eyes had darkened to the color of shadows slipping around one of the window shades. It started to rain once more.

"Don't worry, dear," he said. "Between Vincent and my

guns and karate moves, we'll be fine."

Her brow furrowed and she said, "I'm glad he'll be with you … the best bodyguard there is, bar none."

He agreed but had a feeling that something perilous could be looming on the horizon.

Chapter 4

June 2

Vincent was jockey-like short and on the thin side. But when taking karate lessons from Paul, he had to change into appropriate clothing and it was at those moments that his muscles became well-defined. He had long dark hair, gaps between his teeth and delicate features. Yet, he was an arresting young man of twenty-seven with a softness in his skin, his bearing and his brown eyes. Not a weak softness but a resilience, the hint of reconciliation if called for. All this disappeared when in practice combat with Paul, as their sessions usually ended in a draw.

They met at Joint Base Cape Cod just before six in the morning, both looking well rested but eager. Leon Cassell had arranged for a limo to drive them there from their homes and, as promised, they were allowed to carry loaded pistols aboard the plane.

There was no way Paul would nap during the flight, for the entire upcoming venture was crawling around in his mind like a swarm of ants over a sugary cake. He would wait until he settled in with Fabio before considering the word that was sticking with him: "front". He understood its meaning but wanted to learn as much as he could about how it was related to religion and criminal activity. He wanted Fabio's assessment. And he wanted to be brought up to date on the barber's thoughts about Napoleon. Fabio had once divulged a favorable opinion of him in past conversations.

Paul and Vincent sat next to one another during the flight. Soon after takeoff, Vincent drifted off to sleep. Paul believed it to be an ideal time to read a section of a different book he he'd been putting together. Secretly proud of the way it was written, it concerned one of his and Sylvie's favorite examples of Vincent's unwavering courage. He read the following; it dealt with a visit the trio had made to the island of Elba:

> The next morning, Paul, Vincent and Sylvie left the hotel and hardly spoke during the 15-minute drive to the "rutted road." Vincent stopped the car and all three piled out. Sylvie began taking pictures. From their vantage point, Volterraio Castle was more imposing than Paul had anticipated, certainly earning by virtue of both its appearance and location the title of Elba Island's Guardian. It was perched on the summit of a rocky cliff that angled perfectly skyward and contained nothing but a colossal mass of boulders. There were no paths to climb, no living or dead tree stumps to help during any ascent. Paul thought it

remarkable that the only vegetation was either around his feet or, as viewed against the morning's darkening clouds, clinging to the castle itself. Blades of yellow grass brushed against his legs clear up to his knees, while the castle appeared smothered in green, brown and yellow, like a camouflaged fortress. Paul knew its construction dated back to the 11th century's Pisan period and that it had likely dwindled to half its original height. Still it looked indestructible to him and there were other words that swept through his mind: powerful, formidable, graceful, dignified. Even timeless.

He hadn't yet discussed it with the others, but Paul had every intention of inspecting the castle up close, to glance over an entire sea as the Tuscans had done to spot invading Saracen pirates; to see its underground tunnels firsthand; to walk among its walls much like Napoleon two centuries ago, before the erosion and crumbling began. Then he wanted to observe the blackbirds he'd read about. They had been delivered there as a trick and he understood they were still nesting there among the ruins. In the dim light, he could barely make out a few circling about. Theirs were the only sounds he heard. Much smaller than normal, they gave the illusion that the structure was bigger than it was, as viewed by the French, the Turks, the Saracens or any other enemies.

And who knows, he mused, perhaps they might stumble upon something left behind, something hidden centuries before and now exposed, like the box that Napoleon allegedly carried on his frequent visits there?

He removed his sunglasses, which were no longer needed in the gathering dusk. He then asked Sylvie to wait in the car and lock the doors.

"You ready?" he whispered to Vincent.

"If you are. What looks like the best route to the top?"

Paul tweaked his chin. "Let's check around," he said. "You go that way and I'll go the opposite." He pointed to his left and right. "If you find a halfway decent approach, give a holler. I'll do the same."

"Got it," Vincent said. "Incidentally, why are we whispering?"

"So we might hear echoes of Napoleon's voice. The rumor is that he routinely spoke out loud in Italian up there."

They both chuckled nervously. As Vincent went left, Paul headed right. He passed giant rock after giant rock on his left. Interspersed among them were formations that brought to mind the stalagmites of caves he had explored. He stopped occasionally to survey possible routes to the castle high up. Minutes later he looked back and saw that their car was no longer visible. Up ahead, several rocks formed a mound nearer the road, narrowing it some. Paul rounded the mound and stopped short. What the! He thought his heart would race out of control!

Twenty yards ahead, three men were leaning against the back of a black car. They rose to attention, hands on hips, legs apart. Red hoods covered their heads. The eye and mouth slits were overly large, revealing dark skin and mustaches. All three moved slowly toward him.

Paul had the presence of mind to notice that the car's back bumper contained no decal as was the case back at the museum. But of more immediate concern was what to do. Turn and run? Strike up a conversation? Say, "Excuse me?" He might have done so had they not been wearing hoods.

Suddenly Paul heard Vincent's voice from behind and slightly hillside. He held a pistol in each hand. "Back off!" he screamed at the men. He leaped onto the road and swiftly positioned himself in front of Paul.

The men kept coming.

"Stop or else!" Vincent's voice was louder and firmer as he straightened both arms toward the hooded men, now ten yards away.

They stopped.

"Put your hands behind your head, all of you." Without taking his eyes off them, Vincent twisted his mouth to the side and said, "Show 'em, Paul, in case they don't understand."

Paul showed them and they did so.

"Now, one by one, throw your guns on the ground," Vincent continued. "And don't try anything funny. I've shot these pistols many times before. Shake your heads if you understand me."

They shook their heads, followed Vincent's command, and within seconds, five handguns lay on the ground.

"You in the middle," Vincent said, "only one gun?"

The man didn't respond.

Vincent tipped his pistol in his direction and the man reached into his back pocket.

"Easy now," Vincent said.

The man flipped a small silver handgun onto the road.

"Thank you, gentlemen. Now, all of you—on the ground, face down, hands behind your head."

They spoke for the first time, each saying, "Si".

Vincent handed one of his pistols to Paul and said, "Keep them covered. Every second." He picked up the men's guns and hurled them far up the cliff, one at a time. He then walked over to their car and shot out its tires.

"Let's go," Vincent said. "There's enough room to turn our car around. And you guys? We're walking backwards so don't dare get up until we're out of sight. Get it?"

As they inched away, Paul remained stunned over Vincent's skill in taking control of the situation. Sylvie was right. What a bodyguard!

"Why didn't you whisper to me that you'd be doubling back?" Paul asked.

"Because I figured if we were somehow being watched, they'd see that and I didn't want them to. Besides, it wasn't necessary for you to know."

At the car, Sylvie bolted out. "I was so worried! I didn't know what to do. There were four shots. What happened?"

"Nothing," Vincent said. "Just testing my gun."

They got into the car, Sylvie in back. Vincent maneuvered it around and they sped off through a heavy rain that lasted but a few seconds. It reminded Paul of his boyhood days' vacations in southern Florida.

"You carry a gun, Vincent?" Sylvie asked in disbelief.

"Around here? For sure."

"Back in Paris, you don't seem like the gun

type."

"But away from Paris, I can even swallow swords."

"If you don't mind, Vin, let's level with her."

Vincent's expression didn't register disapproval and Paul explained what had transpired, ending with, "Let's get out of here fast and I don't mean this place. I mean the whole damn island. Screw it!"

"Don't fret, Paul," Sylvie said. "Maybe they're trying to throw a scare into us."

Paul had heard her utter that line before, Still, he couldn't tell if she meant it or was merely trying to console him in his moment of uneasiness.

In the hotel lobby, the conversation was totally one-sided. Paul's words gushed out as if he couldn't wait to get rid of them: "When I took on the assignment, I never bargained for this kind of stuff. I've hunted for stolen treasures all over the world, six continents, never faced this. I'm calling Leon. Let's see when the plane can get here. I'm sure you're wondering about St. Helena. That's still open but I've got some deep thinking to do. I'll let the two of you know what's going on as soon as I know myself.

It was 11:30 when Paul got through to Leon. With uncharacteristic emotion, he summarized the conversation he'd have with Fabio. The more he spoke, the more fired up he became. This eventually eased up, however, when he came to Guy's suggestions. Leon, in turn, stressed the importance of Paul's being the principal investigator in an historical investigation; and of keeping Vincent close at hand.

"But as you can imagine," Paul said, "I don't have good vibes around here anymore and I want to leave. I met with Clive Weaver and that's enough. He was helpful—a little strange—but helpful. When can the plane arrive?"

"I understand, Paul. It can leave here anytime you want."

"Is now too soon?"

"Not at all. Ansel can be there in, say, six hours. Is that okay?"

"Okay."

"And Paul? I say this like a father. Anything worthwhile has its distractions, and some are more serious than others."

"Serious?" Paul countered. "You mean deadly. Yeah, that's it: deadly serious."

Paul dwelled upon the many times he had spoken with Fabio and Drinkwell about Napoleon. Were they still supportive of the life the emperor had led?

He also understood that the forerunners to Drinkwell's "histarians" dated back to the emperor's era and often heard Fabio proudly mention that Napoleon was really of Italian heritage, having been born on the island of Corsica, three-hundred miles from mainland Italy.

Chapter 5

June 3

Paul shifted around in his passenger seat more than usual. The same for glancing out the window. And he summoned up what he had read about Calabria:

Geographically, it forms Italy's "toe", a long and narrow peninsula surrounded by the Ionian and Tyrrhenian Seas. It is separated from Sicily by the Strait of Messina. Nearly half of the area is mountainous and hilly, while plains occupy only ten per cent of the region. Three mountain ranges are prominent: Pollino, La Sila and Aspromonte. Its Sila National Park is said to have the purist air in Europe. Calabria's economy is characterized by widespread corruption, tax evasion and organized crime, which is run by its local Mafia syndicate.

The JBCC airplane landed at the Lamezia Terme International Airport, a ten minute drive to Fabio's barber shop. Ansel had phoned ahead to rent a car for Paul and Vincent to use.

"I could have arranged for a limo as usual, but I thought you might be driving around some," Ansel said. "I'll hang around here at the airport for when you're ready to leave. St. Helena will be some kind of trip, but we'll take care of it. As you know, we'll land on Ascension Island and from there, the Royal Mail Ship will sail you to Jamestown. That's about seven-hundred miles or thirty-six hours away. There's no airstrip there and there never will be, because their authorities decided not to allow anyone to land a plane there. Something to do with the British and Dutch skirmishes centuries ago. So visitors have to sail into it, not fly into it. Pretty grueling. Sound familiar?"

"Sure does," Paul said, "but nothing we're embarking on will be easy." As he spoke, he thought that during the sailing he'd begin making notes for the book he'd write. And he didn't know why it came about, but he also decided that the note-writing should have a title: "Discovery".

That way, I could discover this and I could discover that.

It was five-thirty when Paul and Vincent approached Fabio's barber shop which was located near the center of one of the plains. Vincent found a parking spot half a block from the shop and they both noted a small blue car in a driveway off to the side. Darkness had not set in yet, the weather was calm, and as they moved along briskly, Paul commented on the muffled sounds of birds scrambling for branches within the clusters of trees that lined the sidewalk. Their walk was no more than thirty yards.

Hanging from the door's interior was a sign that read in Italian: CLOSED FOR THE DAY. They entered after a single knock and found the same scene as during Paul's last visit more than eighteen months before.

Fabio himself was sitting in one of its two large leather chairs, leafing through a magazine. A mirror spanned the back wall, below which was a counter of neatly arranged scissors, combs, brushes and a radio. Loud music was blaring. Paul counted three spittoons scattered about. Four empty chairs lined one other wall, each separated by a small table stacked with newspapers and magazines. The third wall contained photos Paul recognized, having been to the country on several other occasions: The Cliff at Tropea, Pollino National Park, and views of Calabria olive tree plantations from the air.

Fabio had not looked at the mirror when Paul barked, "Hey, paisano—you want a haircut and shave?"

Spotting Paul's image in the mirror, Fabio fumbled his way to a position between the two men and shook Paul's hand with a machine-like whipping motion.

"It's been a long time, Paul," he said.

"Yeah, it has. And this is my associate, Vincent Broussard. My bodyguard, too."

"You don't need a bodyguard, my friend … but hello, Vincent. Pleased to meet you."

"Likewise," Vincent said.

They shook hands as Paul continued, "You know, I should

have added 'confidant' to 'associate and bodyguard'. And I say it to emphasize that everything we're about to discuss will definitely stay secret."

The barber was about age fifty, and in both build and appearance resembled the late James Gandolfini of *The Soprano's* fame. His smile was arresting and nearly ear-to-ear. Gray-peppered hair was not as fluffy as eyebrows that curved around square rimmed glasses. He wore a collarless white shirt that hung loose at the waist and, in contrast, tight patch-pocket trousers tapered down to brown suede loafers.

"I'd wager you're as anxious to talk to me as I am to you," Paul said.

"Somewhat—and really—that's the way you put it the last time you came here. I remember it well even though it was what? Two years ago?"

"Almost. Anyway, shall we go to the back room as usual?"

"No need for that. I'm through working for the day, the sign is up and we can talk right here. Do sit down." He pulled three chairs into a circle.

"Let's cut right to the chase," Paul said, "because we can't stay very long."

"I know because on the phone you told me you'd be 'in-and-out', but can't you change your mind? You won't stay for dinner? Good place down the street."

"No, we'd better not. It's just that we're leaving straight for St. Helena from here and we'd like to get an early start."

Paul tried to ignore Fabio's hard look.

"I'll level with you, Fab. You know Thatcher Drinkwell?"

"Not only know him, but we've had some dealings. Good ones, like ours. And we share the same feelings about Napoleon. Nice guy, that Thatch, but get ready for his loose-leaf binders."

"Loose-leaf binders?"

"Got a million of them. They contain all kinds of quoted material and he'll drown you in it."

"Like how many?"

"Maybe ten at a sitting. But it's all so worthwhile. Lots to say and he's totally reliable. Know what I call him?"

"What?"

"The quoter. He'd probably offer quotations to the world if given the chance."

"Okay then. Once these preliminary talks are over—with you, with him, maybe with a couple of others in Buenos Aires and Gibraltar—Vincent and I can proceed with our travels, exploring the status of international religions as I once mentioned to you. In countries like France, Germany, Switzerland, Britain, and some of the Balkan countries. But first, let me clarify: I'm really not that anxious to do the talking. More the listening. As I said on the phone, I'd like to hear your views again on the question of fronts. My understanding is that in your mind there's been a connection between them and Napoleon. So why don't you start?"

"Well, first of all," he said, "when I was more active on the organized crime scene, I was expected to voice my opinion about the emperor and religion during his time in power."

"But why did you need to voice your opinion? Wait though. Okay if we make some notes?" Paul and Vincent already had a pad and pencil in their hands.

"Certainly—go right ahead. Anyway, to answer your question. Voicing my opinion? Because some of our dons believe strongly that Napoleon and religion often went hand-in-hand."

"Oh?"

"Goes back many, many years. They thought, and still do, that he used religion as an excuse for many of the things he did. Like firing people, taking land, extorting, smuggling, prostitution and so on."

"But aren't those the types of things the dons of the time did? Why need religion?"

"Made it all easier … almost acceptable to the ordinary class."

Paul bent over to tie a shoelace—one that didn't need tying, but it gave him a chance to digest what he was hearing.

He straightened and said, "So if I interpret it right, religion was really a front."

"You got it."

"Any religion?"

"The major ones—Catholic, Protestant, Jewish. I don't know much about the others, like any of the Arab ones, but those three I can talk about, because I've listened in on our dons going on and on about how Napoleon felt about them and how he treated them. Not one-hundred percent favorably, but maybe seventy-five percent.

"Understand, Paul, I'm no expert on this, but church-state relationships were constantly strained throughout his reign. I do know there were continual disagreements between him and Cardinals, Archbishops and even two or three Popes. Eventually, I guess he realized the importance of religion in increasing obedience and in his control over the French people. Before that though, things got so hot that one Pope even excommunicated him. But the church reversed it just before he died at St. Helena.

"Regarding Protestants, he had a generally favorable attitude toward them. For instance, Lutheran and Reformed churches began taking part in public ceremonies. That had never happened before. And overall, Protestants considered themselves emancipated and integrated while he ruled.

"Now, what can I say about the Jews?"

Paul looked up and said, "You know, Fab, my fingers are tired. I wish I had my computer here."

"Me too," Vincent kicked in, flapping his hand.

"But go on," Paul said. "Not the Jews?"

"Well, Napoleon enacted laws that emancipated them in France. Actually they became equal to other Frenchmen. He canceled old laws that had forced them to live in ghettos and that limited their rights."

"Rights like what?" Paul asked.

"Rights to property and worship and most occupations."

"They had been deprived of them?" Vincent asked.

"Most of them. So the Jews began admiring him. In the middle of his control, he designated Judaism as one of the official religions of France, along with Roman Catholicism and Protestantism. He even declared all debts with Jews to be reduced or entirely eliminated."

Vincent eyed Paul closing his pad and followed suit.

"So he used religion as a major front, you're saying."

"Major, major, major. For good things and bad."

"You know, Fab, I take it that you think highly of him and what he accomplished."

"Overall … right. Not about everything he did, but most everything. It was his ulterior motive for many of the things he did, or didn't do. And that's the way fronts work. They're really an ulterior motive. They were around then and they're still around now. In fact, **moving** around. The famous Columbian Cartel? It's spreading to Eastern Europe now."

"Yeah, I've heard. And what about cruise lines?"

"What about them?"

"Think we should investigate?"

"Absolutely. Many are in cahoots with pirates and serve as fronts for prostitutes that the pirates supply."

Paul's blinking appeared like a kind of language that needed no expression. He had heard enough. He and Vincent got up and proceeded to shake Fabio's hand. Paul then said, "Before we're off, I have two conclusions about meeting with you. One is that you really know your stuff about what was covered and two, that I never in a million years knew how eloquent you are with the English language."

"Thank you, but I've had lots of practice, and don't forget … I lived in the Chicago area for over thirteen years."

Suddenly, what sounded like distant gunshots rang out. Four of them in a row, ten seconds apart. Soon after, a car with a muffler problem was heard speeding away.

"What's all that?" Paul shrieked. "It's over near our car."

After a moment's stare at one another, all three headed toward the front door. Fabio was about to fling it open but was restrained by Paul, who whispered, "Wait. Let me check first. Stand back."

He withdrew the Beretta .45 from his shoulder holster, crouched down and eased the door open. He inched out further and peeked to each side. "No one anywhere," he said. "Let's check near the car. I'll have us covered." He pulled up the Stealth from his ankle rig and led the way with a pistol in each hand.

"I'll be covering, too," Vincent said, waving a pistol for them to see.

Paul couldn't believe that Fabio wasn't also brandishing a gun.

The changes over time. Going straight for sure.

At the car, each of them poked around with unbelieving eyes. All four tires had been shot flat!

They stood with mouths half-open, shaking their heads in silence.

"Don't even check the doors," Paul finally said. "In fact, let's move away. We don't want anything exploding."

As they were sprinting back to the shop, he said, "Save your talk till there. We've got some deciding to do."

Inside, they sat in the same circle of chairs and Paul began the discussion. "First, I must apologize. That was meant as a warning to us, not you. Yours is the blue car out there, right?"

"Right, and no need to apologize."

"Well, let's call it like this. Because of me, you've become entangled. They're probably against what I plan on doing—how they know, I have no idea—and they think you might get in their way. They probably followed our car here and now they know. Incidentally, you don't pack a gun anymore?"

"I have one in that top drawer over there, but I think I should pack it on me now."

"With your history, yes, you should."

Fabio got up, pulled out a Walther PK 38 from the drawer and slid it into a side pocket of his pants. "For your information, men, I also have a Sigarms .45 and a couple of rifles in the back room."

There was a pregnant lull in their conversation during which Paul pictured himself as a protector, not the other way around. He eventually said, "I think we should stay with you for the night and then scram in the morning. So let's leave for dinner and I'll contact Ansel for a new car. You have anything to sleep on out back?"

"Yes—two cots, as a matter of fact. Plus there's a bathroom and shower there."

"Couldn't be better. Let's go out and eat now."

They were ushered to window seats at the La Fortuna Ristorante. There was plenty left to talk about, but words were few, their wine glasses kept empty. Paul couldn't really tell but he reckoned there was little talk among the other diners. He didn't understand why but wondered if repeated glances in Fabio's direction had anything to do with it.

When they finished eating, Paul picked up the check and moved closer to the window to check the bottom line. He happened to look outside. And then he flinched!

A beat-up black car with a dangling tailpipe was parked across the street. He made out a driver and one passenger.

Paul informed the others and after he paid the check, they hurried out a back door to Fabio's car in a rear parking lot. Their shared guess was that the car out front was the same one they had heard driving off the previous night.

They returned to the barber shop and its back quarters and Vincent elected not to shower but Paul did. While doing so, he scrubbed his scalp more vigorously than ever, as if to erase the remnants of a bad dream.

In the morning, Ansel arrived with another car and they departed for the airport. Paul couldn't tell if Fabio had looked more depressed than he, himself, felt. However, he was more consumed with the vision of four blown-out tires and its implication. Even more so with his recollection of Guy's recent comment—that religion involves not only a belief but also the conduct of clerics and religious institutions. And that all of it can serve as fronts for practically anything on earth.

Chapter 6

June 4

The sailing from Ascension Island to Jamestown was expected to cover seven-hundred miles. Both men napped a good portion of the way, but Paul took time to write down the first legitimate set of Discovery Notes that he would refer to when writing his upcoming book. He didn't count the few words he'd previously written about front groups. He also took along the last three books he'd written: *Napoleon's Final Defeat*, and the mysteries, *Diamonds and Pirates* and *Spying for Keeps*.

And although he had been to St. Helena two years before, at one point he scanned through the familiar flyer he obtained outside the ship's galley. It was titled *St. Helena and Napoleon* and was one in a pile available to all passengers:

> St. Helena, A British island in the South Atlantic, is situated 1,200 miles off the southwest coast of Africa and 700 miles southeast of Ascension Island. The Portuguese discovered St. Helena in 1502 but it became part of Great Britain

in 1673. The island is approximately ten miles by seven miles in size or about half the size of Napoleon's former home-in-exile, Elba. Rough and mountainous, it is composed mainly of volcanic wasteland. The highest peaks—Diana's Peak and Mount Actaeon—rise more than 1,000 feet above sea level. An area of past volcanic activity is Sandy Bay, which contains fertile soil, ideal for the island's fruit and vegetable production. Three columns of Basalt in this area are called Lot, Lot's wife and Asses Ears.

The island's only port and village is Jamestown, the Capitol. Its population is about 5,600, principally Europeans, Africans and East Indians. Its main bay is called James Bay.

The chief crops are flax and potatoes. For a century or more, the flax was used to make mailbags for British Post Offices, but this process has declined because of the availability of cheaper synthetic materials. Other industries there include fish curing and the manufacture of lace and fiber mats.

For many years, it was an important port of call for Portuguese sailors to replenish their supplies and to receive medical attention. At one time, both the British and Dutch claimed the island as their own as they visited it on their voyages to India. In 1659, the East India Company colonized the island. Fourteen years later, the Dutch attacked and took over the island but the British retook it within six months.

Napoleon Bonaparte, of course, was its most famous resident. After his defeat at Waterloo, he signed a second abdication at the Élysée Palace. Three weeks later, he surrendered himself to the captain of the H.M.S. Bellerophon, which took him to Plymouth. From there, he embarked on the H.M.S. Northumberland bound for St. Helena, arriving October 15, 1815. He was allowed a retinue of thirty people. Napoleon stayed at a small house, the Briars, while his eventual home, Longwood House, was being readied. Shortly thereafter he moved into Longwood and lived there until his death.

Three frigates and eight other vessels continually patrolled James Bay or were kept on standby. Gun emplacements and guard posts were established throughout the island.

A year later, Sir Hudson Lowe, was appointed governor of St. Helena and it quickly became apparent that he and Napoleon had little respect for one another.

Napoleon died there on May 5, 1821. The cause and manner of death remain in dispute. Some claim he was poisoned by arsenic, either intentionally or by accident. Others state he died of

> stomach cancer as did his father. He was buried in the island's Sane Valley where his body remained until 1940. It was then transported to Paris and currently lies in the Hotel des Invalides.

With thoughts still churning in his head, Paul next wrote the Discovery Notes, including what he had previously jotted down. It took him well over an hour to ensure that they were all-inclusive. He looked forward to doing so because it was the solution to the problem he'd otherwise face: how could he interrupt his daily plans in order to write a novel? There was only so much time in a day.

> Tired of travel unless for different reason. Will not give up karate work. Want to search for "the progress and legitimacy of religion". To write book about it. To visit with variety of people, like Fabio Calderone, Thatcher Drinkwater, Joe Gomez, Juan Saltanban, maybe others. Then to countries and places like Germany, France, Gibraltar, Switzerland, Japan. Considering investigation of cruise lines. Will continue to make notes like these during travels—then use them later in writing the book. Should be non-fiction. Met with Guy Martin of "Herald Tribune". Writes weekly column: "The Influence of Religion and Napoleon Bonaparte". Lunch with Guy at Bonfiore Restaurant. He inquires about Sylvie. He

proposes additional purpose to trips: combine churches and pastors with related criminal activity. Digital world now. Says some pastors accept prostitutes provided by mobsters. Suspicious-looking guy spotted at nearby table. Eye-to-eye visits recommended. Leon Cassell mentioned (Vérité). Also JBCC and pilot friend, Ansel Stone. He will provide limo for anywhere. Am allowed to be armed with pistols during flights. Rainy downpour when leave. Reading of religion and Napoleon and attending church services through the years. Accumulated snippets. The "List of Five". Napoleon's quote regarding priests. Arrive home. Description of yard. Imagine what inside looks like. Dial Sylvie. She agrees with Guy. "Cover for Crime". About the Mafia. About Fabio Calderone from Calabria. He spent 13 years in Chicago. Great friends. Was once expert on fronts. Now is barber replacing murdered Rocco Stratta. Phone call to Fabio. "In-and-out" visit proposed. General reasons for upcoming visit in Italy. Vincent Broussard and Thatcher Drinkwell mentioned. Also histarians. Munching on crackers. Sylvie calls. Vincent best possible bodyguard. Vincent description. Leave for Calabria. Vincent sleeps. Reading about past visits to Elba and its Volterraio Castle. Dwelling upon Fabio and Thatcher regarding religion and Napoleon.

Thatcher's histarians mentioned along with where Napoleon was born. Calabria description. The airport (Lamezia). To begin writing notes during upcoming sailing. Reminder that such writings to be called "Discovery Notes". Arrival at barber shop. Fabio sitting in chair before mirror. His description. Says he knows and likes Drinkwell. The latter's loose-leaf binders. Mention of preliminary meetings, then countries to be visited. Few notes made. Fabio says dons of both eras believed Napoleon and religion closely related. That he used it as a front---good or bad. Fabio considers various religions, fronts and cruise lines. Gunshots heard. Discovery of our car's shot out tires. Decision made to stay the night. Fabio's guns. Assured of cots in rear room. Dinner at La Fortuna Restaurant. Quiet talk. Beat-up black car seen through window. Depart for airport in morning.

One or two miles out from the dock at James Bay, an early morning shade still held the extent of a fleeting cooler temperature that had arrived during the night. Paul had some difficulty reaching Leon by phone. The contact was weak and filled with static, but eventually they could hear one other. Paul had estimated that they could finish their work there by 2 p.m. and asked him to arrange for the Royal Mail Ship to begin sailing them back to Ascension Island at that time. Leon no sooner had agreed than the phone went totally dead, but Paul felt assured that Leon understood.

On deck, he was again struck by what could be seen of the island … the resemblance of a massive black iceberg with an irregular upper border and a slit down its middle. There, at its lowest level, a collection of white buildings stood out like a row of dice.

Traversing the ramp, the two men—each with luggage and brief case in hand—were drawn to a nearby corner. A prominent street sign read: "Napoleon Street".

"That's it," Paul said, "and there's the red car, just like Leon arranged. I hope the guy in it doesn't insist on doing the driving. I know my way around pretty well."

"You mean he lets **us** have it?"

"Yeah, we don't need any company at this point."

The man apparently saw Paul and Vincent in the rearview mirror and emerged from the car as they approached it. He indicated he was instructed to relinquish it and handed over the keys.

"You don't need identification?" Paul asked.

"No, I was given descriptions and you match them. All I need is your names."

"Mine is Paul D'Arneau and this is Vincent Broussard."

"Good enough," the man said, consulting a card. "And when you're ready to leave, just park the car near here and leave the keys under the mat. He turned to leave and added, "Have fun and good luck."

At the wheel, Paul could have predicted what they would see en route to the Farm Lodge Country House Hotel. They swung onto a metal-lined road, past "Jacob's Ladder"—a 700-step climb to a fort above; past a bird sanctuary, an elongated tree-fern thicket, rows of sunflowers and several redwoods.

They came to a steep slope and on higher ground, stark contrasts came into view: lush pastures, flax plantations and sea cliffs. But then Ladder Hill, turtles at the Governor's House, and the Half Tree Hollow neighborhood. Nostalgia over past visits alongside the anticipation of seeing Thatcher again made Paul's emotions feel twisted into knots. But he came to the same conclusion as he had nearly two years before: that the hotel's name was a misnomer, for it was merely a five-room structure surrounded by tropical gardens. A plaque near its entrance indicated that it was built in the late 17th century as a British East India Company planter's house. They had no real trouble being registered, although a crabby owner and receptionist kept mispronouncing the names that Leon had phoned her about. Their twin room was modest and clean and each freshened up but left the luggage largely unpacked.

Paul wanted the discussion with Drinkwell to include histarians—perhaps at the very beginning—so he removed a thick folder from his briefcase. It contained funds of information including a write-up about histarians that Leon had given him years ago. Paul had never "used" them, nor did he recall much about what he'd read and wanted to brush up on their availability, their promises and their locations. He rummaged through the folder, located the write-up and read the following:

Histarians are individuals, male or female, who are located in practically every region of the civilized world and can provide information that cannot be found any other way. Very few people know of their existence. They give out facts only to other histarians or to those who come highly recommended. Very often they provide insights that are contrary to what history has recorded, so they are properly named. Not "historians" but "histarians".

Most of them prefer to remain anonymous. They never offer a definitive opinion without checking with others of their kind … they are constantly doing so … that is, checking or verifying … in addition to delving into things with their own critical eye.

Some who have heard of them claim they possess mystical powers, but they have nothing of the sort. They simply do exhaustive research … "private collections from private collectors" they call it. Their information sources are never revealed, but their conclusions always turn out to be right. It's superfluous to put it this way … but totally right and totally accurate. And they act fast, providing answers within a day or two—even sooner.

They have sort of a code they live by …

"canon" might be a better word: "Never release information unless you would die over its accuracy." So they rely on solid facts, not on opinion alone … although they will express an opinion of other histarians, usually more than three or four. Four is the general rule. Any of them who violate the above mentioned canon are discharged from continued service and strongly punished in one way or another. This also applies to those found guilty of "leaking" secret information to outside sources—an extremely rare phenomenon.

Finally, they rarely give out much by telephone or over the Internet … only in person.

It was ten a.m. when they arrived at the island's Police Service Building, situated on a quiet side road and straddled by a small neat park. Inside the building, nothing seemed to have changed since Paul and Vincent were there two years before. A simple glance was sufficient to take it all in: ordinary metal desk topped with a **Constable Drinkwell** nameplate; red leather chair behind the desk; two wooden chairs before it; a filing cabinet at each side wall; an overhead camera; a holding cell in the rear. The room smelled old but scrubbed, antiseptic. From the ticking in a closet-like room, Paul assumed it contained the usual electronic equipment associated with police departments.

A man was sitting in the red chair, his head lowered as he used a pencil to sift through a stack of papers. Even when he licked the tip of the pencil, he never looked up. He wore a short-sleeved khaki shirt and a dapple of sunlight shining through a window landed on his left chest and accentuated a small badge.

He was of average height and weight with sharply defined features on a weathered face framed in black hair. The faded tattoo of a bird could be barely made out on each muscular forearm and suspenders gave the impression of pulling him down.

Paul faked a cough and said, “Excuse us, but hello again, Thatch. We finally made it.”

The constable looked up and blurted out, “Why Paul … and Vincent! Hello again … good to see you!” He reached over, shook their hands and motioned for them to sit. “Sorry for the long trip—exhausting as usual, I’m sure.”

“That’s okay,” Paul said. “Did a lot of catching up. You look good. Feel good?”

“Most days, yes. Sometimes no. Nothing serious though. And you two?”

“Most days serious. Sometimes good,” Vincent retorted, and they all laughed.

Paul then explained their in-and-out necessity and followed with: “And how are the histarians? Still a congenial bunch?”

“Still are, and that’s a good description of them.”

”You still their mover and shaker?”

“Not exactly ***that*** but yes, I can count on every one of them … or they don’t belong. Some of them even have Mafia friends … well not exactly friends, but men they can trust. These kinds of histarians sometimes use them to gather information and vice-versa."

"Oh? What's vice-versa mean?"

"It means the same Mafiosi ask them for information in return."

"And do the histarians give it to them?"

"Yes, but only if it doesn't hurt anybody."

"But how do the histarians know that?"

"They confer with other histarians and together as a team, they research the bejesus out of it."

Paul quickly decided he had set the stage for what he wanted to be assured of. "Well, Thatch, as we go country-to-country, if we feel the need for histarian assistance, can you accommodate us? Or would they prove to be necessary in the first place?"

Drinkwell thought for a moment, his eyes stopped blinking and he said, "Are heart beats necessary? Of course I'd accommodate. Just call me anytime, and remember not to mention any sort of advice over the phone. That's the code."

"But wouldn't an histarian break the code when he calls back later with the info I might need?"

"No. Doesn't work that way. He or she would travel to wherever you are and speak to you in person. Or if they're too far away, they have other histarians do it."

"I see, but if they consult with one another … sometimes four people, I understand … how can their consultations be by phone?"

"They never are. They're in person to one another and the

advice eventually ends up with the histarian nearest the individual seeking the advice. That's how they're trained to operate."

Paul felt relieved, almost pacified. "Well," he said, "that clears up one thing by traveling here. The other has to do with Napoleon. You and Fabio Calderone are on the same wavelength, he says."

"Fabio? Good old Fabio! Yes, we share the same views about that military genius. Too bad he ended up as he did. Didn't deserve it."

He reached into a bottom drawer and needed both hands to haul up an overflowing box and place it before him. It nearly obscured his vision.

Paul narrowed his eyes. The loose-leaf binders!

"Tell you what," Drinkwell said, moving the box aside. "Let's make a deal. We'll trade. I'll take some notes about what you say, and you listen to what I have to say about Napoleon. People insist I talk my head off in front of visitors, but I can't help it. No one around here listens to me. Not even my wife at home. So I should open some of my binders?" The cords of his throat weaved about in his loose collar.

"Sure, go ahead," Paul said. He almost added, "We expected it. But as for me, I have nothing more to say, really. So the stage is yours, Thatch." It was hard for Paul to flash a what's-first expression, especially while wishing he had a cracker to munch on. Instead, he crossed his legs and uncrossed them into reverse position.

"Good. But before my Napoleon papers, maybe something about birds, right out of the book I've written: *The Birds of St. Helena.*"

"Sounds fine," Paul said. Vincent nodded.

Hardly looking into the box, Drinkwell pulled out one of the binders. "Here we go," he said:

> Not many seabirds here. They shun us and I don't know why. There are plenty off Ascension but we only have Tropic Birds and Black and Brown Noddies. Some call the Fairy Tern a seabird—I don't because it nests not only on cliffs but also on trees and on some of our buildings. You may spot some … they're interesting birds with translucent wings and eyes that seem too big for their heads. As for land birds, most seem to fly around Jamestown primarily. I maintain they're social creatures—they like to be around people. We have ten species here, only ten in all, like Waxbills, the Common Myna, the Malagasy Fody, and Swainson's Canary. But my favorite is the Wirebird. Can't miss it. It prefers to live on a ridge above Longwood House, but some come down and race around the grounds. They have long spindly legs and no way will you catch one—they're too quick and fast. They'd rather run than fly. I would have named them Ground Wirebirds.

Drinkwell stopped reading. "I should have offered you some coffee," he said. "Would either of you like a cup? It could counter my putting you to sleep."

Paul waved off the offer. "No, no—not at all," he said. "It's very interesting. Migration and all that."

"Well, I didn't get into migration or, more important, when and how certain birds were released here and decided to stay, and don't worry, I won't. In fact, that's enough on that. It's putting *me* to sleep!"

He inserted the binder back into the box, removed a host of several others and opened the top one. "Now about Napoleon," he said. "You want my thoughts, correct?"

"Correct."

Paul still felt that justification of Napoleon's mindset might give his book a certain glitter. But there were three other things of importance: one, that Napoleon understood the power of religion as a front; two, that he may have cavorted with organized crime figures of his day; and three, that most of today's mobsters still look to him with total reverence. All three would be helpful to Paul in his journeys to other countries.

"My thoughts then," Drinkwell said. "You know, I couldn't put into words what you might otherwise gain from the following articles about him. I have five in mind—one or two short, the others not so short. I'll just read one after the other. Agreeable to you?"

"Agreeable," Paul answered, readying himself for some selective background knowledge.

"I took this first account from the diary of the Comte de Las Cases, who was part of the small entourage that accompanied Napoleon into exile. The Comte wrote:

> We were all assembled around the emperor, and he was recapitulating these facts with warmth:
>
> For what infamous treatment are we reserved! This is the anguish of death. To injustice and violence they now add insult and protracted torment. If I were so hateful to them, why did they not get rid of me? A few musket balls in my heart or my head would have done the business. And there would at least have been some energy in the crime. Were it not for you. And above all for your wives, I would receive nothing from them but the pay of a private soldier. How can the monarchs of Europe permit the sacred character of sovereignty to be violated in my person? Do they not see that they are, with their own hands, working their own destruction at St. Helena? I entered their capitols victorious and, had I cherished such sentiments, what would have become of them? They styled me their brother, and I had become so by the choice of the people, the sanction of victory, the character of religion, and the alliances of their policy and their blood. Do they imagine that the good sense of nations is blind to their conduct? And what do they expect from it? At all events, make your

> complaints, gentlemen; let indignant Europe hear them. Complaints from me would be beneath my dignity and character; I must either command or be silent.

"Powerful," Drinkwell said in a sepulchral tone. "At least I think so."

Paul made an entry in his notepad.

"He was certainly controversial," Drinkwell emphasized, "but I admired the man for the good things he did. For what's labeled as less-than-good, I'll leave up to others to decide. But not for some who occasionally pop in here: the mariners, the astronomers, the weathermen. Anyway, let's carry on. In articles number two, three and four, there's the hint of a kind of paranoia or abnormal regression … because he speaks in Italian. Or could it be that the effects of arsenic are working on him? In the first of the three, we have—and pardon my Italian—'*A questa casa. O in questo luogo tristo, non voglio niente di lu'.*"

> I hate this Longwood House. The sight of it makes me melancholy. Let him put me in some place where there is shade, verdure, and water. Here it either blows a furious wind, loaded with rain and fog, che mi taglia l'anima; or, if that is wanting, il sole mi brucia il cervello, through the want of shade when I go out.

"For the next one, I'm no psychiatrist, but you be the judge":

> Man loves the supernatural. He meets deception halfway. The fact is that everything about us is a miracle. Strictly speaking, there are no phenomena, for in nature everything is a phenomenon: my existence is a phenomenon; this log that is being put in the chimney is a phenomenon; my intelligence, my faculties, are phenomena; for they all exist, yet we cannot define them. I leave you here, and I am in Paris, entering the Opera; I bow to the spectators, I hear the acclamations, I see the actors, I hear the music. Now if I can span the space from St. Helena, why not that of the centuries? Why should I not see the future like the past? Would the one be more extraordinary, more marvelous than the others? No, but in fact it is not so.

"And the next is somewhat long, but exceptional. You'll hear grandeur and grandiosity. The first half of it is like a history lesson. Also, as an example of possible paranoia, you'll see that he never uses "I" or "me"; rather, he uses his own name!"

> You want to know the treasures of Napoleon? They are enormous, it is true, but in full view. Here they are: the splendid harbor of Antwerp, that

of Flushing, capable of holding the largest fleets; the docks and dikes of Dunkirk, of Havre, of Nice; the gigantic harbor of Cherbourg; the harbor works of Venice; the great roads from Antwerp to Amsterdam, from Mainz to Metz, from Bordeaux to Bayonne; the passes of the Simplon, of Mont Cenis, of Mont Genevre, of the Corniche, that gave four openings through the Alps; in that alone, you might reckon 800 millions. The roads from the Pyrenees to the Alps, from Parma to Spezzia, from Savona to Piedmont; the bridges of Jena, of Austerlitz, of the Arts, of Sevres, of Tours, of Lyons, of Turin, of the Isere, of the Durance, of Bordeaux, of Rouen; the canal from the Rhine to the Rhone, joining the waters of Holland to the Mediterranean; the canal that joins the Scheldt and the Somme, connecting Amsterdam and Paris; that which joins the Rance and the Vilaine; the canal of Arles, of Pavia, of the Rhine; the draining of the marches of Bourgoing, of the Citentin, of Rochefort; the rebuilding of most of the churches pulled down during the Revolution, the building of new ones; the construction of many industrial establishments for putting an end to pauperism; the construction of the Louvre, of the public granaries, of the Bank, of the canal of the Ourcq; the water system of the city of Paris, the numerous sewers, the quays, the embellishments and monuments of

> that great city; the public improvements of Rome; the re-establishment of the manufactories of Lyons. Fifty millions spent on repairing and improving the Crown residences; sixty millions' worth of furniture placed in the palaces of France and Holland, at Turin, at Rome; sixty millions' worth of Crown diamonds, all of it the money of Napoleon; even the Regent, the only missing one of the old diamonds of the Crown of France, purchased from Berlin Jews with whom it was pledged for three millions; the Napoleon Museum, valued at more than 400 millions. These are monuments to confound calumny. History will relate that all this was accomplished in the midst of continuous wars. Without raising a loan, and with the public debt actually decreasing day by day.

"Really though—isn't that something? History, his own money, improvements, dealing with religion, including Jewish? But let's not dwell on all that. I'd like to give a sample of the love letters he wrote. I'm sure you know he had many lovers through the years: Josephine, Marie Louise. Desiree, Pauline, Marie Walewska, Mademoiselle Georges, Giuseppina Grassini, Madame de Stael. And, most important, Lady Ashley Beckett, near whom he was later buried. I don't want to get into that, either, except to remind you that she was a top executive with the East India Company and was constantly smuggled into seeing him right here on this island. Here's a letter he wrote to

Josephine. It exemplifies a certain sensitivity in the man, as if it were written by a poet":

> To Josephine: I have not spent a day without loving you; I have not spent a night without embracing you; I have not so much as drunk a single cup of tea without cursing the pride and ambition which force me to remain separated from the moving spirit of my life. In the midst of my duties, whether I am at the head of my army or inspecting the camps, my beloved Josephine stands alone in my heart. Occupies my mind, fills my thoughts. If I am moving away from you with the speed of the Rhone torrent, it is only that I might see you again more quickly. If I rise to work in the middle of the night, it is because this may hasten by a matter of days the arrival of my sweet love. Josephine! Josephine! Remember that I have sometimes said to you: Nature has endowed me with a virile and decisive character. It has built yours out of lace and gossamer.

"Now I'll finish these binder pieces with a surprise. It's a long quote taken from your own book!"

"My book?"

"Yes—*Napoleon's Final Defeat.* I can't resist reading it to you because I like hearing the words myself. You probably know most of this by heart, and it doesn't add to what you're here to find out, but okay to go forward with it?"

Paul wrinkled his nose as if trying to sniff the essence of what Drinkwell was saying, while the parallel creases above Vincent's nose became more pronounced.

"I can't guess what part of the book you have in mind, so tell me," Paul finally said.

"The introduction."

"All of it?"

"All of it. They're your words. It's you speaking. Not only informative but lots of poignancy between the lines. Go forward?"

Paul ran a finger around his collar before responding: "Oh, alright … go forward."

> I have visited neither Longwood House nor the emperor's former grave, but I have read about them, studied photographs and film and consulted with other historians who have made the difficult voyage to St. Helena. What follows came from a distillation of all the above. The principal characters in Napoleon's entourage on St. Helena were Louis-Joseph Marchand, his personal valet; Count Charles Tristan de Montholon, his aide-de-camp; Henri Bertrand, his grand Marshall; de Montholon and Bertrand's wives; Count Emmanuel Las Cases, his secretary and literary advisor; Gaspard Gourgaud, his orderly officer;

and confidant, Franceschi Cipriani. In addition, three or more physicians attended Napoleon during his six years of exile (1815-1821), the most important of whom were Francesco Antommarchi, Barry O'Meara and Alexander Arnott. It was Dr. Antommarchi who performed the autopsy on the emperor in Longwood's Billiard Room and Dr. O'Meara who coaxed him to spend time gardening.

If someone were spiking the emperor's wine with the intention of murder, that person logically came from this group. But we must also toss in the British governor of the island, Sir Hudson Lowe. Their mutual antipathy was a poorly kept secret and, in addition, Lowe was in constant fear that Napoleon would escape captivity.

The property's well-maintained gardens are said to be a near duplicate of those that existed during his exile. They feature the original pools, trees and various flowers reportedly seeded by the emperor himself.

The Billiard Room, the first you come upon at the front entrance, was also the one that served as a reception room, map room and a retreat where Napoleon would spend endless hours playing billiards. It is painted in its original green color with black Greek design background. In one of the shuttered windows is a small round cutout through which he allegedly spied on the English Guards. The room contains two display cases containing among other things: the Legion of Honor and Iron Cross of Italy; one of his snuffboxes; a lock of his hair; billiard balls; a small infantry sword; miniatures of the King of Rome; and a Sevres medallion showing Napoleon and Marie-Louise, his second wife and the one who bore him his only child, a son. The room also contains a white marble bust of the emperor, the wooden world globe he used for some of his writings and the billiard table.

Some of the other rooms are: a living room where Napoleon died on May 5, 1821 in his small canopied campaign bed. Here we find his death mask, portraits of Marie-Louise and his first wife, Josephine, and several furniture pieces; a study containing more original furniture and copies of Napoleon's frock coat and hat; his bedroom with its simple furnishings; the bathroom containing the large copper tub in which he would soak for hours, often reading and writing; the valet's bedroom stocked with personal letters, books, medallions and drawings; the library displaying samples of Napoleon's reference books; and the Will Room where he drew up his will in April 1821.

Within the beautiful Valley of the Tomb, a metallic fence surrounds the burial area and a cement slab is positioned atop it. A variety of trees

> adorns the valley, and I cannot improve on the government of St. Helena's concise commentary regarding their historical significance: "His tomb remains there to this day although his body was later exhumed and taken to France. The twelve cypress trees that surround the tomb were planted in 1840 in memory of Napoleon's twelve great victories. The Norfolk pines were planted when France became the owner of the valley, the olive tree was planted by the Prince of Wales in 1925, and the wild olive was planted by Prince Phillip in 1957. In 1921, an olive tree was planted in the name of Marshall Foch to mark the centenary of the death of Napoleon.

Drinkwell caught his breath throughout a protracted silence. At the end of it, Paul said, "I can't believe I wrote all that."

"And you did a wonderful job," the constable said.

Both men looked at Vincent, who stifled a yawn as he chimed in, "Very, **very** wonderful."

"I realize you're in a hurry to leave," Drinkwell said, "but let me share some random thoughts about Napoleon and gangsters and religion. For two centuries, he served as a stabilizing factor for gangsters' activities. Saying it another way: early on during his rule, he was their hero and this carried on for generations. He tolerated religion, no matter the denomination, and so did the gangsters. Not as many today, but plenty enough. The bottom line is that the common denominator among many of today's criminals is a warm feeling about the emperor.

"And a few comments about religion alone. Specifically, about its value beyond a belief, or praying, or heaven, and so forth. There's a flood of new scientific evidence from all parts of the world that faith strengthens resilience to stress, including illnesses. Like diabetes and heart disease in your country and Mexico and Japan and Greece and Thailand and Saudi Arabia, for example. Even in secular Denmark. How do I know all this? From talks with my histarians. Understand, these aren't secret talks, so they can be out in the open. And why am I telling you this? Because it may come in handy in your worldwide discussions."

Each man craned forward and put his palms over his lips as if in prayer but really in silent contemplation.

"So that's that," Drinkwell said. "You have great patience and I thank you for it. I hope you've taken something of value from your visit with me, especially about histarians and the relationship between Napoleon and religion."

"That we have, Thatch." Paul did some underlining in his notepad. "The two most important sentences were when you spoke of Napoleon rebuilding churches that were destroyed during the Revolution and his building new ones; plus the sentence about his being styled a brother because of the character of religion.

"But before we leave, I'd like to get back to the histarians you just mentioned. Why did you become one and even become their leader?"

"The answer isn't complicated, Paul. Twofold … to know I'm helping out in worthy causes and to satisfy historical curiosity."

Paul arose slowly from his chair as did Vincent. "In-and-out, Thatch," Paul said. "I'm sorry to say it but …"

"I understand."

"Please accept our appreciation, and let's keep in touch."

The three men shook hands warmly and the two visitors left the building. Walking toward the car, Paul gazed skyward as his memory was tweaked. He remembered an earlier time when he read extensively about weather patterns and he'd forgotten little of it. He held Vincent back by the shoulder and said, "See those clouds up there? They're low. Well, there are three types of low clouds and just bear with me. I'm not losing it, but as I say, bear with me. One is the stratus cloud that makes a heavy, leaden sky. Two is the nimbostratus, the real rain clouds. And three are the stratocumulus ones that spread out in a rolling or puffy layer. What's up there are clearly stratus clouds, so there's no sign of rain."

Paul flashed a triumphant smile and let Vincent's shoulder go.

"You should have been a professional weather forecaster," Vincent said. "One who could mow down a complainer with a karate chop."

They drove to the hotel, collected their belongings and checked out at 11:30. Their decision about what to do next was easy because they were both hungry. Well remembering Ann's Place, a restaurant near the dock, they headed there. It hadn't changed one bit in two years: quaint, in the middle of an expansive garden and featuring a variety of popular "Helena" dishes such as curry, pumpkin stew, fishcakes, pilau, black pudding and coconut fingers.

It was noisy, jammed to overcapacity and filled with pleasant food aromas. They each ordered fishcakes and black pudding, and initially raced through the meal as though they were late for a job interview. But when Paul checked his watch, he realized they could make the two p.m. sailing time with ease, and they slowed down.

They set sail at 2:10 p.m. The ship was faster than customary and they arrived on Ascension Island at 8 p.m. the next day. Paul was enormously pleased that the St. Helena excursion was worth the time and trouble. He had received the information he wanted: assurance of histarian help and evidence of Napoleon's use of religion to further his agenda.

Near the end of the sailing, he and Vincent agreed that its many hours of inactivity were more stressful than those filled with uncertainties on land. Paul tried hard to ignore any negative thoughts except for two: he was hoping to have used his karate chop even though the reason why might have involved more than one assailant. "Where are they?" he dramatized. "I'm ready for them. I can duke it out with anybody—wherever and whenever."

It was a feeble attempt to block the second thought: worry about the near future.

Chapter 7

June 9

Next up was Joe Gomez in Argentina. Paul wanted to get a bead on pirates and prostitutes, and Gomez was his man.He was the longtime police chief of Buenos Aires, was fluent in three languages, and had frequently assisted Paul in matters involving not only the city proper but also the likes of Juan Peron and his wife, Eva … better known as Evita.

The phone call to the chief was brief and to the point.

"Joe, it's about the three P's we've talked about so much: prostitution, pirates and Peronism."

"I'd love for you to come down again, Paul. You say you're calling from Ascension Island? That would be … uh … a three-hour time difference. I'm here in my office till six every day, but don't hesitate to contact me by cell phone. At any time, day or night, and I'll come for you."

"Terrific. Vincent will be with me again, and a three-hour time difference registers zero in this scattered brain of mine."

The flight from Ascension Island began at 2 p.m. and ended at the EZE Airport in Buenos Aires six hours later. Paul and Vincent disembarked and Ansel taxied the plane away for refueling. He said he'd be back shortly. On a wall behind the airport's main counter was a large picture of Eva Peron and opposite it, on the counter, was a stack of handouts. Paul took one. He and Vincent then sat on a bench in a side waiting room and he read it. It was titled *The Enduring Legacy of Eva Peron,* was written by Alexander Kathryn Mosca and had been published by Kates-Boylston Publications fifteen years before:

> The massive crowd wailed plaintively … refusing to believe that their beloved Evita could be gone from them forever at the age of thirty-three. To Argentina's poor, she was thought to be saint-like, but to the elite, she was more like Satan incarnate.
>
> She was one of the most complex, paradoxical and enigmatic women in history, who, more than most, embodied a litany of extreme opposites: earthy/ethereal—sacred/profane—good/evil—puritanical/promiscuous.
>
> Fueled by a desire "to be someone", a yearning stoked by a childhood of poverty and shame, she hungered for the respect and acceptance denied her as a child of illegitimacy when such a stigma held grave societal consequences.
>
> Early on, while working as an actress, she was

Eva Duarte. She met and married General Juan Peron, the future president of Argentina. As his wife, she was afforded great respect and wielded much power, a perfect position from which to avenge the many deprivations and humiliations she had suffered at the very same hands of those she now ruled.

It is difficult to reconcile the disparate Evitas that seemed to inhabit her being.

Her complicity in offering asylum to the heinous Nazis, a commiseration born more out of greed than a shared ideology, contrasted dramatically with the unabashed tenderness and utter lack of concern for her own health, when allowing a tubercular to kiss her face, or when comforting a sick or orphaned child.

Her charitable foundation granted favors for the needy and built many hospitals. Yet, as she championed these very human causes, her detractors point out that she simultaneously helped herself to vast sums of money and precious gems—obviously not having a conflict of conscience and ambition.

She envisioned one day being VP on her husband's presidential ticket, a position that would enable her to satisfy her fever for power.

But then, the first signs of illness were evident

in 1950 when she fainted at an official function. From that point on, uterine cancer, surgery, and radiation dominated her life, although she continued a grueling public schedule.

She died in 1952 and for the next 14 years, her well-embalmed body was transferred from place to place—including Spain. Finally, in 1976 she was entombed, without fanfare, inside the Duarte family mausoleum in the Cementerio de la Recoleta, Buenos Aires' preeminent cemetery. Her gravesite, on which a plaque is inscribed with the words, "Don't Cry for Me" in Spanish, is positioned among the most famous names in Argentina's history. It is a peculiar irony that her body now lies eternally surrounded by the country's elite, the very people she so hated in life.

The myth of Evita persists until today, kept alive by a spate of books, a play, a movie, a song and by an enduring interest in this passionate woman who lived a short life of stunning contradictions and loomed larger than life.

The world's attention she captured during her lifetime is now eclipsed only by the iconic status she has realized since her death.

Both men had napped during the entire flight and at the conclusion of reading the handout and putting it in his pocket, they gobbled down sandwiches in the terminal's luncheonette.

Soon after, Paul was sufficiently alert to notice a heavy-set man staring at him from behind a door in the next room.

Paul got up and in a loud voice announced to Vincent: "I need to use the john. Back in a minute."

Familiar with the layout of the airport from previous experiences there, he left through a nearby archway, doubled around and ended up six feet behind the man. The man swirled around, gun in hand, and in one nearly continuous motion, Paul sprung forward and leveled karate chops to the man's wrist and mid-section. The gun fell to the ground as the man cried out and collapsed in pain. Paul was tempted to help him up and interrogate him but quickly realized the gun-toter was in no shape to move or give answers. Paul did, however, examine the man's face, found it contorted and covered in sweat, and concluded that he was of Spanish descent. Ready, willing, able—*and hired*—there in Buenos Aires. He picked up the gun and deposited it in a trash can upon returning to Vincent's side. Paul gave a detailed explanation of what had transpired, even going through the motions of a karate chop, and received the usual praise and a stern warning:

"I've got to tell you, Paul. There'll probably be the same kind of thing at every turn, maybe in every country. I'm afraid the search is alive and whoever is calling the shots means business."

"I agree. Let's just keep our guard up," Paul offered. He tried to appear casual but deep down could hardly hide his concern. He rubbed the "decision scar" under his chin.

When Ansel arrived, Paul gave him the same explanation and asked him to notify the authorities that someone had some kind of seizure and needed help. He then called Gomez on his cell phone to notify him of their arrival.

The police chief showed up at the airport within a half-hour and firm hugs were exchanged. "It's been quite a while," he said. "Welcome, for the fourth time, to the Paris of South America."

He was still wearing his light blue uniform with gold and silver badges prominently displayed. Tall, trim and gray at the temples, he looked and spoke more like a Brooklynite than a South American.

"And a reverse welcome to you, Joe, if there **is** such a phrase."

"Thanks, Paul, and I hope the trip wasn't too tiresome."

"It would have been, but we slept all the way."

Paul determined they could have done some talking right there, but he wanted to flee a scene containing a floored body in an adjoining room. He also decided not to tell Gomez about the gun-toter and the karate chop.

"Can we go to your office?" he asked.

"Sure enough," Gomez replied, picking up one of their luggage pieces and Paul's overstuffed briefcase.

On the drive there, they passed by the Recoleta Cemetery where Evita's body was located. Nearby was the Plaza de Mayo and Casa Rosa where she reportedly spoke from its balcony. Paul couldn't help but remember the movie starring Madonna:

Don't Cry for Me, Argentina. At the same time, it seemed to him that during every occasion when he called on Joe Gomez, Evita came into the picture.

The office was located on the second floor of a tall brick and mortar building. Outside, it was encompassed in a blend of low-level trees and assorted flowers. Sprinklers were operating in the early evening hour and Paul thought that as they passed along the entrance walkway, any flower aroma would have been subdued by the water spray. But such was not the case. Somehow, the aroma was enhanced and Paul commented on it.

"It drifts inside sometimes," Gomez said, "and I enjoy it. I don't know why but it makes me feel young again."

Inside, his office was spacious but cluttered. "Pardon the mess," he said, "but believe me, I know where everything is." They sat in a triangle of straight-back chairs.

"May I offer you a glass of wine?" he asked. "I keep a bottle of our Classic Argentina Malbec over there." He pointed to a small refrigerator on a corner table.

The two visitors nodded.

Gomez removed a bottle from the refrigerator, poured the drinks, handed them each a glass and returned to his chair. He asked the others to rise for a toast, but before he could give it Vincent interceded with, "To Buenos Aires, to its police chief, and to Eva Peron. God rest her soul."

"Hear, hear," all three said. And Gomez followed with, "Thank you, Vincent, but you could have left me out."

They sat back down and Paul began: "I hate to say we're in

a hurry, Joe, but to be honest, we are. I call it an 'in-and-out' visit. The reason is that there's so much on our plate … so much traveling to do. And I apologize."

He waited for a response, hoping it wouldn't be a negative one. It finally came: "You know your schedule best, so don't worry about it."

"Then let's get started," Paul continued. "Why we're here is the same as it was for our trips to Calabria and St. Helena and, coming up, to Gibraltar."

"I'm honored to be included, Paul."

"Well, that's been the history between you and me, and I'm proud of it. But we're here to get your take on certain things, and I'd rather it be in person than by phone … for a number of reasons that I won't go into. As I said when I called, it boiled down to my longtime intention to explore the status of religions in diverse countries. What I call 'the progress and legitimacy of 'religion.' But then I was talked into adding how it's related to crimes. A whole bunch of crimes like drug dealing, illegal weapons, loan sharking, forgery, extortion, bootlegging, financial fraud. Even selling human organs and vicious murders. I can't stress the relationship enough, Joe. Some pastors who are aware of certain criminal activities, for example, accept prostitutes provided by mobsters, and in return the pastors keep their mouths shut about the whole thing. And I, myself, coined the trilogy of prostitution, pirates and Peronism. Can we discuss them one at a time?"

"Yes, let's. To begin with, as you know, the first one is legal throughout our country, but **organized** prostitution isn't.

Like brothels or pimping or prostitution rings. Usually, whores become whores because they need the money for survival."

"Wait!" Paul exclaimed, nearly jumping up. "I just thought of something. Would it help by speaking to those prostitute gals who got arrested? What were their names—Marlene and Velda? I don't know the full story, but are they out of prison yet?" Paul checked his watch. "No," he said, "Let's not after all.Would only eat up time. Maybe you can speak for them now and then later we can get together with them."

Gomez looked confounded and said, "Understand Paul, I've never … uh … frequented them—Marlene Kesler and Velda Conklin—but I do know their history and I can combine it with piracy. They were accused of developing a prostitution ring and then using it to work with known pirates who forced their way onto cruise ships."

"And passengers paid good money for a night's screwing?" Paul asked.

"That's about it. Sometimes all day."

"Paul, maybe we should include Somalia," Vincent said.

"Ah, yes … pirate-land. We'll see."

Their wine glasses were half empty except for Paul's. His wine was gone.

Gomez noticed. "More?" he asked.

"No, better not. So in other countries, we'll study what you just said. But how about here? Is this arrangement very common?"

"I'll say. Very much so. I'm investigating it all the time."

"And religion, per se? A very religious country or just so-so?"

"**Very** religious."

"Religious but with a caveat, don't you think?" Paul had used the word advisedly and sensed that the chief understood.

Gomez gave a brief nod. "I'm beginning to feel guilty," he said, "but there's just so much I can control."

"Don't feel guilty," Paul said. He reached over to pat the chief's hand. "Your reputation is unequaled, or we wouldn't be here."

Gomez took a swig of his wine, finishing the glass.

"Moving on, Joe, to the Perons. Especially Eva. Could you talk about her?"

"I could talk about her all day, even though I have mixed feelings about her. But because it involves some serious stuff, I wouldn't want to mess up. Better I read from an article I kept about both of them. It was apparently written toward the end of World War II. Someone gave it to me years ago, but I forget who. After you called and indicated we should include them in our discussion, I found it on a closet shelf. And here it is."

He removed a folded sheet of paper from an inside pocket, unfolded it, and read as follows:

> Juan Domingo Peron spent most of his youth in the region of Patagonia. He graduated from a military academy and by now (1944), has become Vice-President of Argentina.

Strictly speaking, throughout his career thus far, most observers feel his political skills outweigh his military skills. Not long ago, he stayed on good terms with Jews and Nazis but this has changed as the war is nearing its end.

Six years ago, he went to Europe simply as a military observer, spent time in Italy, Spain and Germany and while in Italy, became impressed with Benito Mussolini. It is not clear why he chose these countries, but they so happen to form the Axis alliance in Europe. Some of its leaders have come to be known as war criminals and have sentenced many innocent citizens to death. Those who escaped such cruelty sneaked away to Argentina and to other South American countries. Why here, you may ask. Three reasons are given (and rather weak ones). One—our country was colonized by Spain. Two—Spanish is our official language. And three—much of our population is of Italian or German descent.

Meanwhile, Peron has been associating with one Eva Duarte, and the general consensus is that their marriage is not too far off. She has had a successful career in radio, movies and the theater and soon won the affection of the Argentine people. Born in 1919 as an illegitimate child, she became a prostitute to survive and to obtain those roles. She also became a mistress to army officers.

> And due to her ties with prominent Nazis, it is alleged that she has paved the way for the prevalence of fascism across Latin America.
>
> Known as "Evita" by her adoring followers, it is alleged that because of her ties to Nazis, Switzerland would come into the equation. She and a longtime friend and a Swiss diplomat were to arrange a relationship between the Central Banks of Argentina and Switzerland, business contacts that would eventually advance both Argentine commerce and the relocation of Hitler's henchmen. The bottom line is that her flirtations with the Nazis will no doubt facilitate a formal Swiss-Argentine-Nazi collaboration. And there is no doubt that when she and Juan Peron marry, they will in effect become Argentina's "Populist Power Couple".

Paul and Vincent had been motionless as they listened. Paul was the first to comment: "That's the second article in the past hour. I read one and now I heard one. Both very interesting but this one was better—more informative. Has more facts than I was aware of—facts that will come in handy for us."

"I agree," Vincent said.

"But I'm not totally clear on something," Paul said. "Why is so much attention still being paid to Eva Peron. Even to this day. The only thing I can conclude is that since her shenanigans were felt all over the world, could she have been a role model for other cheaters and money-hungry leaders? To say nothing of the reasons for her sexual performances."

"And in this connection," Gomez said, "do you know what the strangest thing she demanded was?"

"No. What?"

"To be paid not in money but in diamonds."

"Wait. I vaguely remember …" Paul removed the handout from his pocket, found the sentence he had in mind, and read it: "… she simultaneously helped herself to vast sums of money and precious gems—obviously not having a conflict of conscience and ambition."

"Gems. Diamonds. That was sixty-five years ago, Paul. I'm told that some are still hidden in a gold box over in the basement of the Pink House. You remember that place?"

"Oh yeah … very well."

"I even read a book you wrote about it, where you went on and on about cobwebs and spiders. I'm in the book a lot, too. And so is Marlene Kesler."

"*Diamonds and Pirates*. I remember a good deal about what I wrote."

"Tell us some of it," the chief said, "Go ahead. It's interesting."

"Well, you asked for it. At the Pink House, we walked toward a single basement door that was enveloped in vines. Two thin cobwebs spanned the width of the door. It looked as though it hadn't been opened in years. You unlocked the door and we had to bend our heads to enter.

"As I recall, we found a small carton labeled *Eva's Personal Effects* in Spanish. It was in an adjoining room. And here's the important point: against the opposite wall were about ten large cartons. From what we could see, the words *Not to be Displayed* were scrawled across them.

"We ended up opening the small carton and sifted through a collection of items: clothing, cosmetics, silverware, candles, photographs, medals, epaulets. But no gold box of diamonds."

"She must have had more of all these things," Gomez interjected, "but these probably had special meaning for her."

"I remember agreeing," Paul said, "and I suggested that the gold box we were looking for could have been there at one time. Or that maybe it was in one of the big ones against the wall. But we never opened them to look. Stupid. And you mentioned that I went on and on about cobwebs and spiders. I don't know what came over me, but I sure did."

"I can underline that," Vincent said.

Paul stiffened to attention. "Want to hear some of it?" he asked.

Gomez hesitated but Vincent responded with, "Go ahead. I do know you once made a study of them, so for me anyway, it's worthwhile hearing again."

Paul then said that all cobwebs were made by spiders and dust particles. He followed with a detailed description of various classes of spiders, spending the most time on black widows, cellar ones and the jumping kind.

When he had finished his little spiel, Gomez said, "Just a reminder or two: the reason we never opened the ten big cartons was because we smelled the exhaust fumes of a car outside, so we beat it out a back door. But before that, what we'd deduced was that someone could have entered there recently and stolen the gold box. Even someone like Marlene. She might have stored it there but then wanted it for a purpose. Who's to say whether or not she was the 'someone' in the first place."

"And her getting a key would have been easy," Paul said. "Remember what she did for a living? But why store them there? Because she idolizes Evita and was trying to be like her in every way?"

"You captured it," Gomez said. "And I know I'm skipping around but I've never bothered to check for the diamonds since then, and I guess nobody else has or word would have leaked out about it. So should we take a look again?"

"Absolutely. Right now?"

"No. I think it's too late and we'd be rushing things. Perfect for overlooking them. I'd vote for the morning. Can you stay over? You know, the Sheraton Buenos Aires across the street, where you've stayed before."

"Okay, we're game. And Joe—I'm so sorry we didn't look inside the other cartons. It might have helped prove that she was getting paid in diamonds."

"Amen. Now I have one last question before you check in at the hotel. Are you still interested in spiders?" Gomez gave Vincent's knee a tug.

"I hate them but, yes, they're interesting."

"I would think so. Look at your Hollywood. Didn't they

make a movie called 'Spiderman'?"

"Uh-huh."

"I thought they did—and it was a box office success."

The next morning, Paul and Vincent rushed through breakfast at the hotel and, on the way to checking out, were met by Gomez who was waiting for them in the lobby.

"Good sleep?" he asked.

"Pretty good," Paul said. "I wish we weren't in such a hurry, though."

"If I were your father, old buddy, I'd tell you to slow down. Just about everything in this world can wait."

Paul's expression reflected full acceptance of the advice.

On the drive to the Pink House, Paul said, "We'll just check those ten cartons, and then we're off to Gibraltar. That meet with your approval, Joe?"

"Yes. I'm so glad you stayed over. Now we can resolve this thing, once and for all."

At the House, they found neither cobwebs nor spiders at its basement entrance, and none of the three offered an explanation. Inside, they marched right into the room containing the cartons. They opened them individually and in every single carton, they found diamonds and other precious gems arranged in layers separated by pieces of cardboard. On the uppermost cardboard, one or another of the following inscriptions was printed in Spanish:

Switzerland—designer labels from Chanel
Damiani—handmade in Italy since 1924
The German Cross

"The three nations!" Paul said breathlessly. "I could have predicted it. So now we have our answer. For some reason, Switzerland wanted it that way, and the same for Italy and Germany. All three wanted full credit, so Evita obliged."

Paul didn't say it but he felt that what they had uncovered was conclusive evidence that she had dealt with the three countries in an illegal way. A way that involved payoffs.

Gomez drove them to the airport and, after good wishes and hearty handshakes, they took off for Gibraltar by way of Ascension Island where they landed to refuel. Paul thought it surprising that the island was exactly midway between Buenos Aires and Gibraltar. He couldn't determine why, but he took it as a good sign.

Chapter 8

While Ansel and Vincent were tending to refueling at the island's Wideawake Airfield, Paul sauntered into a small building which, from previous experience, he knew housed a computer that was available to British soldiers, but also to the general public. He was familiar with what he planned on reading but wanted to refresh his memory.

"What the hell," he murmured as he sat before the computer, "might as well. All I do is read or listen." He downloaded the following:

> The Rock of Gibraltar is a limestone promontory of the British overseas territory of Gibraltar. The territory has a population of about thirty thousand. Most residents are descended from Italian, Maltese, Portuguese and Spanish settlers. Others are descended from British military personnel who were formerly stationed there. Almost all inhabitants live in apartments in the

town of Gibraltar and the workers are primarily employed by the government, by dockyards or in jobs related to the tourist industry.

As for the Rock itself, it is nearly fourteen-hundred-feet high and is located off the southwestern tip of Europe on the Iberian Peninsula. It is considered Crown property of the United Kingdom, forms a peninsula that juts out into the Strait of Gibraltar and borders Spain. Occupying nearly all of Gibraltar's 2.3 square miles, most of its uppermost area is covered by a nature reserve where about two-hundred-fifty Barbary macaques reside. These animals—the only wild population of monkeys in Europe—along with a labyrinthine network of tunnels—attract numerous tourists every year. The underground tunnels are known as the galleries and the Great Siege Tunnels.

These underground tunnels have a unique history. They were first dug in the late seventeen-hundreds. The British commander wanted to create the potential for cannon fire upon Spanish batteries in the area below the north face of the Rock. The siege lasted about four years, and during that span the British had constructed six such embrasures and mounted four cannons.

The so-called Galleries were constructed later on. Comprised of an entire system of halls, passages and embrasures measuring nearly a thousand feet long, they too are a popular tourist attraction. From that location, visitors are able to view the Bay of Gibraltar, the isthmus and Spain itself.

All told, the Rock contains over one hundred caves. The most prominent and most visited is St. Michael's Cave, situated halfway up the western slope of the Rock. Within it is another area called Cathedral Cave, thought to be bottomless and therefore an underground link to Africa. This has never been substantiated. Cathedral Cave now serves frequently as an auditorium for concerts, ballet and drama presentations. The beauty of its crystallized surroundings draws raves from its numerous attendees. They are particularly drawn to a centuries-old stalagmite that became so heavy, it dropped and landed on its side at the far end of the chamber.

From a military standpoint, it was fortified by over thirty thousand British soldiers and sailors during World War II, thus playing a key role in the defense of shipping routes in the Mediterranean. In 1942, during the war, the Allies launched an attack from Gibraltar against German and Italian forces in North Africa. And as recently as 1997, it was revealed that Britain had concocted a secret plan to hide service men in the Rock's tunnels in case the

Germans captured it. It was named "Operation Tracer" and had the radio capability to report all enemy movement. A six-man team remained under cover for over two years before they were disbanded and returned to civilian life.

Such a history of sieges and military action is responsible for the popular saying "Solid as the Rock of Gibraltar." Technically speaking, it is not based on the solidity of the Rock itself but rather on the action and dedication of the servicemen assigned to it.

Juan Carlos Saltanban, the last of Paul's confidants, lived and worked less than a stone's throw away from The Rock. Paul and Vincent landed at Gib Airport and, after phoning Juan and being told he would anxiously await their arrival, they walked the short distance to his complex on Catalan Bay. They wanted to talk to him primarily about his Synchronic Action Device or SAD, and whether or not it might assist in their "Cover for Crime" adventure.

Temperatures had dropped into the low fifties as they breathed the fresh nippy air of early summer and came upon the complex. Paul well remembered its shabby gray exterior when he was there before, but now found it painted a glistening green that smarted his eyes. And as they approached the same set of ebony doors that opened onto an elongated balcony, he hoped that the SAD had been improved upon; that it had become the more sophisticated instrument that Juan foresaw.

The doors were unlocked, but once through them, a loud bell resounded throughout the balcony, though no one answered its call. As he looked down over the railing, Paul was as impressed as he was in 2013, only more so. The number of interconnected rooms had doubled and each was occupied by a female worker who was working at a computer. They wore green blouses whose backside bore an emblem depicting a black silhouette of The Rock. Paul couldn't swear to it but they seemed to be acting in unison.

The contents of each room hadn't changed: a beech-colored swivel chair with a waterfall seat edge and contoured backrest; teak side tables that held a computer, printer and copying machine; a huge shredder; and a table with a glass top, below which a powder-coated steel frame rested on cubic pillars.

Paul, more won over than before, suppressed a smile as he whispered to Vincent, "They look and act like robots."

Vincent echoed the thought.

Paul didn't say it but wondered if Juan was controlling his workers with his SAD. With what Paul had in mind, he hoped so.

Suddenly, Juan's voice emanated from an overhead speaker: "Welcome, gentlemen. I shall be there in a minute on the dot."

Paul was tempted to respond but held back, instead deciding to use the minute in a silent reconstruction of their past. As they took seats on a side bench, Paul so informed Vincent and then began a brief reconstruction as if he were writing it all down.

> *We first met four years ago at a scientific symposium in Berlin. I was taken with his grasp of science and intrigued with his refusal to use words that had contractions. When asked about his background, he stated that he was once the president of Radonia in South America but soon gave up politics and moved to his present location because he liked the protection it was afforded by the nearby Rock. He even composed a song titled, "In the Shadow of The Rock."*

Then Saltanban appeared out of nowhere. "Greetings," he said.

"Good to be here, Juan," Paul said.

"Thanks for having us," Vincent added as he introduced himself.

Their handshakes were forceful.

"Come down to my studio," Juan said, leading the way along the balcony, its right wall that of glass partitions through which plush meadowland and attractive hillside homes could be seen.

They entered the hallway to a pair of rooms. As he led them past the first one, Paul noticed that its door had a steel beam across the front with a padlock at the end of it. They arrived at the far room, tiny and crowded with stacks of papers on several tables and on the floor itself. Three wooden chairs were scattered about, two of them tilted by the paper stacks. Juan cleared his throat and said with a touch of fanfare, "What is it you Americans might announce? Voila, my cubbyhole?"

In the bright light, Paul felt that their host hadn't changed, except his goatee was grayer and his stoop was slightly more pronounced. Tall and hefty, he was closing in on age sixty and was no doubt using dye to darken a head of curly, dense hair. He wore square, wire-rimmed glasses that were attached to a red and blue chain. On each finger was the expected gold signet ring, a "J" in script on the left as you faced him and a "C" on the right. Paul recalled once asking him why there was not simply a "JC" on them and the response was, "No, no. These are for 'Juan Carlos'. Your way is reserved for someone more important than I—Jesus Christ."

Paul also recalled his reference to Radonia. And asking him how he got started in telecommunications before the short stint in politics. Not much varied from the way he expressed it years ago. He spoke of his interpreting smoke signals; of the Sumerians who developed the first known system of writing; the Romans who started the first newspaper; the English who introduced the first known pencil; the French who developed photographs; and the Canadians who put the first radio together. Next he dwelled on three Americans who invented the telegraph, the telephone and the phonograph: Morse, Bell and Edison.

He said, "The telegraph was a very important instrument during your Civil War for both your press and the armies of both sides. And it helped at your stock exchange and at your railroads."

Paul became more attentive than he expected because he'd suffered through it all before.

"You have heard enough?" Juan asked.

"No, do continue."

"How about you, Vincent?"

"Do continue."

Paul appeared as though he was strengthening his resolve to seek all he could from Saltanban, while Vincent looked like someone suffering from an unfulfilled promise.

Saltanban went on: "What did I plan on next? Ah … the telephone! You know, two funny things. One, the sound a telephone makes is a bell, and Alexander Graham Bell discovered it in the late 19th century. And two, one never thinks of it, but at the beginning there were no switchboards. They came during the next year. Then came dial phones, service between countries, and the thing that I am most interested in. Do you know what it is?"

"Public speaking?" Paul said. He paused before saying: "I am sorry … no, **I'm** sorry … but I couldn't resist. Keep going."

"Alright then. I am most interested in commercial satellites. Think of these as relay stations. But I have said enough about these devices. I am afraid I ramble once again. Some other time perhaps I might further discuss the radio and the phonograph. So now, you understand, it is all related—all these forms—and all these countries that somehow wanted to—how do you say it—wanted to get into the act. Anyway, we are now up to what I am most interested in: plans about advanced telecommunications."

During all the speaking and all the listening, Paul had his mind set on the SAD in the other room. But, not wanting to rush things for fear it might disrupt Juan's eventual cooperation—and the reason for their visit—he played along. "Meaning what?" he inquired.

"Meaning what? I must get even more technical. Bell Laboratories discovered the transistor; Xerox the copier; and Corning Glass the first optical fiber that could be used for long-range communication. Fiber optics, you know, uses a laser to send signals through glass or plastic. Sending signals? Ahh! My company used to deal with fiber optics and satellites primarily, but we have more recently concentrated on cybernetics. I wanted to advance knowledge about how information is transmitted by the control mechanism of machines and the nervous system of human beings, and that is where my Synchronic Action Device comes in. Should we go see it now?"

"Yes," Paul said, "but before that, how about computers? You never said anything about them, but where do you feel they're taking us? Do you feel the same way about them?"

"Because you told me when you called that you would be investigating international crime, I have definite thoughts about computers. The crime-computer link. I am concerned. The Internet with its encrypted messages can be such a tool of secrecy that crime of every kind will become electronic and will take place once the decision is made. Drug operations, fraud, embezzlement, prostitution, blackmail, government conspiracies, military coups, murder. Much is possible now, but it can get worse, all due to computers. In the matter of terrorism, for instance.

"And even in business or education or government work, face-to-face meetings may no longer occur. A computer will be a sword with a double edge. Email. The Internet—an Information Super-Highway, but one that is filled with—what are they called? Potholes? It is the secrecy that is my worry. Split second. Cheap. Yes, computers are good but can become evil. I am afraid the whole planet has an analog intelligence dealing with a digital threat. That is how I view it. End of ramble. Now let us go see my model—the SAD."

As they left for the next room, Paul nearly voiced amazement over his host's knowledge, but instead asked, "Is it bigger now?"

"No, smaller."

"Smaller?"

"Yes. The information it was feeding me was unclear. But by removing a wire here, a switch there, it now gives me clarity. What did you say you wanted it to do?"

"I'll follow your question with a question. Can it help identify a specific telephone caller from a church to a specific criminal?"

"No, it does not work that way. I would need names to begin with. And then the SAD would verify the names. And if you have an address, it can verify that, too."

Paul rubbed the palms of his hands. "Perfect then," he said. "It's got me thinking, Juan. We don't need you. Just lend us your model."

Saltanban's empty facial expression was brief and he led them to the next door, removed the padlock and lifted away the steel beam.

There, on a table in the center of the room was a box with a sliding front panel and a golden handle at the top. He slid the panel aside and proudly revealed a device the size of a small sewing machine. It sported row upon row of miniature screws, nuts, bolts, washers, dials, clips, hooks, pins, needles, knobs, levers, tubing, eyelets, springs, brads, clasps, staples, hoses, chains, sprockets, cables, valves, blades, belts, bushings, drills, rods, grommets, pumps, compressors, wheels, shafts, hammers, buttons, fasteners, discs, latches, graces, tacks, hinges, cords, locks, and plugs.

It was a toss-up as to who was the more impressed—Paul for the second time or Vincent for the first time.

"You're right," Paul said, "it's smaller."

"And smarter," Juan said. "So you think I can be of service to you. I mean me and my model here?"

"No doubt about it. Eventually, I hope we'll have some names and addresses that will need verification. I'll let you know."

They returned to Juan's studio, he summoned one of his workers for coffee and doughnuts, and while consuming them, the three men shared a mutual satisfaction with the past half-hour.

At the ebony doors, Juan said, "Gentlemen, I will be

waiting for your call and I hope I can be of service."

Paul led the warm handshakes and said, "Juan, when the time arrives, I know you'll be playing a key role in our grand design."

PART TWO

Chapter 9

June 13

It was time for the second edition of Discovery Notes, beginning with the trip to St. Helena. On the flight back to his home in East Falmouth, Paul again relied on his memory plus snippets he had occasionally written on scraps of paper:

> Arrived at James Bay. Call to Leon to assure us of later trip back to Ascension Island. Difficult connection. Napoleon Street and red car. Creditable man passes it on. Drive by familiar sights on way to Farm Lodge Country House Hotel. Easy registration. Write-up about histarians. Arrive Police Service Building. Constable Thatcher Drinkwell. His description. Discussion re his accommodation re histarian role. He promises accommodation. The way histarians work. Napoleon and Fabio Calderone discussed. Loose-leaf binders mentioned. He reads re birds. His thoughts re Napoleon. What Comte wrote. Nap's

words. My read of Napoleon. Drink. on Nap., gangsters and religion relationship. Why current gangsters revere Nap. Why Drink. became histarians' leader. Re. clouds. Ann's place for lunch. Sail back to Ascension. Value of trip as positive. B. Aires and Joe Gomez. Article re Eva Peron. Armed man spotted. Given karate chop. Gomez arrives. Described. Drive past key sights to his office. Bldg described. Wine. Explanation of 3 P's. Marlene, Velda, pirates and cruise ships. Gomez reads Peron article. Evita still role model for current money-grubbers. Her preference for diamonds over cash. Pink House, gold box, cobwebs and spiders. Ten cartons containing diamonds from 3 foreign countries. To Gibraltar and Saltanban. The Rock in article. SAD mentioned. Description Salt.'s complex. Reconstruction of past. Salt. Appears. To his studio. His description. Extensive Salt. talk re communication, etc. The SAD seen and described. What it can and will do. He promises cooperation.

Paul now had the experience of his last twelve days to assist in writing the book, but he wasn't ready for it yet. He had phoned Leon about supplying the limo to drive Vincent from Joint Base Cape Cod to his home near Harvard Yard and to drive himself to East Falmouth.

Arriving there at mid-afternoon, he couldn't wait to settle

in at his man cave desk and review his priorities. But uppermost was a call to Sylvie at her workplace, even before he unpacked and freshened up.

"Paul!" she shouted, nearly separating the receiver end of the phone from his ear, "I was about to make my usual call."

"I'm back, darling," he said, "and what's this about your usual call?"

"I've phoned there every day, and boy, continual no-answers are tough to take."

"Well, here I am and I'll save going into everything until you get home."

"Okay, but at least you can tell me now—are you happy with the way things went?"

"Yeah, very much so. Each man—Fabio, Gomez, Drinkwell, Saltanban—they all provided what I asked for: advice, information . . whatever … you name it. So how about dinner out, Syl? We can go over it all at the restaurant."

"Sounds good. I should be home by 5:30."

Each made the sound of a kiss into the mouthpiece and then Paul unpacked and freshened up. As he did so, it dawned on him that he hadn't had a solid meal in ages. But, except for obtaining a supply of crackers, he kept away from the kitchen, not wanting to ruin what awaited them at Bonfiore's.

At his desk, he munched and thought. Thought and munched. Munched and thought. He wanted to get straight how he should proceed. And where. He settled on those countries where he'd had the most experience, knew his way around, and had made alliances with key law enforcement personnel in all of them. Not with religious leaders for there were too many of them. Since the better part of his confidants had stressed the relationship between some pastors and some gangsters, wouldn't his securing information from law enforcement make solid sense? For law enforcers generally knew who the gangsters were. And the gangsters obviously knew who the pastors were—which ones were partaking of the prostitutes that the gangsters were supplying.

First of all, though—what countries? He narrowed them down to seven and listed them in his pad, stabbing the air with a pencil as he went along: Switzerland, France, Italy, Germany, England, Hungary and Greece. It was difficult for him to keep all things straight, especially when he realized that some of them worked closely in law enforcement with nearby countries. Like Ireland, Romania, and Bosnia-Herzegovina. He looked over both lists and his spirits cratered. Seven and three. Ten in all! But they were all in Europe, and he believed that what occurred there reflected what occurred in the rest of the world. And there was more that crossed his mind—possibilities that upcoming events might force them to visit even more countries. It was in this connection that histarians would play an important role, ones whom he would consult at a later date. He would keep an open mind.

Even so, if going to the seven main countries—one right after the other—wouldn't it become boring? Much of the same at every stop. But our questions might vary, depending on the country. Also, when we **do** *consult with histarians, they'll easily detect boredom and weigh it in their recommendations. So keep your spirits up, fella!*

He took time to ratchet up his resolve, then added to a second pad the additional things he had in mind, not necessarily in order of importance because one was as important as the next. He summarized them in a condensation of words but knew precisely what the words stood for:

—The original main reasons for the visits: legitimacy of religion, its relationship to criminal activity, and the Napoleonic influence on both.

—The five things that make a church healthy—(1) love, acceptance and forgiveness; (2) hunger for personal growth; (3) shift from traditional to contemporary worship; (4) prayer; (5) service and active volunteerism.

—The five questions that must be asked from a criminalistics and forensic science perspective: (1) what types of crime prevail? (2) how successful are the perpetrators? (3) in what ways are their criminal activities related to the States? (4) how might such criminals be identified? (5) how should the States handle all of it?

Then he wrote in capital letters: BOREDOM. There was such an element in his thinking because of expected repetition in one country after another. Would he and Vincent become bored and if so, how would they counteract it?

> *And if* **yours truly** *can get bored, will readers of the book get bored ... if I write one in the first place? But whether I do or not, this is all interesting material and I should save what I learn for a later date.*

He finally scribbled slowly: WILL THE SEARCH FOR ME CONTINUE AND REACH A HIGH POINT? Once again, he had the feeling that something perilous might be looming on the horizon.

An hour after he had entered the room, he put down his pad and went to a window because he needed a break. He looked out over the evergreens onto the fields beyond, their soft valleys and hilly contours blending as if to send a message: “Stay calm, my friend. With God’s help, it will all come together.”

Chapter 10

June 14

After landing at Switzerland's Zurich Airport and making their way to the far end of the main terminal, Paul expected to see what he had always seen at the terminals of most other visited countries—a descriptive article usually enclosed in a waist-high glass cabinet. Such was the case here, and side-by-side, he and Vincent stopped to read what was on the three large pieces of paper that were spread out before them:

> Welcome to Switzerland! To acquaint you with its characteristics, the following has been taken from the booklet, *Central European Waterways* by Vantage. Some of the booklet's renditions have been eliminated. Our goal is to give you the essentials:
>
> Each of Switzerland's eight regions has its own history. Landscape, cuisine, architecture and even languages become changed as otherwise invisible borders are crossed. A landlocked country in the

cultural and geographical heart of Europe, Switzerland has a distinct character and dynamism. While the country is admired for the beauty of its Alpine environment, its people are respected for their industry and technical ingenuity, as well as their social responsibility and direct democratic system of government. It is one of the world's richest countries, located in the Alpine region of central Europe. It covers some 15,950 square miles and is inhabited by 7.5 million people, 22 % of whom are non-Swiss. It borders Germany to the north, Austria and Liechtenstein to the east, Italy to the south, and France to the west and northwest. The mountainous country has engendered a robust spirit of independence and enterprise and a zealous work ethic in its population.

Though divided by religion, and with diverse cultural roots, the Swiss are remarkable for their strong sense of unified nationhood. Its national character has also been molded by its neutrality. Having avoided many of the major conflicts that shaped the culture of other European nations, it stands slightly removed from the wider world. Although it is a neutral country, it maintains a citizen army to defend its borders. National service is compulsory. However, except in time of war, the Swiss army has no active units and no top general, although regular training takes place. The last mobilization occurred during World War II. Today, the only Swiss mercenaries are the Swiss Guards who defend the Vatican and act as the papal bodyguards in Rome. Switzerland maintains the European headquarters of the UN and the world headquarters of the International Red Cross based in Geneva, and sees its role in international affairs as a largely humanitarian one.

Regarding the famous Swiss Alps, at altitudes above 9,800 feet, mosses and lichens cover a desolate rocky landscape, above which are snowfields, glaciers, and permanently snow-covered peaks. Forests are closely monitored and protected. Clearing hillsides, which increases the danger of avalanches, is forbidden. Also, most Alpine flowers are protected and it is forbidden to pick them. Edelweiss, the symbol of Switzerland, grows among rocks at altitudes up to 11,500 feet.

The country is divided into 26 cantons or territorial districts, and three main linguistic regions. The German language predominates (75%); then French (20%) and Italian (5%). As for religion, 46% of the population is Roman Catholic; 40% Protestant; and 6% practicing Jews and Muslims.

In 1798, having conquered northern Italy and wishing to control routes between Italy and France, Napoleon invaded Switzerland. Then for fifty years, even beyond his fall in 1815, internal religious hostilities transformed what had been until then a loose confederation of cantons into a union ruled by a federal assembly in Bern, which was chosen as the Swiss capital.

In the early 1930s, Switzerland's pacifistic stance and democracy were threatened by Nazi and Fascist sympathizers among its population. Later in that decade, as war seemed imminent, its economy accelerated, fueled partly by the booming army industry in which the country was involved and by the fact that Swiss banks played an important role in international finance. In the next decade, with Nazi Germany to the north and east, France under German occupation to the west and Fascist Italy to the south, Switzerland was surrounded. Invasion seemed inevitable, but it never took place as the country demanded its neutrality. It was not directly drawn into World War II but played a part in the conflict. It acted as a secret meeting place between leaders of the Allied and Axis powers and set up anonymous bank accounts for German Jews. Swiss banks also provided currency for the purchase of military equipment and exchanged large amounts of gold that were pillaged by the Germans for currency needed by the Third Reich. Unlike all other European countries, Switzerland remained untouched by the upheaval of war and detached

> from the postwar new world order.
>
> With respect to gold, the country was rocked by the "Nazi Gold" scandal when it was alleged that Swiss banks were holding gold looted by the Nazis and the assets of Jews who had perished in the Holocaust. Under strong U.S. pressure, Switzerland agreed, in August 1998, to pay $1.25 billion in compensation to families of Holocaust victims and to certain Jewish organizations—leaving a severe impression on the national psyche.

It took a full five minutes to read the message. When it was over, Vincent said, "I have just one question."

"Go ahead."

"You think the welcoming message in other countries will be just as long?"

"Probably. But it sets the stage—and that's fine with me. We'll take whatever we can get."

"So we read them all?"

"We read them all."

Then, as they turned away, Paul said, "The flower that was listed—Edelweiss? It reminds me of the show tune from the Rogers and Hammerstein musical, *The Sound of Music*. I guess I have lots of memories like that."

Vincent looked at him quizzically and said, "Pardon me for asking, but do you mean that with all that's in there, a white flower is what sticks in your craw? Whoops! Sorry. That implies something unfavorable. Not 'craw, but 'mind'."

"Yeah, but so do a lot of other things … religion, the Vatican, the Red Cross, gold, the Nazi and Fascist stuff, Napoleon, Swiss banks. We know a lot about them already or we can figure them out ourselves, but the article gave us leads to pursue."

Vincent countered with: "And as we do, let's take everything in, including the surroundings. You told me that when you were here last, you didn't because you had too much to accomplish. This time, though, let's have a **slow** look around. What's the rush? That way, we might be able to cut unnecessary corners as we go along from country to country. Learning from our mistakes."

"But what happens to our in-an-out approach then?" Paul began jangling change in his pants pocket.

"That's your approach, not mine," Vincent replied with an imploring smile. "I say let's take it easy. Relax and enjoy the roses. Nobody gave us a deadline, so it's an artificial one."

Paul removed the hand from his pocket, gave his lower lip a few taps and said, "You know, Vin, you drive a hard bargain."

"Hard enough for you to agree?"

"Hard enough."

Outside at the far end, Paul had no problem spotting the limo that Ansel had promised would be there. But he spotted something else. Behind the limo was the airport annex building and from a third-floor window, rays of the early afternoon's sun reflected off the barrel of a rifle that was aimed directly at him!

As though struck by an unanticipated sidewinder, he nearly fell over but then dropped his briefcase and luggage piece, crouched down, and yanked out his Couger .45. All in one motion. The rifle disappeared.

He straightened up, returned the .45 to its holster and with unbroken eye contact, he asked Vincent, "Did you see all that?"

"I saw your maneuver but not why you went through it. Why, in heaven's name?"

"Some guy was pointing a gun in our direction from up there." Paul pointed at the window. "I hope he took off. Was I quick enough?"

"I'll say. Looks like he did."

"Did what?"

"Take off."

Paul said, "Well, here we go, Vinny Boy. Pointed handgun, pointed rifle. What's ahead? Upcoming is the first of seven cities. Maybe it'll be a prototype for the others."

He felt bogged down in indecision as he added: "As for firearms, we have to be alert, so let's just carry on. As for cities, we know what we're after, but how the hell do we proceed? I mean … we have our list, so do we just read from it at every stop? In other words, do I read out loud as to why we're there?"

"No. The list is for **us**," Vincent answered. "You should pick out key parts as we go along. Or I have another suggestion: why not make copies of the list and hand over one copy to whatever person in whatever country? Seven countries, right? So make ten copies, just to be safe."

Paul picked up his luggage pieces, stared at him and said, "Vin, you make good sense. As usual. Let's do it like that."

They headed back to the terminal and into a transit lounge. Two copying machines were visible off to one side. There, they hailed a Delta steward and Paul received advice on how ten to twelve copies of a single sheet might be made.

"But wait," the steward said. "I'll do it for you."

Paul reached into his overstuffed brief case, located the sheet and handed it over.

The job was completed in two minutes, with an obvious shortcut being taken. He accepted the ten paper-clipped copies, slid them into the inside right pocket of his blue blazer and, reaching for his wallet, asked about cost.

The steward said, "Did you fly Delta by any chance?"

"No, we had our own private plane."

"But if you didn't, would you have chosen Delta?"

"No doubt about it."

"Forget the cost then. Good bye and good luck."

As the steward walked away, Paul uttered a drawn-out "per … fect" under his breath as he perused every line of the top sheet.

Paul had called ahead to the office of a longtime acquaintance, Kris Stuyvesant, one he believed to be the most respected police commander in all of Switzerland. Originally from Amsterdam, he was the one Paul felt everyone turned to when it came to Swiss law enforcement. His office was located in Lucerne, twenty-six miles away and located at the north end of a lake with the same name. Vincent drove slowly over narrow cobblestone streets so they could take in all the sights: frescoed houses; an abundance of fountains named after military and political heroes; the Fraumunster and St. Peterskirche churches that featured Europe's largest clock face and beautiful Chagall stained glass windows; the famous Chapel Bridge; and in the distance, the snowcapped Alps.

Having been there before, Paul was familiar with the many squares that were full of old buildings, cafes and restaurants. He also knew that from a geographical viewpoint, Lucerne was divided into two divisions that followed the banks of the Reuss River. They headed for the northern bank and once there, Paul pointed to an unassuming three-story brick building with a sign attached to a supporting column: FEDERAL DEPARTMENT OF JUSTICE AND POLICE. They parked out back and walked around to the front entrance. For some reason, as they climbed up a single staircase, Paul kept a hand under the left side of his blazer and over the .45 in the shoulder holster there.

They passed through three secretary's offices before reaching the commander's. At all three, Paul recognized the women seated at their desks, nodded to them and received a nod in return. The last secretary ushered them into the commander's office as if she had been expecting their arrival. Kris Stuyvesant was sitting in front of a computer and bounced up to greet them.

"Ah … Paul!" he said, "I thought you would never show up."

"Me, too. But please don't ask why," Paul said.

"Welcome, and this must be Vincent?"

The ensuing exchange was mutually warm and Vincent stole the spotlight with his comment: "You've got quite a country here."

They took seats on swivel chairs that surrounded a Tristen occasional table near the center of the room. In appearance, the room didn't seem to fit the level of the commander's authority and as before, Paul wanted to tell him so, but this time he thought better of it. In essence, it lacked the essentials of a working office except for the computer and possibly five television screens that were aligned with one another. They flashed scenes from different locations in Switzerland. Printing, copying and shredding, however, were no doubt the responsibility of the secretaries. Large in size but simple in furnishings, a small desk looked mismatched with the expansive wall behind it, although squeezed on its top were three retro style phones with flash, redial and push-button features. Hanging on the other walls were pictures of Swiss landmarks, all with the Alps in the background.

But Paul's opinion of the office's highlight—before and again now—was a liquor console that was finished in warm rustic honey while grained and peppered with knots and nail holes.

"Your brass entertainment console. Still have it … eh, Kris?"

"Still have it. I keep it for you, Paul. Both of you would accept a drink I assume." He spoke with a slightly Dutch accent, his words selective and beckoning. Around sixty, he was tall, graying blond and handsome, with bright blue eyes that appeared to stare through everything before him—people, places, things. He wore a tan shirt without medals or medallions, its collar open, sleeves rolled up to the elbows.

"Yes," they said in unison.

The console was an impressive structure with a front that dropped down to become a bar and revealing a roomy cabinet for spirits and two drawers for cocktail napkins and more. The lower cabinet's double drawers were set with a slide hatch and square escutcheon of antiquated brass and concealed a removable wine rack and shelf.

"Cocktail or wine?" Kris asked, as he approached it.

"Wine, and make it Chardonnay please," Paul said.

Vincent nodded. "Good, I'll join you."

While he poured the drinks, Paul noted an obvious physical change in the man and remembered one of his comments. He was more hunched over than before, no doubt molded by many hours spent assessing news reports before the TV screens. And when Paul once complimented him on twelve successful years of leadership, Kris thanked him and said with a toothy grin and helpless gesture, "But it's those assistants out front who deserve the credit. I'm just a fixture around here."

They took tiny almost negligible sips of the wine during several exchanges of small talk. Kris then said, "So … shall we get down to business? You told me on the phone why we're meeting and that you would be doing the same thing in six other countries. Do I remember correctly?"

"Yeah," Paul said, "and I wrote a list of the items." He took out the stack from his pocket and handed over the top sheet. "As you can see, Kris, the first item speaks for itself. Come to think of it, they all do."

He allowed the commander to examine the sheet. "Well," Kris finally said after folding it and putting it into his shirt pocket, "the top two deal with religion and that's out of my league except for its tie-in with criminal activity. But I can comment more completely on the third. And if you want a suggestion, the most knowledgeable person to see about religion in Switzerland is located at a church not too far from here. Church of St. Leodegar and its top priest, Father Morton Heg. Nice man, easy to talk to. He's been around a long time, the spiritual advisor to many of us. After we finish, I can call him if you wish."

"Would appreciate it—thanks. And as for that first item, the crux of the matter is that crime and religion are sometimes interconnected."

"Interconnected?"

"Yeah. One's a front for the other."

Paul paused to let the comment take effect, then added, "I don't mean to imply anything, Kris, but can you speak reliably for the rest of law enforcers in Switzerland?"

There was no hesitation in the answer: "I'm in direct contact with most of them on a regular basis, so I would say 'yes'. You want me to begin?"

"Not yet, if you don't mind. First let me outline what I

already know about crime—then you can take over. I won't refer to notes, so you can assume that the stuff I cover is well ingrained in yours truly."

"In me, too," Vincent said in a sideline glance at both men.

Paul knew there would be a chance for repetition but couldn't separate what he was thinking from what he might have referred to in their recent phone call. Thoughts were exploding from his mind. For one thing, he had to admit to himself that he was more interested in the religion element than the crime element. That the former overshadowed the latter. The latter was merely a means to an end. After all, he had been a criminal investigator for many years, so crime analysis was nothing new. But religious concerns had been piling up in his subconscious, alongside possible means of evaluation. And his final rationalization was that the best way to evaluate international religions, to put a stamp of approval—or disapproval—on them, was through the knowledge he could receive from law enforcers, not the other way around. For priests, pastors and other members of the cloth might not be as open to scrutiny.

"You said you wouldn't refer to notes," Kris said, "but do you have any with you? I've been told that during many of your travels, you've given lectures."

"I've cut back on them, but once in a while, I'll give one. And to answer your question—yes, I have some notes with me."

"Well then, instead of an outline, could you refer to the notes … to be more complete. Do you have the time to do it like that?"

Kris checked his watch while Paul looked at Vincent who gave a half-nod.

"But so much of it would be elementary to you," Paul said.

"Maybe. Maybe not. A review wouldn't hurt anyway."

Paul reached into his briefcase and withdrew a folder of notes. Leafing through them, he said, "Okay, you asked for it and we have the time. And come to think of it, I'll pretty much read what I have and ad lib every so often … if I think it's required. I don't have much on Switzerland crime so …"

Kris interrupted: "No, that's what **I** will cover. After all, it's why you're here."

Paul found the notes he wanted and asked, "You don't think if I stick to these and mostly read, that it'll be too stilted?"

"Stilted?"

"Yeah, too formal?"

"Your lectures were well received?"

"Can't complain."

"Then, one will be well received here, so do go ahead. It's too bad you have an audience of only one … uh … I mean two."

"But I've heard it before," Vincent said.

Kris went to a closet, returned with a small lectern and placed it on the table in front of Paul.

"Whoa," Paul said, "real fancy."

He placed his notes on the lectern, slid his chair back some and began reading: "So, about organized crime—a few years ago, I wrote an essay about the subject and I'll touch on four areas: its origin; its dynamics; its worldwide organizations; and its typical activities. Some of what I'm about to say comes from a book written by Martin Roth—*The Writer's Complete Crime Reference Book.* And much from a 2008 *Wikipedia* article. Credit where credit is due. But before the four areas, some preliminary definitions. Criminal organizations are groups run by criminals, most commonly for the purpose of generating money. No surprise there. Some of them, such as terrorist organizations are politically or religiously motivated."

Paul's first ad lib came at this point. "Notice the word 'religiously' …"

"Father Heg will hit on that later," Kris said.

"So I'll skip ahead," Paul continued. "Gangs sometimes become disciplined enough to be considered organizations. These gangs are often called 'mobs'. The act of engaging in criminal activity as a structured group is referred to in the United States as racketeering. You may have heard of *RICO*—which stands for *Racketeer Influenced and Corrupt Organizations Act.*

"Now regarding Origins, if we refer to Robert Sullivan, Editor for *Mobsters and Gangsters: Organized Crime in America, from Al Capone to Tony Soprano*, New York: Life Books, 2002, and take a global rather than a strictly domestic view—that is, on the part of any single country—it becomes evident that even crime of the organized kind has a long if not necessarily noble heritage. The word 'thug' dates to early 13th century India, when thugs or gangs of criminals roamed from town to town, looting and pillaging. Smuggling and drug-trafficking rings are as old as the hills in Asia and Africa. And defunct criminal organizations in Italy and Japan trace their histories back several centuries. In *Organized Crime, 2004*—and this is the last time I'll cite sources—Paul Lunde states that 'piracy and banditry were to the pre-industrial world what organized crime is in modern society.' It's a question of precursors to what exists today. He also states that barbarian conquerors, whether Vandals, Goths, Norsemen, Turks or Mongols are not normally thought of as organized crime groups, yet they share many features associated with successful criminal organizations. They were for the most part non-ideological, used violence and intimidation, and adhered to their own codes of law.

"Today, crime is thought of as an urban phenomenon, but for most of human history it was the rural world that was crime-ridden. Pirates, highway men and bandits attacked trade routes and roads, at times severely disrupting commerce, raising costs, insurance rates, prices to the consumer. And the same thing is happening now! The pirates are at it again, not in cities, not on back roads but on the high seas. I've written three books about it, the latest being *Diamonds and Pirates*."

Paul was surprised to see Kris taking his own notes!

Or is he drawing pictures? But he appears to be four-plus attentive.

"Next we have Dynamics. In order for these groups to prosper, some degree of support is required from the society in which they live. Therefore it's necessary to corrupt some of society's respected members, most often achieved through bribery, blackmail, payoffs, and so forth. Judicial officers, police officers, and politicians are especially targeted for control by organized crime via bribes. Even clergy members serve as fronts for criminals who supply them with sexual favors.

"Lacking much of the paperwork that is common for legitimate organizations, criminal ones can usually evolve and reorganize much more swiftly when the need arises. They are quick to capitalize on newly-opened markets, and quick to rebuild themselves under another guise when caught by authorities. This is especially true in cases of human trafficking.

"The newest growth sectors for organized crime are identity theft and online extortion. These activities are troubling because they discourage consumers from using the Internet for e-commerce. E-commerce was supposed to level the playing field for small and large businesses, but the growth of online organized crime is leading to the opposite effect: large businesses are able to afford more electronic band-width and, therefore, superior security. In addition, organized crime, using the Internet, is much harder to trace down by the police even though they increasingly deploy cybercops. Since police officers and law enforcement agencies in general operate on a national level, the Internet makes it even simpler for organizations to cross boundaries and even to operate remotely for the most part."

Paul paused to straighten out his notes on the lectern, noticed that Kris was writing faster and asked: "You getting anything out of this, Kris?"

"Much more than I imagined. I didn't realize you had such

a grasp of the subject."

"For the most part though, what you're hearing is what I've accumulated from other sources—but thanks. Now in the past, mobs that wanted to expand put themselves in competition with other mobs. This often led to violence—turf wars over drugs, prostitution and so on. Today though, they're working together more and more—hence the rise of global criminal groups. My book, *Global Shadows*, deals with this. Examples are the Sicilian Mafia in the States having links with similar groups in Italy, such as the Camorra, and with the Irish Mob in the States. Then there's the Japanese Yakuza and Russian Mafia often working together. The FBI estimates that global organized crime makes $1 trillion per year.

"We move on to number three: Notable Organizations. And there's much to say about this category. Perhaps the best known are the Sicilian and American La Cosa Nostra, most commonly called the Mafia. A member of the Mafia is called a 'mafioso', and kinship groups within the Mafia are called 'mafiosi'. While we're on the subject, a few other terms: members of the Mafia are bound by 'Omerta' or the code of silence. It's simply a way of saying, 'If you talk, you die'. And there's the 'Black Hand'. When the Mafia first settled in the U.S., they were referred to as this because their hands were often stained by the tar paper in which they wrapped the remains of those who opposed them. Nasty stuff!

"Then there's the Neopolitan Camorra; the Calabrian 'Ndrangheta and the Apulian Sacra Corona Unita, all similar Italian organized crime groups. Some others are the Mexican and Colombia Drug Cartels, the Indian Mafia and the Chinese Triads. And on a lower level in the criminal food chain are many street gangs such as the Latin Kings and biker gangs like Hell's Angels.

"Too much for one sitting, Kris?"

"No, keep it up. I feel like a student listening to his teacher."

"And liking what he hears?"

"I wouldn't say liking the content, but liking what he's learning."

"I'll pick up where I left off then. Let's see: I'd be remiss if I didn't list some world leaders throughout history who have been accused of running their countries like a criminal organization: Adolf Hitler of Germany; Idi Amin of Uganda; Mobuto of Zaire; Ceausescu of Romania; Franco of Spain; Hugo Banzer of Bolivia; Kim Jong Un of North Korea; Milosevic of Serbia and Yugoslavia; Fujimori of Peru, and Than Shwe of Burma. Corrupt political leaders may have links to existing organized crime groups, either domestic or international. Or else may simply exercise power in a manner that duplicates the functioning and purpose of organized crime.

"And to complete the picture, in addition to traditional crime groups that are out to make money, there are those out for political or ideological gain. I speak of terrorist groups such as Al-Qaeda, Hamas and ISIS.

"Just a word about the organizational chart of a crime family or syndicate—say in New York or Chicago. It mirrors the management structure of a corporation. At the top of the pyramid is the boss or Chief Executive Officer. Below him are an underboss or Chief Operating Officer and a general counselor or consigliere. Note the words 'Executive' and 'Operating". They're different. Then follow ranks of vice-presidents—called capos—and soldiers.

"And here's how some criminals operate—two main ways. They infiltrate and victimize legitimate industries. They engage in a wide range of illegal activities. They victimize the industries through the use of extortion or theft; hijacking cargo trucks; robbing industry goods; committing bankruptcy fraud (also known as 'bust-out'); or insurance and stock fraud (that is, inside trading). They also victimize individuals by car theft, burglary, and credit card fraud. Some defraud national, state or local governments by bid-rigging public projects; counterfeiting money; and smuggling or manufacturing untaxed alcohol (bootlegging). Some of the industries they've had great success in are: food products, real estate, restaurants, garbage disposal, produce, garment manufacturing, bars and taverns, securities, labor unions, vending machines and the waterfront.

"What might I say about Typical Activities? Just a summary—organized crime groups participate in a wide range of services and goods, such as smuggling of guns into a country; murder for hire; illegal dumping of toxic waste; casino skimming; using non-union labor while pocketing the wage difference; and on and on.

"I'll end with a brief note about so many people in our country who are jailed for indefinite periods of time. In Chicago, for example … about 70,000 men and women, all members of gangs, are incarcerated at the Cook County Jail every year. Most are poor or mentally ill and don't have enough money for bail. They're just awaiting trial, but in the meantime, they do get some medical attention. It's become a mental health facility."

Paul then puffed out a breath, pushed the lectern gently in front of Kris and said, "There, now it's your turn. And I do apologize for my many lists, but I wanted to be as complete as possible. Also, I never covered forensic science, one of my favorite topics, but it definitely fits into the fight against organized crime."

"And once he gets going on that, watch out!" Vincent said.

Paul wasn't entirely pleased by the way it had gone because he was looking at his notes more than at his table mates who were an arms' length away. He felt uncomfortable.

"I don't really need a lectern," Kris said, "because I won't use extensive notes, but as long as it's here, I'll just place a five-by-eight card and the sheet you gave me on it." He reached into his shirt pocket, removed the folded card and sheet, unfolded them and placed them side-by-side on the lectern. He then commented, "After you called, Paul, I gave it some thought and decided that the best way to handle what you're after is to break it down into categories. And now that I've heard what you had to say, I'll eliminate some of what I planned on covering if it's duplication. Is that all right?"

"Definitely all right."

"Good. You'll notice that as I venture forward, most of the

criminality is what I'm aware of in Switzerland and in the specifics we share with neighboring countries, particularly Germany, France and Italy. Not only are we juxtaposed geographically, but in a sense, in law and order affairs. "

Already Paul detected a definite formality in the way Kris expressed himself and hoped it would continue because it sounded so clear-cut.

Chapter 11

Kris picked up his card and said, "We've got the five questions that need answering from a criminalistics and forensic science standpoint. That happens to be my Number 1 category. The other categories are—Number 2: statistics, immigrant criminality, and types of convictions in Switzerland; Number 3: Napoleon and the Perons. Their influence and culpability; Number 4: stem cell research; and Number 5: any lingering questions you might have. Do you have any?"

"As a matter of fact, Kris, I do. But I'll wait till you finish."

"Fair enough. Let's see, your five questions are: What types of crime prevail? I'll cover that in my categories. How successful are the perpetrators? Not very, but there's much recidivism. In what way are their criminal activities related to the U.S? I have no idea. How might such criminals be identified? We work very hard at it, and one thing stands out. One would think that criminals are close-mouthed all the time. Not really; not when they're caught. Some **do** squeal. And how should the U.S. handle all of this? Again, I have no idea. So it's five categories and five questions, with some definite overlapping. Hope it's not too confusing."

"Not yet anyway."

"Okay. Number two—dealing with statistics, immigrants, and convictions. One at a time, and I'm reading from my card. Last year in this country, our police registered a total of about 526,000 offenses. Of the main ones, 44% were thefts; 41% were murders and attempted murders; and 3% were rapes. Regarding immigrants, there was a conviction rate that was 12 times higher among so-called asylum seekers, while the rate among other foreigners was twice as high compared to Swiss citizens. Overall, the types of convictions were—and here comes another list—homicide, bodily injury, rape, sexual contact with children, theft, robbery, receiving stolen goods, embezzlement, fraud, narcotics possession, and violation of traffic laws.

"Next, about Napoleon and the Perons. You've no doubt heard about the effect Napoleon has had, and still has, on criminals worldwide. Switzerland is no exception and I won't go into detail as to why."

"You needn't," Paul said. "It's well-known everywhere."

"But I want to consider the Perons some. First is Juan, the former president of Argentina. He was very fond of Italy's Mussolini who, along with Hitler, was responsible for many deaths in Europe. Juan spent six years there—in Italy, Spain and Germany—countries that made up the European Axis Alliance during World War II, and he may have helped some people escape to his home country. Today, who honestly knows how they returned the favor, but that whole period, with Juan in the middle of it, is very suspicious.

"As for his eventual wife, Eva, she was a popular prostitute all over the place. The world, I mean. Probably because of that, she had connections with many Nazis, including those in this country. And somehow she worked deals between the banks of Switzerland and her own country. Plus get this: as an example of outright collusion, our bankers helped the Nazis secrete vast amounts of money and gold that were stolen from innocent Jews. Many people still think there was a poorly disguised Swiss-Argentine-Nazi collaboration, which the Perons facilitated. And that's enough about them. Makes my blood boil."

"Good summary, Kris," Paul said. "Pretty much matches what we already know about them and the dirty part of their lives. A friend of ours expressed it this way: 'They helped make Switzerland a safe haven for valuables after thievery by the Nazis and their French counterparts'."

"To a tee," Vincent said.

Kris flashed a gracious smile as he said, "Thank you and oh, I forgot one thing. Although it's a shot at my country, I've got to say it. Some historians believe that Switzerland not only hid investments for other countries but, as a result of such deception, no taxes were paid. By anyone. And they end up saying that Nazi Germans and the Vichy French are the real culprits. Echoes how your friend expressed it.

"But let's get to Category 4: stem cell research. It's

strongly related to Jewish money; to Argentina and therefore the Perons; and to those taxes I mentioned. Here's how I tie it all together. Indirectly, much of any so-called Swiss money that might have been directed toward stem cell research could be considered of Jewish origin. How so? Well, before killing the Jews, the Nazis stripped them of their money and had it secreted right here. Then future stem cell research originating here could be regarded as being financed by those deceased German Jews. Ultimately, their descendants—those who settled in Argentina—might have had a legitimate claim on anything positive relating to stem cells in the future. So that possibly the Swiss could have used this as a bargaining chip if some countries made it difficult for those Swiss banks that helped outside citizens dodge taxes."

Kris wiped a line of sweat from his brow. "What an interwoven nightmare," he said. "I hope I didn't mess up the way I presented it. Was it clear enough?"

"Well done, Kris. And don't worry … I won't ask you to repeat it."

"Better not, or I won't refill your wine glasses."

"Nah, please don't even think about it," Paul said. "It's too early for more than one."

"That's a relief. I don't have much sweat left."

It was the first time in the past twenty minutes that they shared a laugh.

"Now for lingering questions," Kris said. "Are there any?"

Vincent shook his head "no" while Paul replied, "I only have one: during the war, why wasn't Switzerland invaded by Germany?"

"Everyone asks about that. We were spared because every Swiss man was armed and trained to shoot. Thank God."

Paul was the first to rise. As he did, he asked, "You'll call Father Heg then? We can go to the church right now, if he's available."

Kris went to one of his phones, made contact with the priest, explained the situation, and received a warm go-ahead for the meeting to take place in several minutes.

Kris told them that the priest's office was in a back wing of the church, and he gave them the address. "You have to go through the church to get to it and he works alone—no secretaries, no young clerics, just alone while he works, reads and prays. I hear that sometimes he even prays with other priests over the phone."

Back in the limo, Paul thought that much of what Kris had said was not germane to what he and Vincent were seeking. Also, that he himself knew as much about Switzerland crime as the commander did. Giving him credit, however, he thought the man was more into administrative details than the everyday problems of crime commission and punishment.

Let's depend on Father Heg's input for making the trip worthwhile.

They drove slowly through town, at the foot of the Alps, past the Jesuit Church, which Paul understood was the first large

Baroque-style church ever built in Switzerland. At the Church of St. Leodegar, there was adequate parking space out front. As they exited the limo, Paul stepped back to observe the church's tall twin towers, its metal-covered pyramid roof and three arched entrances situated under a canopy.

They made their way through the atrium and nave, observing all they could without stopping, past all the side altars and up to the high one. To the right was an open door to what Paul felt was the wing. They entered cautiously, circled around and found it to have all the earmarks of a secret passageway: narrow, dimly lit, low ceiling, the faint smell of moisture. Up ahead was another open door and above it was a sign attached at a right angle to the wall. It read: **THE REVEREND FATHER MORTON HEG**. Paul was taken with the sign's formality—large, bold lettering, light pink background. He thought it incongruous to the overall surroundings of the passageway.

They ambled in and walked up to a jam-packed corner of an expansive wing. The other corners were empty. Before them were the usual essentials of an office: computer, printer, copier, shredder, several phones. And an abundance of bookcases whose shelves were filled to capacity.

The priest was writing at his desk—more of a table really, with a long mirror attached to its backside. He glanced at the mirror, sprung up, twisted around and extended his arm between them. Their handshakes lasted throughout an opening run of silence. Father Heg was the first to break it.

"Welcome … welcome, gentlemen," he said, ushering them to a nearby bench. They sat but the priest remained standing. "The commander spoke highly of you," he said, "then indicated why he thought I could be of assistance … what some of your questions might be. Please, how might I help?"

Paul seemed preoccupied with the priest's appearance. He was a towering presence, augmented by a close-fitting black cassock beneath a Roman collar. He stood with legs spread solidly on the floor, like an athlete ready for action, about to lunge. He had a ruddy complexion, an overgrowth of white hair and deep-set dark eyes that pierced slowly between the two men.

Before answering, Paul decided to hand him one of the sheets because he thought, in truth, that it would simplify matters. At least he hoped so. In addition, while the priest examined the sheet, it would provide time to formulate the opening questions.

Important stuff in a make-or-break session. Successful trip or a waste.

"All right, Father. First, thank you so much for this meeting. I hope we're not interrupting more important things on your schedule."

"Not at all. I welcome important interruptions. Can you imagine the times Charlemagne and Napoleon were interrupted? And look at the decisions they made. I'm not suggesting I have their stature but you **do** understand?"

"I do, but before we get to why we're here in Switzerland, I'd like to ask what I consider a basic question. It's one I asked

Kris, only here it applies to priests, not law officers. It's this: Can you reasonably speak for all the clerics in your country?"

The answer came after a moment's hesitation: "I would think so … definitely for Catholics and most likely for my Protestant and Jewish cousins. Excuse me, but that's what I call the clerics in other religions … 'Cousins'."

"What about Catholic ones?"

" 'Brothers'."

"Sounds rational to me," Paul said. He smiled thinly.

"Now, to answer why we're here. We're trying to get a sense of how religion is working around the world and whether or not it has strong ties to criminals. In other words, do they work together for various reasons, and if we're talking criminals, how can the reasons be other than bad? Kris gave an excellent assessment of the criminality side but said little about the religion side. That's where he came up with your name, Father, and it didn't take him long. Immediate, really."

Paul knew what was in the sheets by heart but, nonetheless, he looked one over. "Should I lay out specifics, or can you take it from here?" he asked. "You've got the sheet to help you."

The priest sat back down and examined the sheet again. "Yes, I can take it from here," he said. "Those five ingredients for a healthy church are certainly all-inclusive, and I can honestly say that churches all around our country demonstrate and honor them more than those in surrounding countries do. And that's not being critical … it's just the way it is."

Paul began taking notes, as did Vincent. Father Heg

noticed, removed his own scratch pad from one of the desk drawers and flipped to a middle page.

"After Kris called me, I jotted down some notes about what was straight in my head and what I researched a little, especially for statistics. I'll elaborate on the main religions here. There is total freedom of worship among our 46 % Roman Catholics, 40 % Protestants and roughly 10 or 12 % Jews and Muslims. Let's look at each of these."

The priest appeared as though poised for a sermon.

"As for our Catholic churches, they're organized into six dioceses and two territorial abbeys, comprising about 3 million people."

"Let me stop you there," Paul said. "Could the leaders of any of those churches be involved in criminal activities? Could they be hiding crimes and somehow getting rewarded? Serving as fronts?"

"I really couldn't comment on that."

Paul had to arrive at a decision. "Couldn't or wouldn't?" he asked.

"I'm not sure what you're driving at, so I'll just say 'both'."

"I understand," Paul said. He really didn't … not fully, anyway. But, no matter how clear the answer, it was his first attempt at getting a priest to admit to "monkey business" by religious hierarchies. And he promised himself that it would continue, there and elsewhere.

"Shall I go on?" the priest asked.

"Yes. Sorry, Father. I hope I didn't ruin your train of thought."

"No, not at all. That about sums up Catholic churches. Now for Protestants. As I said, about one in four of our population identifies itself with that religion. Most of its parishioners still refer to their churches as 'Reformed', but I won't bother you with why. It involves a complicated history of name-changing that began in Zurich and then spread to Basil and Bern—and even to some cities in Germany and France. The only reason I bring this up is to point out that for centuries, even though there was no change in their name, they were still called 'Reformed'. But there was **no** reformation. The only change was that what began as a link to our state districts had finally begun to loosen. The grip had been like a vise but was now like a handshake. A government versus religion battle for many, many years."

Paul and Vincent had put their pens aside and now Paul decided to probe further: "So if religion was involved in crime, so was your government?"

But Father Heg wouldn't bite. Instead he said, "Sorry, I didn't hear you well. Is what you asked of any importance?"

Talk about a curve ball. This guy's a pro!

"Not important," Paul said. "Sorry once again."

The priest turned to another page. "Now for Jews and Muslims," he said. "I have to confess that I didn't write down much about them. And why is that? Because I don't **know** much about them. But I can say a little. First, our Jewish community: way back, it was made up of settlers from Germany and France. All of them, except for physicians, were not treated well. They were considered resident aliens and required special permission to marry, for example. Or their businesses were heavily regulated. Naturally, they wanted some form of emancipation. Then after Jews from Russia came in, things improved somewhat. And I guess that's enough about their early history."

He flipped to a third page. "Let's mention the Holocaust. Prior to and during the Second World War, we gave refuge to about 23,000 Jews, although our government decided that we would serve only as a country of transit for them. Imagine! But I'm proud to say that these Jews were protected during the Holocaust due to Swiss neutrality, although they didn't receive the financial support from the government that non-Jewish refugees received. And besides that, many more Jews were prevented from entering in the first place. Then about ten years later, we looked after Jews from Egypt, Hungary and Czechoslovakia. What about Israel, you ask? We were and still are supportive, while maintaining our neutrality. Currently, our Jewish population is well represented in the textile and clockwork industries as well as in manufacturing and wholesales. Continuing on the plus side, many international Jewish organizations have located here and we have thriving synagogues, kosher restaurants, Jewish bookstores and other signs of a flourishing Jewish life. But on the negative side is whether or not former Jewish money is hidden here and, if so, is it intended for later use in more advanced stem cell research?

Some say that there are Swiss swindlers who might intercept such money and use it as future bargaining chips.

"As for Muslims? Can't say too much. That community is comprised of several nationalities. What I have written down here is that it's represented by people from Turkey, the former Yugoslavia, Lebanon, Morocco, Algeria and Tunisia. Twenty years ago, there were only three mosques; now there are ninety spread around our country. And I know firsthand that the so-called Federation of Islamic Organizations has worked very closely with Catholic and Protestant churches not only on religious matters but also political ones. They definitely work hard for a better voice in the issues they hold dear."

He closed his pad and reinserted it in the drawer as though it was a sign of finality. "Anything more, gentlemen?" he asked.

"No," Paul replied. "You've been most informative." He withheld saying "helpful".

In the limo, Paul had to turn on the wiper blades for, although a brief rain had stopped, it had left the windshield dimly shaded. A shade he equated to Father Heg's keenly shaded remarks.

What garbage!

He expressed it that way to Vincent, adding, "It was like filler for a screen play to hide certain weaknesses."

"And uninteresting fillers, too. In fact, I stopped taking

notes."

"We both did, remember? Yet there's one thing that caught my eye … I should say 'ear': his mention of stem cell research. Almost in passing. That has always been of interest to me and bears looking into. And the rifle guy is still out there somewhere."

"Don't you wonder if he and the one in Buenos Aires know each other?" Vincent asked.

"Yeah, I do," Paul said, fidgeting in his seat. "And funny that both threats took place at airports. For now though, it's one country down, six to go."

Chapter 12

June 14

At Sicily's Catonia-Fontanarossa Airport, Paul and Vincent both decided Switzerland was history and that they would visit three other countries—this island belonging to mainland Italy; Germany; and France—then fly home to check with close friends about their take on what had transpired thus far. The friends would include forensic scientist Walter Sparks; fellow investigator David Brooks; and journalist Guy Martin again. That would leave England, Hungary and Greece to visit afterwards.

As usual, they headed for a limo that Ansel had provided, and on the way, Paul said, "Vin, I just thought of a change of plans. I've already been to the prison here to confer with Warden Rossi. Just two years ago, in fact. I wrote a chapter about it in one of my mystery books, *Spying for Keeps*."

"I remember. Covered a lot of ground. Instead of yourself, the hero is a guy named Jim Hunter."

"And it's unbelievable how what Hunter said is what we're looking for now. Why don't I refresh my memory, read what I wrote, and substitute that for another visit? What I did was to combine what I personally learned from the warden with what Jim Hunter went through during the invasion of Normandy."

"So we've wasted time by flying here?"

"Yes and no. Think about it: all the remaining countries are within a 5-to-6 hour flight radius. Not bad." He checked his watch. "It's five-thirty, so let's register at a hotel, relax a bit, and count this stop as a vacation that came up as a surprise. Then we'll leave for home in the morning. The hotel I have in mind is amazing. It's called *The Magnifico*. I happened to bring that mystery book with me and I can read what I wrote there. The hotel's right across the street from the *Ucciardone* prison."

"I get it, but didn't you call ahead to the warden about when we'd arrive?"

"Yeah, but I can call again to explain. He's my friend and he'd understand. I don't even have to say where I'm calling from."

"Call from here?"

"Why not?"

Paul flashed a c'est tout dire smile and continued: "The hotel even has live entertainment. There's an auditorium that reminded me of the many times I lectured aboard the Queen Mary cruise ship. During the day, lectures were given by various authors, and during most evenings, they enlarged the stage for performers … like musicians, dancers, magicians and ventriloquists. Here, not only do hotel residents attend but others also come from far and wide."

Soon after settling in at *The Magnifico*, Vincent took a nap while Paul phoned Warden Rossi about the change of plans, then read the chapter in his mystery book, *Spying for Keeps*.

Ten minutes later, he felt totally relieved as he showered, shaved, and made a few notations in his scratch pad. When Vincent awoke, he, too, read the chapter:

> At the airport, Jim was afraid the upcoming five-city challenge wouldn't yield much. And he hadn't even started yet! Still, he would plow ahead with his "formula of information". He reviewed its questions over and over as if he were about to take a college exam about them. He even reviewed them with Camille:
>
> —types of crime
>
> —success rate of perps
>
> —their identity
>
> —relationship to U.S.
>
> —handling of info
>
> With all this in mind, he wanted to honor Frank Merriday's expectation of arrests in the U.S.
>
> They taxied to the hotel, but before entering Jim glanced across the street in the direction of the massive nineteenth-century prison. Its rows of intertwined walls—moldy, crumbling and nearly

windowless—appeared never-ending as they wrapped around adjoining streets. Wide stretches of dirt and crushed stone ran along barbed wire fencing; and several carabinieri police officers brandishing machine guns were stationed atop domelike turrets. At street level and astride the front gate were two officers dressed in dark blue jackets with badges in front and insignias of yellow flames on their shoulders. The shiny purple stripes on their trousers were as straight as the rifles they steadied upright at their sides.

In contrast, the hotel's exterior was what one might expect of a successful business establishment: an off-white concrete building with an overabundance of windows and doors, surrounded by beautifully manicured gardens. The interior was furnished in a minimalist style using precious materials such as Wedgwood, white marble, and a mix of designer objects and traditional elements like the old brick arches that decorated the lounges. After registering, they refused any assistance and lugged their luggage to an assigned room that was more simple than elegant.

"See that minibar?" Jim asked. "But let's wait till later. Are you as anxious to see the warden as I am?"

"I think I'm more inclined to wonder if he will

agree to see us. And do the guards over there understand English? And even the warden?"

"We'll soon find out. Let's get going. You'll take notes?"

"As usual."

At the prison's front gate, Jim spoke to the carabinieri softly, slowly and distinctly as he introduced himself and Camille, and expressed the importance of speaking to the warden about European crime. He expected some resistance but received none. Not only that, but they in turn introduced themselves! Their English was broken but understandable, and they happened to be brothers—Enrico and Tony Albano.

"Go in. Long way down," one said, while the other opened the gate wide. "Our warden … he is Roberto Rossi. He is good man. Come from your country."

Jim couldn't believe how easy it was but reasoned they were more taken with Camille than with giving full attention to their request. And, believing that the men's noses must have become accustomed to a smell resembling that of a fish processing plant, it dawned on him that a harbor was nearby. Also nearby—to the left of the guards—was an alarm device and telephone, both embedded in a crevice that was sagging with decay.

They sauntered down a deserted hallway past a series of closed metal doors to their left, and to their right, soggy and flaky masonry. It seemed to take forever to reach a wooden door on the left. A simple sign was posted beside it: WARDEN. They knocked gently and walked in.

Warden Rossi had no secretary to screen people wishing to see him. He was standing by his desk as if he were expecting visitors. As they came in, he remained speechless while pulling over three chairs that were stacked not far from a door that fronted a large sparkling-clean office with bright lights but sparse furniture. The warden arranged the chairs in a semi-circle and said, "Please. Sit. Make yourselves comfortable." He continued in fluent English: "Enrico and Tony just called me, gave me your names and said why you're here. You may not be aware, but you'll be making my day."

Jim introduced Camille as his fiancée and, after handshaking, she began taking notes.

"Making your day? How's that?" Jim asked.

"I see so few people except for the carabinieri outside and inside. Inside … they come to ask for time off all the time. I give it to them. Nothing else. I should have taken time off myself, like for the rest of my life, but … a different story …

excuse me."

"We understand you were born in the U.S. May I ask where?"

"No, not born there, but raised there. Born here in the province of Potenza. My parents were killed in a car accident when I was just a baby, so I was raised in New York by my aunt and uncle. Went to grammar and high school there. Came back to Italy when I was eighteen. Couldn't find a job in the U.S."

"You came here?"

"No. To the province of Potenza—then here."

"You must have connections with New York then?"

"Yes. I still have friends there and in New Jersey and Pennsylvania. We communicate regularly."

"Ideal!"

"What's that mean?"

"You'll see. It has to do with the relationship between crimes here and crimes there. I've been hired to move about in some countries ... learning the extent of crime; how successful the criminals are; *who* they are; and what could be done to identify them. Also what their connection is to criminals now living in the United States. All of this is to facilitate arrests. And as long as I'm at it,

I might as well explain my Plan-C."

"Your Plan-C?"

"Yes. It's what I used in a job I had helping the Allies. I have my own Plan-C machine to listen in on selected phone calls in order to decipher messages. I refer to it as 'Charlie'. It's more reliable than the German Enigma-I or even the Triton Enigma our military uses to direct U-boat operations in the Atlantic. The unique thing about it is that it can also give a person's approximate location."

"Location too? How's that work?"

"Sorry, but I can't give that out."

"I understand … I think."

"And I used Charlie over and over again while helping out in the war still going on, but … thank goodness … that's coming to a close. It's what helped in monitoring enemy secrets. So I asked myself: why can't I use the same machine to monitor what's going on among disgusted Nazis, the Mafia, new gangs and old gangs? I could be identifying criminals; give their location; determine who gives orders; who carries them out; and so forth. Then arrests could follow."

Rossi began taking a few notes and had a look of satisfaction that he made no attempt to hide.

In the same vein, Jim was thrilled with what he and Camille had stumbled onto there in Palermo.

And in a decrepit prison, no less.

Can our having picked Palermo possibly cut short the number of destinations we planned on?

"How long have you been the warden?" Jim asked.

"Thirty-three years," Rossi grumbled.

He was a rotund man with scant white hair, pasty face and, on removing his tinted glasses, probing eyes that had probably seen everything. His light tan jacket, open shirt collar and faded blue jeans were hardly those associated with the right side of the law. Silently, he leaned down to his desk's lower drawer and removed three glasses and a bottle of wine.

"I know it's early in the day, but believe me, what you're here for deserves a toast. Nothing better for that than a small swallow of Vega Sicilia. May I pour?"

"Good idea," Jim said. Camille nodded. Their expressions told a brief story of payment for information.

The toast took less than a minute and Jim then decided to reveal why they were there instead of at a police chief's office.

"Your chief here in Palermo refused to talk to

us. Said he was too busy."

"De Giovanni? **Bastardo**! I'm not surprised. He's part of the problem we have on the island."

"How so?"

"Well, no one's been able to prove it, but everyone agrees to it. He's on the take. 'Kickbacks' as you might say in your country."

"Involving crimes?"

"Involving crimes. Rapes, murders, loan sharking, forgery, just about everything illegal. Especially prostitution, where women are used in the kickback. Even youngsters are forced into it, and he does nothing about it. Every time he mentions, 'going to church', he means 'going to a whorehouse'."

Camille's note taking had reached a furious pitch. Jim noticed and signaled with his eyes that she should take a break. She stuffed her notepad back into her purse as if her hands were becoming contaminated.

"Not a pretty situation," Jim said to Rossi. "Can we go into details about specific crimes … maybe their prevalence and the possible identities of certain people who are escaping the law? And any who have some relationship with the U.S.? Incidentally, that's why I was happy to hear about your history back in the U.S."

"When you said, 'ideal'?"

"Yeah, and I'll be saying it again."

"I'm afraid I'm confused. Why again?"

"Pardon any imposition, but I anticipate repeating the word after you go ahead and talk about suspected Sicilian criminals and even what you know about crime on the mainland. I hope you're willing to do that. But only after I hear what you have to say about something else."

"I have a better idea. You ask the questions you want, and I'll give you my best answers. So what's the 'something else'?"

Long ago, Jim had learned that to test a person's honesty and integrity, a diversionary tactic helped. In this case, the warden's knowledge of World War II was central to the diversion. His understanding of the stages of the war, if compatible with what Jim himself knew, would make what the warden might indicate about criminals more legitimate.

"Can you give me a rundown of key events in the war that's still going on, starting at the beginning?"

"I'm confused again. How does that help in what you're trying to find out?"

"Because as we all know, history reveals that the overall crime rate increases during times of war. And maybe by reviewing the current war, some criminal elements might stick out, if not the names of criminals themselves."

Jim held his breath and saw that Rossi also did.

"Well, I've followed the war effort from the beginning," Rossi said, "and I'm willing to comply, but only in a special way. And that's because my memory isn't what it used to be."

He went to the only bookcase in the room and pulled out a book titled, *Notable Events of World War II.* He opened it to the third page.

"I used to know much of this by heart, but now would I be honoring your request by selecting the most meaningful chapter titles involving what went on chronologically?"

Jim continued to be impressed with the warden's command of the English language.

Doing it the way that Rossi suggested wasn't exactly what Jim had in mind, yet was better than nothing. And he thought that perhaps he might detect something in Rossi's expressions as he picked from the list of contents.

"Fine," Jim said, "so, yes, go ahead."

The warden then stated, as he pointed down the page at the chapter titles: "From 'Versailles' to 'The Battle of Britain'; from 'The Rise of Hitler and Mussolini' to 'Pearl Harbor'; from 'Roosevelt, Churchill and Eisenhower' to 'Montgomery, MacArthur and Patton'; from 'Midway,

Guadalcanal and Rome' to 'D-Day'." He slammed the book shut and looked for a response from Jim first, then from Camille. The silence was louder than a hush.

"I didn't get anything out of that, really," Rossi finally announced.

"Neither did I, so let's move on," Jim said. "The Mafia's a good subject to start with. Take as much time as you want, but give us a rundown. Both Camille and I will be taking notes, if you don't mind."

"Okay … and if I'm not familiar with that subject, I don't know my name. The Sicilian members have been usually based around here—in Palermo and Trapani—but now they're expanding to the eastern cities. As you know, they have ties to the States that date back many years, only they're getting even stronger now. You certainly know how a Mafia family is organized with its capofamiglia or boss at the top and below him, a consigliere or counselor and a sotto capo or underboss. Next there's a capodecima or group leader and the uomini d'onore or men of honor. Under them are ruthless aspiring members of the hierarchy. They run errands, double-cross each other, bomb cars, kill and kill—targeting judges, politicians and other public figures, hoping they might soon become men of honor themselves.

"Then there's the Omerta, meaning 'manliness' in Sicilian. It amounts to a code of silence when law and order question them. They have a code that they live by: if a Mafioso or his family or close friends is slighted, he stands ready to use violence to defend his honor.

"Now let me give you the names of a few alleged Mafioso leaders." He went to his desk, returned with a folder and sorted through some papers. "Here we are," he said. "Most have been recently murdered, but maybe you can pay a call on their relatives, if you think it would be helpful. *You* decide.

"First we have Vito Cascio Ferro. Listen to his advice on protection rackets. It says a lot. 'Don't ruin people with absurd demands for money. Offer your protection instead. Help them prosper in business and they'll not only be happy to pay you pizzo, or protection money, but they'll kiss your hand in gratitude.' It says here that he was arrested sixty-nine times but was acquitted every time. I wonder why. I also wonder how he became a highly respected member of Palermo society while, at the same time, was credited with helping in the growth of the U.S. Mafia. He died just last year. Apparently natural causes, but that's a joke in my opinion.

"Then there's Calogero Vizzini. Entirely

different type. He's an anti-fascist and is now collaborating with the Allies and … get this … was recently made an honorary colonel in the U.S. Army! I think what helped him the most was insisting that after the war, Sicily should legally become united with your country. He's still alive. And speaking of Allies, the Mafia collaborates with them, so many are given positions of responsibility in the Allied civil administration. Something you might investigate … could give you some leads.

"And I'll get off this topic before it makes me sick. Let's end with the awful release of every prisoner here—all seven-hundred of them."

Jim looked up from his notepad and said, "Release of your prisoners? How did *that* happen?"

"It was the fine hand of one Salvatore Giuliano, and it took place just six months ago. They called him the 'Sicilian Bandit'. You deal with him and it's *bacio della morte*."

"Come again?"

"A kiss of death. He wasn't strictly a Mafia member, but he was protected by them and also by the political class. Last year, he kept killing policemen and, as I said, he wound up raiding our prison here and releasing the inmates. Some of them ended up in the U.S."

"But how on earth could that have happened?"

"We have no idea. Some kind of connection between him and one of the prisoners, I guess. They're housed in one-person cells that are arranged in a round pattern. The cells face toward a central observation tower in such a way that our guards can see into all of the cells, while the prisoners can't see the guards. Anyway, it was mass hysteria for over an hour … uh … 'hysteria' … 'confusion', right?

"Pretty close."

"Screaming, shots fired all over the place. Some of the prisoners had guns. We still have no idea how they got them. No one was killed on either side. But over the next month, we were able to recapture many of them. Not the ones who escaped to the U.S., but we have their names. Or the two or three who fled to the hills and, with Giuliano's assistance, formed their own bandit gangs. Guiliano was eventually shot dead by one of the bandits he helped create."

"Fate," Camille said.

The warden's nod was almost undetectable, his face careworn. He said, "I suppose that's the best explanation."

"And what's your opinion about Nazis who've either become disgusted with the war or think it's about over?" Jim asked.

"They're wandering all over the world, and there are lots of them. Here, in Switzerland, in Argentina, in China, but … and I'm afraid to say it … mostly in the U.S.

"We actually know that many of our prisoners who showed up in the U.S. immediately sought out Nazi soldiers there, but we have no idea why. And that's where that Plan-C machine of yours might be used."

"So can you give me a list of the names of your prisoners not accounted for?"

"Sure. They'll no doubt communicate with criminal friends of theirs who are already there in the U.S. That way, you can arrange for arrests of those friends."

Any observer wouldn't be able to tell who looked at the other person first—Jim or Camille. But, in either case, it became apparent that Camille felt it was time to leave the prison. Likewise, it became apparent to Jim that he had learned more than he had expected. The Mafia; the escape of prisoners to the U.S.; the Nazis who left the battlefield; the anticipated use of Plan-C; and probably some other things … subtle things. Regarding the latter, that was the way it always was for him when on a mission: take away what

> you're after but no doubt other findings might come along as a bonus. They might register in one's body language, in kinds of verbal expression, in the sincerity of others. In this case, the sincerity of Warden Rossi and even his carabinieri were straightaway and clear as crystal.
>
> He agreed with Camille's obvious feeling that it was time to bug off. They rose and then the warden did. He went to his desk for a list of unaccounted-for prisoners and handed it to Jim. Seldom had Jim hugged a man in appreciation, but he did this time. He was effusive in his words and Camille followed suit.

Paul and Vincent decided on what pertinent information might possibly be extracted from their readings—if any.

"The rest is irrelevant," Paul said, sitting on the edge of his bed.

"Irrelevant and interesting," Vincent chimed in. "But we ***did*** get some leads … people we might see. Should we look them up?"

"Now I'm thinking not. We might get killed."

"You're right, so I have to agree. And also, Paul, I have to admit something. While you and the warden were talking, for some of the time I was only half listening because my mind was elsewhere—back in Kris Stuyvesant's office. I indicated 'no questions' to him because I didn't want to show ignorance but, between you and me, I know zilch about the stem cells he referred to. You game on doing a little teaching?"

Paul fell back on the bed and, with hands folded behind his head, he felt happy to be given such an opportunity, for he knew much **more** than zilch about the subject.

"They're the body's 'mechanics'," he said, straightening up. "They repair damaged tissues and organs. And because they can grow into any type of cell in the body, scientists believe they hold the key to many new therapies."

"But where do they come from?"

"From fertilized eggs left over from in-vitro fertilization. This is what has caused so much controversy in one religion after another."

"There's that religion word again, but as long as you brought it up, one more thing: I've heard you speaking to others about … how'd you put it … some religious practices leading to forensic cheats? What's that all about?"

"Well, I look at it as a quartet: gangsters, corrupt forensic scientists, immoral religious leaders and paybacks. The gangsters get the lab results they want—such as phony DNA readings; religious leaders serve as fronts; and they along with forensic scientists get rewarded with prostitutes."

Almost as a reward for the information he'd received, Vincent said, "Thanks for that, Paul … terrific. Now let's have dinner and afterwards take in whatever show they have in the auditorium." He read from a folder on the dresser: "It's a magician … Donato Gianolo."

"Good idea. Maybe he can make my headache disappear.

But before that, we've got some time to kill, so I'll summarize what our four contact people had to offer that might help us—and the same for those in the countries we've visited so far. It's really only Switzerland. Here in Sicily it's by remote … I suppose you'd call it … remote from the book I wrote."

Vincent agreed and prepared for a shower while Paul moved to a desk and began writing from some notes he'd taken:

Our Four Contact People:

Fabio (Italy)

—Napoleon used religion as a front

—How Napoleon treated the main religions

—Much regarding fronts

—Regarding cruise lines. Many in cahoots with pirates and serve as fronts for prostitutes that pirates supply

—He recommends that cruise lines be investigated

Drinkwell (St. Helena)

—Raved about histarians

—Admires Napoleon

—Said that today's gangsters still admire Napoleon

—Said that faith strengthens resilience to stress and many illnesses

—Main information: assurance of histarian help.

Gomez (Argentina)

—The prostitutes, Marlene and Velda

—About Juan and Eva Peron regarding Switzerland.

—Eva's being paid off in diamonds

Saltanban (Gibraltar)

—His Synchronous Action Device (SAD)

—How it can help identify and locate callers from churches to criminals

—Explained crime/computer link and how computers can be valuable but also dangerous

Two of Seven Countries Thus Far

Kris Stuyvesant (Switzerland)

—Mentioned criminalistics and forensic science in same breath

—About statistics, immigrants and convictions

—About Napoleon and the Perons

—About stem cell research

Father Morton Heg (Switzerland)

—Said the five ingredients for a healthy church apply in Switzerland

—Described religions and how organized

Roberto Rossi (Sicily)

—Warden of prison. But from a chapter in *Spying for Keeps.*

—Mafia organization

—Explained how many escapees fled to U.S. Gave their names

Chapter 13

The auditorium was packed. They headed for the rear, and as Paul was about to sit he noticed a woman who suddenly appeared near their seats, then moved rapidly up the aisle and disappeared in the control booth.

She was young and beautiful and wore a double-breasted dark jacket with line-backer shoulders, white shirt and tight-fitting blue trousers.

Paul gazed up at the booth with its lighted paneling and a camera lens projecting through an open front. It was not a man operating the camera, but a woman! Not really operating, but standing beside it.

The woman who had paused near us!

Paul nudged Vincent to take a look and at that very moment, the woman aimed a pistol in their direction.

They flipped up their seats and instinctively ducked down.

Suddenly the lights went out and the auditorium was cloaked in total darkness except for a small area behind them near an emergency door, and also along dimly-lit aisles. People scrambled and bounced off each other like bumper cars. A few screamed. They seemed to be scaring one another, but most could make out where the stairs were and began filing up toward the main entrance. At the top landing, beyond the booth, rays of light soon began to appear once the first attendees pushed open the double doors. But the woman was no longer in sight.

By then, their guns had been drawn and hidden in their armpits, arms swung across their chests. All in concert as if they had rehearsed it.

"Quick, out the back door," Paul whispered. They separated its curtain, hurried toward their room, locked the door two ways, plopped onto their beds and sighed in unison. Somewhat short of breath, Paul said, "Good God … I can't believe it … a woman! I guess they recruit both genders. I don't know what you're thinking, Vin, but I've had it around here. Let's head for home sooner than planned. Like **tonight**."

"Okay with me," Vincent said, "and while we're on the subject, we'll still have five more countries to visit. Won't the repetition get to us?"

"Probably, but we've got to push ahead. Maybe we'll be surprised. And who knows … things might change."

"For better or for worse?"

Paul repeated himself: "Who knows? But one thing I **do** know … whoever's behind tracking us won't let up. I'll swear to it till my dying day."

Vincent had a troubled look. “Look,” he said, “don’t use that ‘dying’ word. And I still don’t completely understand. Couldn’t we continue on schedule and wait until we visit more countries?”

“We could, but a female with a gun pointing straight at us is the last straw. It’s all gotten to me, and I definitely need a breather. We were going to see these three guys anyway … get their take on how we’re progressing. Or not progressing. So why not now? And if we learn anything from them, it would be a bonus. Understand, Vin, I want home whether we see the guys or not. And whether I write part of a book or not … which I’ve put off for now. And who knows for how long?”

Vincent rolled over on his twin bed, reached to pat Paul on the arm and said, “Now I completely understand, my friend. Let’s get on with it.”

Vincent, unmarried, accompanied Paul to his house on Cape Cod. It was seven in the morning, U.S. time, and Sylvie was shocked to see them. So shocked that she kissed Vincent on the lips instead of the cheek and had to apologize.

Paul took his time trying to explain what had taken place in their travels thus far, although he didn’t mention the episode involving the *Magnifico Woman*, as he would begin to refer to her. Nor did he mention why they decided to return home at this stage, and she didn’t ask for an explanation because she was no doubt anxious to mention the two-day oceanographic symposium she’d be attending in New Seabury, the next town over. It would begin right after work at Woods Hole that day.

He did say, however, that they would resume their travels as soon as they had paid the three men a visit, beginning with Sparky and ending with Guy Martin. They would then leave for Paris. "So we'll be on a tight schedule ... maybe fifteen or twenty minutes per person. That seem okay to you or would they feel insulted—too rushed?"

"Neither one. And certainly not as rushed as I feel right now." All in all, she stressed her understanding of the tight schedule and next informed Paul of the symposium. He pointed out his happiness over her keeping busy and, blowing repeated kisses her way, watched her leave for Woods Hole.

Soon after, he phoned all three men to inform them that he and Vincent would be stopping by. Each expressed great delight in hearing from him and looked forward to the visit.

The longest conversation was with Guy who said he had some surprising news but would wait until they met before commenting on it. Paul tried to dig the news out of him but was nowhere near successful. He stated that they'd be willing to travel to the Boston office but Guy insisted on lunch at Bonfiore's as before. They set the time at 1:30.

Paul next removed a folder from his briefcase, the one containing two sheets about what he had learned from the four contact people plus the two men in Switzerland. He wanted to condense the summaries into questions he might put to Sparky, David and Guy, so he jotted down the following in one of the margins:

—Legitimacy of religion and its relationship to criminal activity

—About Napoleon

—Investigate cruise lines

—Faith helping reduce stress and extent of illnesses

—Contacting prostitutes Marlene and Velda

—Explain the crime/computer link

—Explain stem cell research

Paul's intent was to present a sheet of these items to each man and have him choose the one or ones he might be able to offer insights about. In the future, he would refer to it as the "Sheet of Seven" and had to smile about it because there were now so many titles to so many things that he couldn't keep them straight.

What went with what? What's most pressing now?

Chapter 14

June 15

The office and forensic laboratory of criminalist Walter Sparks was still located in the Hollings, Connecticut Police Department Building. It was there that many hours were spent by Sparky and Paul as they exchanged forensic views, wore down international challenges and learned from one another. Even Vincent had participated in some sessions. And for years Paul took Sparky's words as gospel.

The two men entered the building, and at its dispatch window they exchanged warm greetings with several long-time receptionists. As was so often the case, one of them announced their arrival as a subdued public address message and then they were buzzed into a maze of interconnecting rooms. Each was filled with hard-at-work employees, traipsing about filing cabinets and computers. Most all of them waved at the men. They proceeded directly to the crime lab and on to the criminalist's corner office. They entered without knocking and eased cautiously between two long benches of wire baskets, microscopes, chemical bottles, latent fingerprint equipment, swirls of glass tubing, and the brothy smell of petri dishes. Vincent's hand accidently knocked one of the dishes slightly off center.

Sparky was sitting at a desk, his back toward them, while inspecting a tagged knife with his usual handheld microscope. "Hi folks," he said without turning.

"Wait now," Paul said. "I think I know the answer because we've played this scene before, but how in hell did you know we're here?"

Sparky finally swirled around and answered, "Because I heard the message from out front. They all register in here. And because I heard the petri dish move. So there."

Sparky rose and, after handshakes, pulled over two chairs and all three sat down.

"So good to see you both. All is well?"

"All is well," Paul said, "although my head hurts from the constant travel and some unexpected things. But let's get to why we're here, and we won't take up much of your time, Spark. After you, we have two more guys to see and then it's back on the trail again, starting with Paris."

Paul was pleased with the criminalist's obliging look and—as a fan of yesteryear—with his recurring appearance—that of a fifty-some-odd throwback to a Western Union clerk in a 1940s B movie: green visor, slicked down black hair parted in the middle, wire-framed glasses, gartered shirtsleeves and faded white suspenders.

"You may wonder about what our purpose is in all the travel," Paul continued. "It's twofold: one, learning about the progress and legitimacy of most religions and how they might be somehow tied to Napoleon. And two, investigating criminal activity, including churches and pastors acting as illegal fronts. What I mean here is: does such a thing exist and if so, how extensive is it, what can be done about it, and does the U.S. inherit such crimes and criminals?"

Sparky interceded, saying, "Yes, I know about your purposes."

"You know?"

"Word gets around. I can even predict what countries you'll be visiting."

Paul wasn't surprised because the criminalist, who was also an histarian, had always been on top of things.

But has he also been talking to Guy or David?

"I figured you could, Spark, but so can I predict that even right now, you'll repeat what I've heard over and over again. You're that fond of saying it; I'm fond of hearing it; and I know it by heart."

"Like what?"

"Like 'It's easy to trivialize trifles, but so often in forensics as in most endeavors, it's the minute little details—a scratch here, a scratch there, an insect here, an insect there—that are the most revealing.' Did I get it right?"

Sparky nodded and said, "It's a draw."

"Always is, but let's not waste time. I have here a folder with six subjects I scribbled on a sheet inside it. Can you pick out which subjects you can help us on? You know, sharing some knowledge that we might not have?"

Paul handed the folder over and Sparky took mere seconds to read the inside sheet.

"The last two," he said, "stem-cell research and the crime/computer link. I doubt that you're ignorant of them, but I can summarize what I know. And that isn't just the result of my training and the issues that I deal with on an everyday basis, but also because I'm an active histarian. Shall I go ahead?"

"By all means," Paul said.

Sparky looked up, searching the air for how to begin. "Let's see," he said. "I won't even mention what stem cells are … but I **will** mention where history places their research. The cells, Switzerland money, some Jews, some Nazis, Argentina, the Perons … all are hinged in several ways. And I say 'hinged' advisedly. First of all, during the days of Argentina's Juan and Eva Peron—back in the '40s—they ignored the obvious when some Nazis got away with murder—literally. Either that or they helped spearhead the entire operation. I think the latter. It boils down to Nazis being allowed to settle there. The Nazis then murdered Jews and hid all their money—down there and in Swiss banks. And here's the important point: it was money that had been earmarked for stem cell research."

Paul had known everything that Sparky said. And it was the second time that he'd sat through an explanation he didn't need or want, the other being during their session with Kris

Stuyvesant. But he stretched out an appreciative smile.

"Next," Sparky said, "the crime/computer link, as you have it worded here. Cybercrime. I could spend hours on this, but I'll give only a few bare essentials. And don't tell anyone, but I'm more interested in this than in stem cells because it's where forensics can play a more essential role. Fact is we can examine for fingerprints and DNA on certain computers. That's the simple stuff. But things are certainly changing when people can execute crimes electronically. At the other end of the scale though, we can now tap in ourselves. It's what the higher-ups call 'digital forensics', but I call it 'forensic tapping'. In other words, the bad guys can use computers for crimes ranging from drug operations to murders, but we're developing sophisticated technologies to counter it."

Sparky pushed a button on his sit-to-stand desk, stood straight up and pushed some papers around. "So what's cybercrime or computer related crime anyway?" he asked. "The simplest answer is that it involves a computer and a network. I don't know whether you've heard about it, gentlemen, but I've been asked by the federal government to assist in what's now become the most modern branch of forensic science in Connecticut. Together with some colleagues of mine, we help in recovering material found in digital devices, often in relation to computer crime. I now get involved in examining for the usual crimes of murder and fraud and prostitution and extortion—but also for cyberwarfare—even cyberterrorism." He pushed the button again and sat back down.

"Excellent, Spark, excellent," Paul said. "You certainly

have a way of covering a lot of ground with the fewest words. Now two or three last things: do you think that what we learn in just seven countries reflects what transpires worldwide?"

"Yes, I do. Seven is enough."

"And as we continue, can we call you if necessary?"

"Yes, naturally. You know that, Paul."

"And may we also call if we need histarian help?"

"No question—yes. I have histarian contacts in many countries, including the ones in your project."

Paul's focus on Sparky doubled in intensity as he exclaimed, "Aha! So that's how you know the countries, right?"

"Sorry, but I'm not at liberty to reveal that type of information."

Chapter 15

Of all the friends Paul had in the investigative and treasure hunting field, Dr. David Brooks was his favorite. They had often shared chilling stories about their investigations and promised each other that they would someday collaborate on a particular case, but it never materialized. The closest they ever got was on a case involving the possible theft of atomic secrets from the Los Alamos National Laboratory. They even flew to New Mexico on the same plane, but when they arrived there they were told that papers dealing with sensitive material had been mistakenly placed but recently found—that no crime had been committed.

Paul often told people of how David bragged about his new attaché case, the one that nobody had ever seen him open. Except Paul. There was not much visible inside with the exception of an Undercover .38 Special wrapped in terry cloth and some extra rounds of ammunition. Hidden behind a retractable panel, however, were a whistle, a small cylinder of Mace and a Scout knife. He also liked the fact that the attaché case announced that he was in his detective mode in contrast to his physician mode.

Then there was the other thing they shared: karate. Their expertise landed them positions at Bruno's Karate Studio where Paul taught percussive *tae kwan do* … kicking, elbows flying, slashing with both hands and feet. David taught *bujutsu*, a form of Japanese martial arts that was based on Zen Buddhism.

Vincent did the driving down a slope that led to the venerable Hollings General Teaching Hospital, a formidable complex crammed into the eastern hillside. Paul's eyes caught its commanding clock tower on the horizon, a reflex he was certain all visitors shared. This wasn't the first time he had admired the hundred-year-old structure, a landmark continuation of the elevator shaft still in use for the administrative section of the building complex. Half again as tall, it sported silent clocks on three sides, shaded by a copper cupola. And in Paul's mind, it pierced the sky like a foundation pile in reverse. Architecturally, it was the only feature of the hospital he liked, tested and timeless amidst a mishmash of wings and additions, red brick against greys and tans and glass.

They headed for David's office and were informed by a nurse they encountered that he was still making medical grand rounds but should be available within ten minutes. She suggested they wait in his office. There, as they passed by a table of books, Paul was intrigued by the cover of one off to the side. He took it up and they both sat on a small sofa. He leafed through the book after noting that it was written by an author whose name he didn't recognize and that it highlighted another man named David. Drawn to a section containing the name over and over again, he read:

> As the headlights of his Mercedes fell across his driveway, David cursed Fitzpatrick Snow Removal. Half-assed job. He noticed a faint outline of tire tracks as he pressed on the remote control and entered his attached one-car garage. Probably Fitzy's truck or maybe a delivery truck making a wrong turn. He was not concerned until he reached the breezeway and spotted light shining through the window of the rear bathroom. He whipped out his Minx and streaked to the left side of the door to the den. Hugging the wall, he tried the door. It was locked. He slipped in a key and, shrinking sideways, flicked the door with his fingers and allowed it to drift open. The light thud of the door on the inside wall sounded heavy in the silence—loud enough, he thought, to rouse any intruder occupied in the back of the house.
>
> David clutched the semiautomatic with both hands and waited a few seconds, trying to breathe only through his nose. He recalled once reading that armed cowboys never peeked around corners from a standing position. He squatted and, ignoring the pain in his knee, eased the Minx into the doorway. His head followed close behind.
>
> He reached around and turned on the light. The

first things that caught his eye were his desk and table drawers—every one had been pulled out. Most of them together with his considerable number of removable bookshelves lay on the floor like a pile of bricks and tiles. Scattered papers, slanted pictures, disturbed books, overturned lamps, puckered carpeting.

Infuriated, David dashed from room to room, flipping light switches, ready to shoot at anything that moved. Disarray, but not destruction, was everywhere. He found the bathroom light on. He checked his watch. It read six-forty and he deduced the visitor must have been there within the last two hours.

He ambled about—more leisurely now, but with Minx still drawn—stepping aside as he flung open closet doors. Convinced no one was in the house, he returned the gun to its rig and, shifting around in the center of the living room, asked himself, "Who was looking for what?" It was a question plucked from coals of agitation, because David was, first and foremost, inflamed over the violation of his personal space. He felt blood bubbling at his temples.

He thought of sitting but was too fired up for that. Instead, he hunched over and crossed his arms tightly on his chest like a tourniquet meant for the adrenaline surge he felt throughout his body. He was even annoyed over the herky-jerky tapping of his foot. Suddenly he stiffened upright. The basement!

David barreled down the stairs as he yanked out his Minx once again. Despite semidarkness, he knew exactly where to pull on the three light chains. There was no one there and his gun collection was intact.

Upstairs, he fixed himself a drink and considered straightening out the mess, but he decided he wanted Elsie to see it. He sat at the kitchen table, sipping while he kneaded his knee. By the last sip he had reassured himself the intruder had never entered the basement, a pronouncement that helped him tolerate the break-in and subjugate its relevance vis-à-vis the question he had initially asked: "Who was looking for what?"

Soon, the real David entered his office, a stethoscope looped around his neck. He apologized for his absence and asked if they'd been waiting long.

"Not long," Paul said. "Sorry to barge in and we won't take much time. We're headed for Boston."

"You're not barging. Never have, no matter what I'm doing. And speaking of that, grand rounds took a little longer because of a case of meningococcemia that needed attention."

"You and your big words. Is the guy alright?"

"It's a gal, and I think she'll pull through," David answered as he removed a long white coat.

Taller than Paul at six-five, he appeared top-heavy with the upper-body contour of a less towering man, perhaps a boxer. Empty-hipped, his trouser legs broke clear to his toes, a sight not lost on most observers. He would offer a dismissive wave. "Helps warm the tops of feet, you know."

Having just turned fifty-two, his uniformly dark hair was neatly parted on the right side. Only his eyebrows and the sliver of a mustache showed streaks of light gray. Soft blue eyes made up for a tendency to keep from smiling. Rather, he preferred a constant check of his surroundings, whether in a room or on a city street, a routine he'd adopted from his practicing the Buddhist concept of mindfulness years before. To those who cared to comment, he would explain that it was a way of managing stress.

Their handshakes were brief, David starting with Vincent, then with Paul, and back to Vincent. "Oopes," David said, "I forgot. I already did that. I'm still making grand rounds." He sat on a chair opposite the sofa. "Well, you two guys are canvassing the globe, eh? How's it working out? Are you learning what you want?"

"Mostly, but we're still not finished," Paul responded. "And why we're here is to fill in some blanks." He handed him the same folder he'd given Sparky. "Inside are six questions I put together. I've memorized them and, as a doctor, can you comment on the faith one—practicing it to reduce stress and the extent of illnesses? If I had to explain why faith is in the six at all, it's because it's part and parcel of religion, and that's one of the reasons we're doing this in the first place. If you remember my phone call to you, David, I mentioned religion and crime."

Paul didn't wait for an answer because David was alternating between reading over the six issues and checking his surroundings.

"And then the Marlene and Velda one," Paul continued. "You've met them and know their history. Would speaking to them give the complete lowdown on the cruise line one? You know what I mean there, of course."

This time David **did** speak up. "First off, about those prostitutes. In my humble opinion, there's a lot to gain in talking to them. You mentioned crime … well they promoted crimes aboard cruise ships. If they know what's good for them, they'll no doubt cooperate and even name the cruise lines involved. Their ships and crews can be approached and given warnings or even citations of some kind to knock it off. Or to appear in court. And secondly we have religious faith and its effect on stress and sicknesses. You know about my involvement with Buddhist mindfulness and its help in reducing stress. I'd say toss in illnesses, too.

"Now, men, did I synthesize too much or should I expound?"

Paul checked his watch and jumped at the chance he'd been given. A perfect opening. "Nothing further," he said. "It's a stupid way of putting it—maybe even grammatically wrong—

but we have to synthesize our visit. Because frankly, David, we're in a hurry. But as has been our wont, we'll keep in touch."

Little more came up before the two men took their leave.

Chapter 16

Paul wasn't in a hurry at all. In the course of dealing with Sparky and David and prior to the upcoming visit with Guy Martin, what was grinding out in Paul's mind was why a quick resumption of foreign travel was necessary and who told him it had to be? "It wasn't" and "No one" were his answers and he felt satisfied.

What would now take the place of a hurry-scurry existence would be relaxing for a full couple of days—watching television, taking in a movie, reading. Especially reading, and Ernest Hemingway was his favorite author.

> *Why didn't I understand? The relaxation is really why I wanted to come home. Seeing the three men is secondary.*

He wished they needn't meet with Guy, but since he had called him he would follow through. But it would be a snappy visit, for as the hours slowly passed, he longed for relaxation even more.

At 1:30 on the button, Guy was waiting for them in the usual booth at Bonfiore's restaurant. Sliding in, Paul dispensed with any greeting, instead mentioning that they soon had a plane to catch for Paris, then to Germany, and couldn't afford to spend much time there. He emphasized that he hoped Guy would understand.

Nodding, Guy said, "Sure do. I've been in that situation myself when I had deadlines to meet at the *Tribune*." He then switched the subject, saying that he hadn't seen Vincent in years and explained why his handshake was firmer than the one with Paul.

They had hardly settled in when Guy produced a stamped envelope and took out a thin strip of paper with a barely legible message scrawled across it. He gave the strip to Paul who squinted his eyes as he made out: "d'arno ——pack in, ma pal, or els."

Paul was furious as he looked at the other two and said, "Son-of-a-bitch. I'll be damned if I'm about to pack it in! Bastard doesn't even know how to write. But why mail it to **you**?"

"My best guess is that wherever it came from … he or they sent it because they know you're mainly on the road, and that you and I are friends. Has anybody suspicious been seen around your house?"

"No."

"See? They have no idea where you live, but I'd keep an

eye out. One of these days they might learn."

"But how do they know we're friends? Doesn't it worry you?"

"No idea. And they're after you, not me."

Paul dropped the slip into his pocket and asked, "So that's the surprise?"

"That's it. Thought you'd be interested."

Disgusted, Paul took a while before saying, "Well now I know, so let's tuck it all away and get to why we're meeting." More and more, he wanted their time there to fly by.

"Agreed," Guy said. He then dominated the conversation as if he were an evangelistic preacher who was giving a lecture and the other two were part of a large audience. Paul let him go on, his mind adrift, his next days pictured bright before him. Earlier, Paul had wanted to learn Guy's opinion of global religion and global crime, but now he tried to appear interested in what was being said about Napoleon Bonaparte. What sunk in with Paul did so in dribs and drabs:

> "Sooner or later, the subject of arsenic has to be considered. My take is that it was fed to him in small doses from 1812 on."

> "Whoever was doing it deliberately wanted him to fail in battle."

> " 'Any suspects?'" you might ask. The usual ones but no real proof. I'm talking about *St.* Helena, not the start of it all during the battles. This is why I believe there was a conspiracy. You know the cast of characters as well as I do. You've written about them. Count de Montholon heads everyone's list."

> "But then there's the governor of the island, Hudson Lowe. I call him Sir Nasty Lowe because of his behavior and fear that Napoleon would somehow escape and return to France to rule again."

> "And don't forget Charles-Maurice de Talleyrand or Lady Beckett, the mystery lady from the East India Tea Company."

Paul had had enough but couldn't think of a way to leave graciously. He even forgot that they hadn't eaten yet, but once remembered, he perked up and hoped that mouthfuls of food would limit Guy's monologue. It did—almost altogether—and after they had rushed through skimpy sandwiches, they left the booth, Guy patting his stomach, Paul relieved, Vincent trailing behind with a toothpick in his mouth. On the way to the front entrance, Paul peered out of a row of windows and saw approaching rays of sunlight about to burst through. It was entirely different from the last visit there when there were no sun rays but flashes of lightning in an ominous sky. He interpreted the improvement as a good sign.

Chapter 17

Alone in his East Falmouth home, Paul paced about while munching crackers, not with thoughts that would stun the universe but with a sense of detachment—detachment from intertwining emotions of uncertainty, doubt and fear. Even without a car, he felt safe for he had all the firepower he might need—on his body and in his basement cabinets of pistols, rifles and ammunition. Vincent had driven to his own home after dropping him off.

On his first day there, he slept and slept, taking naps to quell the drowsiness of previous ones. But on day two, he once again turned to Hemingway's *A Farewell to Arms,* having frequently read the first two pages of the twelfth chapter. Milan is mentioned a host of times and it was to that city that he, as a teenager, was so often taken by his parents who had begun to love its atmosphere more than New England's. Not only that, but they believed Rome represented the "old" Italy while Milan represented the "new" Italy. And so did Paul, who was also of the opinion that Milan was the best "balanced" Italian city, having kept its history intact.

He also believed that most of what was written in the chapter's surrounding pages was beautifully written and too believable to ignore so, even though he skipped a few pages, he would continue to read until "Milan" no longer appeared.

> The room was long with windows on the right-hand side and a door at the far end that went into the dressing room. The row of beds that mine was on faced the windows and another row, under the windows, faced the wall. If you lay on your left side you could see the dressing room door. There was another door at the far end that people sometimes came in by. If anyone were going to die they put a screen around the bed so you could not see them die, but only the shoes and puttees of doctors and men nurses showed under the bottom of the screen and sometimes there would be whispering. Then the priest would come out from behind the screen and afterward the men nurses would go back behind the screen to come out again carrying the one who was dead with a blanket over him down the corridor between the beds and someone folded the screen and took it away.
>
> That morning the major in charge of the ward asked me if I felt that I could travel the next day. I said I could. He said then they would ship me out

early in the morning. He said I would be better off making the trip now before it got too hot.

... They were anxious to ship me to Milan where there were better X-ray facilities and where, after the operation, I could take mechano-therapy. I wanted to go to Milan too. They wanted to get us all out and back as far as possible because all the beds were needed for the offensive, when it should start.

The night before I left the field hospital Rinaldi came in to see me with the major from our mess. They said that I would go to an American hospital in Milan that had just been installed.

... You go away in the morning, baby, Rinaldi said. To Rome, I said. No, to Milan, said the major, to the Crystal Palace, to the Cova, to Campari's, to Biffi's, to the galleria.You lucky boy.

... The next day in the morning we left for Milan and arrived forty-eight hours later.

Sylvie was aware of Paul's attraction to Milan and before she had left for the symposium, she had asked why he went to Sicily and not there. His answer was that he had made extended trips to Sicily twice before and knew his way around that island in contrast to what he knew about the country's large cities. It was enough to satisfy her and she asked nothing further.

PART THREE

Chapter 18

June 17

It was time for Paris and Chet Knight, the young chief police officer at the dome within the Hotel des Invalides. The dome was a former church and contained Napoleon's burial tomb. Paul and Vincent had conferred with Knight on several past occasions, and before leaving Connecticut Paul phoned him to set up the meeting and to indicate why he was traveling so much. He considered Knight to be the one who could give the most accurate and complete information about Napoleon and his legacy.

In another moment of introspection, Paul dwelled on the word "legacy" for the first time. He had thought so often and so much about the military genius, and had listened to what others had to say about him, but now he wondered what "legacy" had to do with any of it. He had an accumulation of questions and answers and ran them through his brain as if it were a spinning wheel:

Why does it matter ... only because criminals

are still fond of him? Maybe. But how does ***that*** *help? By people who might be willing to convince such criminals that Napoleon also had a bad side. What people? Maybe law enforcers and newspaper, magazine, television and radio journalists. So would that decrease criminal activity?*

Paul rubbed his decision scar but could not come up with an answer to the last question.

After he and Vincent arrived at the Charles de Gaulle Airport, he thanked Ansel for the flight and waved off a limo. He'd taken too many by then and wanted to travel differently, so he flagged a taxi and asked to be driven to the Meridian Montparnasse Hotel. Halfway into the twenty-mile ride, he noticed the driver constantly checking the rear view mirror. He asked why.

"Black car, monsieur. Follow us from de Gaulle."

Paul looked curiously at Vincent, then turned around and saw a black car tailgating them. The car's tinted windows masked any view of its interior. Instinctively he wiggled his left shoulder to be certain his Beretta Cougar was there, and it was.

What the hell—country to country! Expect it and be prepared for anything.

"Well?" he whispered to Vincent.

"Same old, same old," was the reply.

An intermittent fast-slow driving pattern continued until they reached Charles de Gaulle Avenue when the car suddenly veered off onto the Malakoff Highway in the direction of the Eiffel Tower. The taxi then slowed to the traffic's pace along the Avenue de la Grande Armée, through the Arc de Triomphe, onto the Champs-Élysées, and past the Hotel des Invalides, the complex which was on their immediate agenda.

As Paul paid the cabbie, he thought it odd that during the second half of the drive, the cabbie had commented no further on the episode, but Paul let it slide. He was getting sick and tired of new worries.

The Meridian had not changed much since their last stay there: lobby décor in pastels, reservation desk spanning an entire wall, archway to a cocktail lounge spanning another, bronze statues of war heroes at every corner, contemporary furnishings and light fixtures, overuse of mirrors and glass, and background music from America's Broadway.

Their room was a duplication of the lobby in style. It was clean, ample and serviceable, but its tenth floor view contained none of the well-known icons of Paris. While Vincent freshened up, Paul sat on the edge of one of the twin beds and began a partial assessment of things as they now stood. He first contemplated the traditional components of detective work, the kind that Guy had brought up. He had never dealt with fronts or investigated the more usual **violent** crimes—murder, rape, aggravated assault and the like—although his quest of stolen treasures had required utilizing many of the same investigative components: interviews and interrogations, undercover operations, overt and covert intelligence, tailing, and archival research. But he fully understood that shedding light on items listed in the Sheet of Seven was not the same as investigating pilfered art.

He also mused about his last Parisian visit, commissioned to locate an art dealer who had absconded with a painting of one Catherine Worlee Grand. It hadn't registered at the time but Paul had skimmed over an article that alluded to her love affair with the noted statesman, Charles-Maurice de Talleyrand. Paul's jaw tightened as he now grasped the irony of that situation, coupled with his belief that if Napoleon had indeed been murdered, Talleyrand had to be considered a prime suspect. Another new worry, and in his subconscious it was barking at him.

They didn't stay there long, soon phoning for a new taxicab. They took off for the Hotel des Invalides, and once there Paul couldn't resist picking up a pamphlet from a stack of them at its entrance.

He said to Vincent: "Sorry, but there's never been a flight when I didn't read up on the place I was going, even if for the umpteenth time."

Vincent gave a nod, which Paul interpreted as, "Go ahead. I can wait."

Glancing through the pamphlet, Paul said he knew most of what was written, but he went ahead anyway:

This Hotel des Invalides is a complex of buildings in the 7th arrondissement of Paris, containing museums and monuments, all relating to the military history of France, as well as a hospital and retirement home for war veterans. Included is the Dome des Invalides, a large former church that contains the burial tomb for Napoleon Bonaparte.

The tomb is often referred to as his sarcophagus. It consists of a casket within a scrolled cover, and is made of red porphyry, a variety of granite, rising high toward a double cupola and pendentives of the dome. An elaborate bronze door leading to the sarcophagus is flanked by two colossal bronze figures that bear symbols of imperial power on a cushion: the crown, the sword, the globe and the hand of justice.

At the base of the sarcophagus is a multicolored, star-shaped mosaic recalling Napoleon's eight most famous triumphs: Rivoli, the Pyramids, Marengo, Austerlitz, Lena, Friedland, Wagram and Moskowa. And circling around are twelve winged statues in Carrara marble, symbolizing victory.

Within various recesses, at two levels and not far from the sarcophagus, are several paintings that evoke themes defined during the reign of Louis XIV; that celebrate the Catholic religion; that show angels holding the symbols of the religious and warrior monarchy; and that highlight a shield with the coat of arms of France.

They entered the dome cautiously, as if they didn't want to call attention to themselves, although scores of visitors looked their way. Paul ran through their faces and recognized none.

Why would I? We're strangers to one another. I hope.

They climbed up the stairs to Knight's office at the far end of a gallery. Paul remembered the stairs well, for the last time on them he had sprained an ankle and it was never the same. He also remembered the smell of the area … light musty but not offensive. So that since then, any time the ankle kicked up or he passed a musty-smelling tree trunk, he pictured the sarcophagus and the stairs.

Paul knocked on the last right-sided door and they entered a small office that appeared rather like a maid's room in a third-class hotel: No windows. Simple desk. Bare coffee table. One floor lamp. Two plain wooden chairs. Small cot. An apparently long bench with no cushions. But there was a shelf containing a single pile of books about Napoleon—seven of them. He read their spines from top to bottom:

The Military Maxims of Napoleon

The Age of Napoleon

The Decline and Fall of Napoleon's Empire

In the Words of Napoleon

Napoleon. Centres of Power

Napoleon Bonaparte—England's Prisoner

The Napoleonic Wars

Officer Knight approached them and was about to offer a greeting when Paul beat him to the punch. "So good to see you again, Chet!"

Vincent gave his usual "Ditto".

"So good to see both of **you**," Chet said.

He led them to the bench, which wasn't long at all, for it was two that were positioned together. He pushed one of them into a right angle with the other and they took seats with Chet on one side and the other two men on the other.

He was dressed in a gray police uniform with a revolver at his waist and a large medallion pinned to his left chest. It contained a photograph of Napoleon. Paul still thought he looked too young, too short, and too thin for a cop. Even too handsome. Last time there he almost told him so, but didn't for fear of offending him. This time, however, he chanced the handsome part but worded it obliquely. "My God," he said, running his eyes over Chet's face, "when will you develop a wrinkle or two?"

"Only when I smile, and that doesn't happen much lately.

It will though, when I get out of here, but that's a different story." Chet framed his hands into a fist and then continued: "On another of your escapades, eh? Or should I say escapes?"

Paul replied, "You must have heard well over the phone … about what we're doing, I mean. And I suppose it would qualify as an escape. And how about **you**? I thought you would have left here by now."

"I should have, but they talked me into finishing out a year. That's about now and I'm beginning to do some packing. Can't wait to leave, and I have a load of offers to consider. Now then …Vincent, you go along with all this travel?"

"Six years worth, and I'm still alive. Doesn't feel like it some days, I must say."

After more small talk, Paul said, "Anyway, thanks for seeing us again—and on such short notice." He removed a copy of the Sheet of Seven from his jacket and handed it to the officer, allowing him to look it over.

Then Paul said, "There are so many things we could get your opinion on, Chet, but it's info about Napoleon that we're primarily interested in. Judging from your books up there, we'll be well served."

"I couldn't promise that but I'll try my best. I think the real authority is a prior over in Gordes—near Marseille. He's not well health-wise, I hear, but if he's strong enough, he might be willing to see you. Worth a try."

Vincent made a note in his pad.

"We know that man," Paul said. "Friar Dominic. He's an historian—one of the oldest. We've been there before … ages ago. He looked pretty weak then. So he's still alive?"

"The last I heard he is, and still active as an histarian. You know what they can do, don't you?"

"Yes, and Chet, your mentioning Gordes over in the east reminds me of my hoping there was something to learn in Bordeaux over in the west. No one there to help?"

"Not that I'm aware of. But it's not about helping, is it? It's their wines, right? Their Haut Brions and their Monton-Rothschilds."

"No, I'm not a wine connoisseur at all. It's simply that I've heard it's a Unesco World Heritage city worth seeing … with all its magnificent 18th century buildings and historic monuments. And it's now only a two-hour journey from here because of a new high-speed train. But we'll save it for another time."

"I see. Anyway, let's get back to what I might have to offer. I don't know as much as I should about helping or hurting criminals, but I can say something about how Napoleon self-destructed … about his defeats. And then a couple of things I learned just yesterday … new stuff. What timing! What a coincidence!"

Paul could have pressed him on the issues but decided to let him have the floor completely to himself.

Chet checked the Sheet of Seven again, and continued. "I'll get to that new stuff in a minute. First though … about those defeats. About how he probably self-destructed. The Russian campaign is a perfect example. There, he abandoned what he had preached: the diamond-shaped formation; the spider web tactic; his square battalion; his envelopment attack. And most important of all: march dispersed, fight concentrated. I'd say the abandonment probably applied in other encounters. But why? Was it because of arsenic in his system? Remember it was being used by him and his men as a recreational drug in small amounts, but was it adding up? Or, unbeknownst to him, was it being given in larger amounts in order to kill him?"

He stood, reached up to the shelf, took hold of the top book, sat back down and opened it. Then he said, "After you called and indicated why you wanted to see me, I did some research and here, let me read you what I underlined in this book, *The Military Maxims of Napoleon,* written by David G. Chandler and published by Lionel Leventhal Limited. It indicates that some things are different today from when certain dictums applied many decades ago. I've left out a few technical words and the end of my underlining refers to his terrible defeat in the Battle of Waterloo":

> To demonstrate the latent perils inherent in too direct or literal application of the *Maxims* to modern warfare, any attempt to apply the Napoleonic dictum "march dispersed, fight concentrated" on a future European … battlefield could well lead to the presentation to the enemy of a very tempting target for a short-range nuclear weapon. Modern requirements are therefore for formations to fight … dispersed as is consistent with achieving their appointed roles, relying on

artillery, minefields, heli-borne firepower (especially against armour) and conventional airstrikes to reduce the enemy's striking force. It has been calculated that a modern company commander has at his disposal, or can call down, as much weight of firepower as a Napoleonic commander … The old saying about every soldier having a "marshal's baton in his knapsack" has thus taken on an unexpected modern meaning. Napoleon had no air element in his armoury—and indeed may be said to have compromised his "C31" capacity (Command, Communication and Control, with Intelligence) by ordering the disbandment of the French Army's single unit on … balloonists soon after becoming First Consul. This ill-judged decision—which well illustrates that there were distinct limits to even Napoleon's powers of intellectual vision—is hard to comprehend. The unit has played an important role in the battle of Fleurs … despite the fact that the Austrians captured one balloon half inflated in a church. (It is still to be seen in the National Military History Museum in Vienna). Had Napoleon possessed such an instrument of intelligence gathering (the equivalent, perhaps, to modern satellite surveillance), the approach of three Prussian corps through the Bois de Paris … would have been detectable from at least 10 a.m.

> instead of 1:30 p.m., with possible incalculable results on the outcome of the climactic Battle of Waterloo.

"So there you have it. Along with Alexander, he must be considered the greatest military leader of all time, but I just can't overestimate the possibility of his self-destruction."

"You make a strong case, Chet, and I tend to agree with you. But now for those new findings. What are they?"

Chet returned the book to the shelf before beginning again. "Well, number one is what I read yesterday in the *Wall Street Journal.* It's about crime, not about Napoleon. I'm not an expert on crime, nor am I interested in becoming one, but this **did** grab my attention, and I thought I'd pass it on to you. U.S. economists are ..."

"Wait!" Paul said. "You get the *Journal* over here?"

"Yes, ever since I arrived. Don't forget that I graduated from the John Jay College of Criminal Justice in New York City. It was there that I started receiving the *Journal*, and I still do. It's mailed to me every day. I bet their circulation department thinks it strange that they mail to where Napoleon's body lies."

"I'll bet a copy isn't addressed to Napoleon, though," Vincent said, tongue in cheek. Neither of the other two changed expression.

"Anyway," Chet said, "according to the paper, many U.S. economists are claiming that there would be less crime if the country moved to a mostly cashless society. They say that it's based on the fact that criminals rely heavily on cash transactions and that if large money bills, like fifty-dollars and over, are eliminated, they would suffer. And why? Well, I never knew this, but only a fraction of paper currency can be accounted for among non-criminals. So where's the rest? In the underground criminal economy. The result would be that many more smaller bills would be necessary to make up for the loss of larger denominations, and it would mean larger and much heavier suitcases instead of small briefcases. Then the newspaper brought in things that could be affected like the number of false invoices and bogus checks—all of which I didn't quite understand. But the whole idea of less available cash? I don't know if it would be a blessing or not, but maybe you could file the idea away."

"Very … **very** … interesting, Chet. Worth filing away."

"And the other thing isn't as dramatic, at least not now in its early stages. I don't know the exact details but I understand that police everywhere can now track gunshots." Chet paused into an obvious thinking mode.

"Meaning what?" Vincent asked as he erased what he had just written.

"It works something like this: when a gun is fired, sensors are immediately placed nearby and high up. This is done by an independent company. So the location of the gunfire is determined, police departments receive audio clips and they can move into action. Sounds simple to me. But promising."

"Another thing to file away," Paul said.

It appeared that Chet was awaiting more comment at the same time that Paul's mind had switched to Gordes and its prior. Finally, he rose and spread three fingers in Chet's direction.

"Uh … they mean something?" Chet asked.

"Yeah, three **important** somethings. One—insights concerning Napoleon. Two—changes concerning cash. And three—sensors concerning gunshots. All well thought out and well presented to us by you. I can't say how indebted we are."

For the first time that day, Chester Knight smiled.

Chapter 19

After a call to the monastery in Gordes to confirm the availability of the prior, Paul and Vincent found that he was still alive and functioning. But before traveling there, Paul thought it best to put together the third set of Discovery Notes. He sat at the desk in their hotel room and scribbled them out:

> Arrived home. Called Sylvie. Said trip was worthwhile. Dinner out. Counties to visit. Reason for visits. What makes a church healthy, five questions to be asked, etc. Question of boredom. And something perilous. Arrive in Switzerland. Article about the country. Mention of what sticks in my mind: religion, Vatican, Red Cross, gold, Nazi and Fascist stuff. Vincent says we should stop rushing. At airport, man with rifle at annex bldg. I show my pistol and he disappears. Vincent says copies of reasons should be given to each contact. Delta steward makes copies. Call ahead to

Commander Kris Stuyvesant. Drive to Lucerne. Various sights. Fed Dept. Bldg. Office described. Kris suggests Father Morton Heg for religion inf. I mention “fronts”. I give small lecture, then he gives his. At Father Heg’s office. He comments on Swiss religion. I mention the two rifle guys. At Sicily’s airport—decision on which countries to visit. Home to confer with contacts, then on to remaining three countries. Magnifico Hotel. Change of plans. To read my book re prior visit to prison with Warden Rossi. Book chapter describes the warden, the prison and hotel described. Rossi gives history of WWII, Mafia. How some prisoners escaped to U.S. I describe stem cells to Vincent. Also how they’re linked to Swiss and some Jews and Nazis. Forensic cheats. Paybacks. Summary of what 4 contact people had to say, plus men in 2 of 4 countries thus far. Packed auditorium at hotel. Woman aims pistol at us. I decide to return home and put off writing the book. Sylvie to attend symposium. We’re to visit with Sparky, David and Guy. List of what we learned from 4 contact people and the two men in Switz. At Sparky’s office. He speaks of stem cell research, Jews, Nazis, Perons in Argentina. Also of crime/computer link, cybercrime, digital forensics, cyberwarfare & cyberterrorism. Says the 7 countries do represent the entire world and that he’s available as an histarian, if ever needed. Meet

> with David Brooks. Mention of Bruno's Karate Studio. Description of Hollings General. David described. Re the 6 questions. Comments on faith to reduce stress. On Marlene and Velda re cruise line. Re his Buddhist mindfulness. I meet with Guy at Bonfiori's. He produces mailed message re "knock it off." Relaxation at home. I read part of book on Milan. To meet with Chet Knight. On taxi drive to Meridian Hotel, past many landmarks, a black car tails us. To Hotel des Invalides and Chet's office. Seven books on Nap. are on shelf. Chet described. I give him copy of Sheet of Seven. Chet recommends Friar Dominic at Gordes. Chet describes Nap. Defeats and reads from book about his self-destruction. Mentions WSJ article re cashless economy creating less crime and re sensors able to track gunshots.

They checked out of the Meridian Hotel, then decided on lunch at a restaurant that Sylvie had often recommended. Once, she quoted James Cameron as saying, "Paris is an air and a scent and a state of mind." She went on to say that the same thing could be said about the gourmet Alain Ducasse Restaurant in the Hotel Plaza Athenee. She explained that the hotel was located just off the Champs-Élysées, within view of the Eiffel Tower, and was a perfect throwback to the classic French style of the early 20th century with its high ceilings, authentic molding, and numerous fireplaces.

The taxi drove slowly along what its driver claimed was one of the world's most glamorous shopping streets with its many luxury boutiques: Chanel, Dior, Lacroix, Valentino.

Vincent looked interested but Paul took little time to notice. Nor, once inside the restaurant, did he comment on the unique table arrangement, brass lamps, and red leather banquettes beneath Art Deco murals. He did, however, pick up one of the menus. Its backside referred to the scent of the dining room as that of "white tea mingled with geranium and freesia that is designed to be calming, relaxing and sophisticated."

He spoke to Vincent as if he were where he really didn't want to be: "Maybe I'm sometimes sophisticated—who knows—but I'm certainly not calm and relaxed. Not right now anyway."

Paul refused a token liquor, devoured a paltry lunch and waited impatiently for Vincent to finish his. At the beginning of the wait, he opened his briefcase and consulted a list of key law enforcers in the four cities that were next on their schedule. Paul knew them well from previous visits when he either led or contributed to the apprehension of notorious criminals. The printed names seemed to mollify the anxiety that had overcome him:

NUREMBERG, GERMANY——EMIL GRONER

LONDON, ENGLAND——CLIFFORD WATT

BUDAPEST, HUNGARY——MARK FERENC

ATHENS, GREECE——GEORGE FRANGOS

Their phone numbers were on a separate sheet.

He said, "Take your time, Vin. I'll be in that side room over there, calling our next four contacts—outlining why we want to see them."

Once the calls had been made, Paul indicated that not only had each one been well-received but also that all four men had assured him that they could provide significant information about religion throughout the countries they represent. So much so that he doubled his usual tip percentage to the waiters and waitresses.

With Ansel at the controls, they then flew to the Nice International Airport, landing there within the hour—two p.m. They were in the region of Provence, north of Marseille, where they rented a car and then drove twenty miles to Gordes, a medieval village perched on the southern edge of Plateau de Vaucluse. Its dry-stone bories tightly set against the base of cliffs had served the Resistance well during World War II. Vincent drove slowly while again following the signs and proceeding north another two miles on a road that wound through rocks and valleys and forests. They eventually arrived at a narrow valley that embraced the Cistercian Abbey Notre Dame-de-Senanque. In a month's time, a purple hue would spread through its fields of neatly arranged lavender and over miles of woodlands beyond; but for now, thousands of gray-green plants lay dormant, ready to reach their full bloom and famous perfumed scent in mid-July. It was 2:45, June 18.

Nearly everything outside the monastery was different from the last time they had visited. For Paul, it was a vivid memory. He had been hired to investigate a series of robberies involving ancient and well-preserved paintings that had been displayed in one of the monastery buildings. He located them within a few days, never levied a charge, and was guaranteed a seat in heaven by the prior.

The security gate to the parking grounds was gone as were the many monks who strolled around on compressed dirt and uneven crushed stone, sure of their footing even while staring at their bibles and mumbling. All of it was now shiny asphalt with yellow markings that designated parking spaces. All previous weed collections had been replaced by patches of deep green grass and shrubs. Most of the patches contained small statues of well-known saints. Two attractive brick buildings lined the rear of the property and were separated by a closed gate. Even the vestibule of the dome-topped main building was different, but more inviting in the mid-afternoon sun. Wider windows allowed the sunshine its freedom as—throughout the inside vestibule—it highlighted freshly painted light-blue walls, darker blue carpeting, pictures of religious events, a water fountain, and several cushioned chairs. Vincent commented on the old musty odor that had been replaced by an uplifting flowery scent not unlike that of the lavender fields they had passed years before.

As they climbed a winding staircase to the third floor, Paul recalled what Guy Martin had once warned him about Friar Dominic. It was almost word-for-word: "He'll feed you information but sometimes he'll slip in something cryptic or ambiguous. Likes to play mind games. Uses double entendre.

Makes me think "schizophrenia". But the vast majority of what he says is legit."

They were waiting less than a minute when a sub-prior appeared out of nowhere. He was middle-aged, wore a white cassock and introduced himself as Frere Rudolph.

"Frere Dominic is expecting you," he said, "so you may go right in." Then as Paul and Vincent regarded one another, the sub-prior disappeared.

"Where'd he go?" Paul asked.

"Beats the hell outa me," Vincent replied, turning his hands palms-up. "You'd think he'd at least open the door for us."

Paul opened the door to a large office. A lanky man with bushy white hair and sunken cheeks stood behind a large table.

"It's a pleasure to meet both of you once more and to welcome you to Senanque," he announced, walking unsteadily toward them to shake their hands. "And before I forget, do call me 'Dom'—nothing more formal than that." A high pitched and loud voice belied his asthenic figure.

He wore a white collar and lavender blouse tucked into black pants pulled high on his hips. A large silver cross hung from his neck. His facial skin appeared tight and smooth as if it had never experienced the sun. But it was his nimble smile that intrigued Paul the most, at one time full and rich, at others taking seconds to form and only moments to disappear. The word "disjointed" came to Paul's mind.

And as before, the number of books surrounding them was

impressive. They were arranged on floor-to-ceiling bookcases and, in perusing their spines, Paul noticed that most of them bore historical titles.

Dom dragged three chairs to the table and asked them to sit. They did and he joined them there. “I’ve been informed you’re interested in Napoleon,” he said. “I’m an histarian, you know, and others of them have hinted at that interest, even though they shouldn’t have. So yes indeed, I can put the Napoleonic era into a word-for-word context that might be of value to you. I’ve read about the importance of the Stone Age through developments in ancient Egypt and in the civilizations of Mesopotamia and Sumeria and Babylonia; in the battles of the Hittites and the Persians and the Assyrians; through the glory of Greece and the grandeur of Rome, as they say; and on into the Middle Ages. And I’ve read and reread the sad details of terrible wars—revolutionary, civil, worldwide; the rise and fall of Hitler and Stalin dictatorships in Europe; anti-colonial sentiment in Africa and Asia; flaming battles for independence in Kenya, Algeria, Mozambique, Angola and Rhodesia; the Mao Tse-tung cultural revolution in China; Israel’s six-day war in Egypt; internal turmoil in Russia, Nicaragua and the Philippines. Skirmishes in the Falklands and Granada and Northern Ireland; the rise of terrorism and the 9/11 attacks; tensions with North Korea, Iraq, Iran and Syria.”

A good deal of what had thus far taken place and what would ensue was **exactly** what Paul remembered as occurring the last time they were in the prior’s presence, especially that lengthy historical recital. The words sounded familiar. The choice of countries and territories sounded familiar. But what it all had to do with Napoleon was puzzling.

*The **same** list we heard before! Does he realize it? Do schizos repeat themselves accurately?*

Dom continued: "So you may wonder what I'm driving at, and I don't blame you. I would do the same thing. Simply this. In all my reading, I don't just read … and, yes, I've read all the books rimming this room. What I do is **study**. What you have just heard is an example of how accurate and how complete my study is. I don't miss much. And I haven't missed the abrupt change in the behavior of an army general like Napoleon Bonaparte. His military and political decisions became erratic overnight."

He reached into his pocket, took out a pill box and swallowed two pills without water. "I'm sorry, gentlemen," he said. "I didn't plan on getting into the subject of histarians, but you know I'm one, don't you?"

"That we do," Paul said.

"Okay then. Aside from my study, it's through the cooperation of many of them that I know so much about recorded Napoleonic history, but even more about so-called Napoleonic truths. And I would recommend that you examine the possibilities and either discredit them or authenticate them. Could you handle that?"

"Certainly," Paul said. "Couldn't we, Vin?" By that time, Paul had grown more and more suspicious of the prior's mental state and the need for them to play along, because some informational "pearls" might be dropped.

"But let me ask you, Dom. You say you get all your information from study and from fellow histarians. Where do **they** get it?"

"Sorry. I can't give out an answer. However, histarian sources go much deeper than the persistent rumors we analyze. I've been here fifty years. Sometimes visitors say things to me that they wouldn't say in public—you know, on the outside." Again, Paul didn't quite get what the prior was driving at.

An example of what Guy had called "double entendre"?

"And do you know who coined the word 'histarian'?" Dom asked.

"No. I don't."

"Yours truly. Me. The others like the word, too."

"Speaking of others, what about monks? The last time we were here, there were lots of them walking around outside. Have they left for some reason?"

"No, they're still here."

"How many are there?"

"Very many, but I can't in true conscience reveal the number."

"Okay—but might I ask where they are?"

"That's permissible. Although anything you might ask is

permissible. It's just that the answer might not be. A question of a chicken or its egg."

Hmm ... now slipping in something cryptic or ambiguous. And what's wrong with telling the number anyway?

"They're at a special prayer meeting in our auditorium. I'd have you join them but once the doors are closed and prayers begin, no one else is allowed in. That applies to me, to the sub-prior, to the sacrist, the circuiter, the chamberlain, the almoner, any of us. And if it applies to leadership, it must apply to visitors. Make sense?"

"It does and maybe I shouldn't have asked."

"No. As I said—anything may be asked."

"Okay then. I'll ask if many people come here to seek your advice."

"Enough."

"And what are they usually seeking?"

"Settling the disputes about Napoleon."

"Disputes?"

Time to draw him out.

"Yes. It isn't simply a case of whether or not he was murdered." Dom removed a manila folder from the table drawer and referred to it as he continued. "You should concentrate on three fronts: his lovers, his last two battles, and his postmortem disappearance."

"Postmortem disappearance?" Vincent exclaimed.

"Yes. After his death, the ceremony on St. Helena is well documented, but what was not recorded is that there was ample opportunity for the body to be stolen."

Paul knew all about such a possibility and about Chet Knight's not bringing up something that might or might not have occurred over a thousand years ago.

"With regard to his lovers," Dom continued, "you know that he had more than most for that era. But one woman stands out. Her name was Lady Beckett and she was a top executive with the British East India Tea Company. Everyone knew she was a female Lothario. The older she got, the more feeble she became and the more she opened up about her relationship with Napoleon. She wrote extensively about that part of her life, calling it her 'ruby years'. Here's one of her quotes."

The prior read from the folder:

> The ruby symbolizes great value, wisdom, costly glories, and prized treasures. It says so in the bible; in Job and in Proverbs.

Vincent continued to take notes and Paul began to do the same.

"I, myself, added some notes to this folder," Dom said.

"I'll read them to you:

> How do the words apply to Napoleon? Prized treasure? If the relationship was as expected, he certainly was that to her. Wisdom? In good health, he had that in full measure. Costly glory? Aha! This is the important one. He had glorious triumphs but at what cost? Thousands of men perished. Great value? On balance, he was all of that.

"That leaves the military battles. You **must** visit his so-called 'First Island of Disgrace', so do go to Elba. I believe you've already gone to St. Helena but now it should be Elba. We think he made a big decision and hatched some sort of plan while he was there. That's 'decision' and 'plan'. The decision had to do with his will. The plan was related to his two terrible defeats in Russia and here in France. Our histarian there can elaborate. Name's Clive Weaver. He's older than I am, which means he should be dead. He was with the British Museum early in his career, then moved to the island forty years ago."

"But wouldn't a phone call do?" Paul asked.

"No, afraid not. Nothing by phone by any histarian. And don't forget, he may have sensitive materials to give you."

Paul snapped his writing pad shut and said, "Dom, a second question. What's your opinion about Napoleon's reputation regarding his influence on criminals—back then and now?"

"They loved him then and they love his memory now. There's no doubt because the evidence is clear. It's in the books and skirts around in the sieves of my mind."

So he ***does*** *have some self-awareness.*

Paul and Vincent were the first to rise and initiated wholesome thanks and goodbyes.

"Do come again," the prior said, "if I'm still here."

While descending the staircase, Vincent held Paul back and asked, "Should we take his advice and go to Elba?"

"I don't think so. We've enough to do."

I could flip a coin. If it comes up heads, this trip to Gordes was worthwhile. If tails, maybe it wasn't.

Overall, Paul also thought that more than enough time had been spent on Napoleon and not enough on religion. He expected it to change during their next stop.

Chapter 20

The flight to Nuremberg, Germany was taking less time than either man had expected. Paul told himself that an overburdening number of European cities to visit would not foil a more streamlined intent, even though there were just so many ways to be met and greeted by colleagues of years past. Two weeks before, he had planned on learning all he could about the progress and legitimacy of religion and how it was possibly connected to traditional Napoleonic teachings. It was to be the subject of the book he wanted to write. This was compounded, however, when Guy Martin highly recommended adding criminal investigation to the mix. Yet, unless unexpectedly diverted, he was now determined to subtract the Napoleon component and concentrate on religion.

But Paul found himself in a quandary concerning their travels: not really looking forward to repeated circulars about a city or country; to scenes of foreign lands; to repeated observations of and by law enforcers; to repeated requests for the enforcers' take on the same things. In addition, waves of anxiety washed over him, but with Vincent's help and companionship, he would go through the same routine each and every time. He understood it all and accepted it.

Their plane touched down at the Nuremberg Airport and, as usual, a container of circulars was prominently displayed on a counter in the main terminal. Both men took a copy and read it. It was titled "The Nazi Era":

> We are not proud of this, but because of the relevance to the Holy Roman Empire and the location in the center of Germany, the Nazi Party selected our city to be the site of giant Nazi Party conventions—the Nuremberg rallies. There is a Documentation Center there for you to enter and examine many walls of photographs. The rallies were held from 1933 to 1938. After Adolph Hitler's rise to power in 1933, they became huge Nazi propaganda events; a center of the Nazis'opinion of excellence; and a tribute to himself. At the start of the 1935 rally, Hitler specifically ordered the Reichstag to convene there in order to pass the anti-Semitic Nuremberg laws, which revoked German citizenship for all Jews and other non-Aryans. Several of the premises that were built for these conventions may be seen there today. They represent examples of Nazi architecture that were related to that madman's dreams.

> Then during the Second World War, Nuremberg was the headquarters of important military production, not only for us but also for them. It included aircraft, tanks and submarines. Also, a certain division of a concentration camp was located there and there was extensive use of slave labor.
>
> Everybody understands that although we were a heavily fortified city, we suffered severe urban devastation and human loss during many bombings by both the Nazis and Allied forces. But our city was rebuilt after the war and, to some extent, was restored to its pre-war appearance. Do experience some of our reconstructed medieval buildings.
>
> Welcome and good fortune!

No sooner had they checked into a local hotel than Paul changed his mind about two aspects of their travels. One was about repeated circulars and the other concerned scenes of foreign lands. It might have been the circular he'd just read in its entirety; he wasn't sure. His condemnation of them had been mentally strong, but not strong enough, for he said to Vincent: "I'm a basket case, Vin. Within a matter of minutes, I've gone from anxious and disinterested to curious as hell. You once stressed we shouldn't hurry all the time so what say? It's early enough. Let's tour around. We've got to start living in the moment. We'll look at places we haven't seen before. We'll read circulars we haven't read before. And you know that list we just went over? We can't do them all, but let's start at the top, then pick and choose."

"Should we rent a car?"

"Why not? I'll do the driving this time … get my mind off things. And who knows—at the rate some bozos show up on our tail, we might never get a chance to travel around again like this."

Paul found a parking space near the Wurzburg Residence. He maneuvered the car into it and began his exit. Suddenly, a panel truck came out of nowhere, sideswiped the door and burst away under the cover of the blinding sun. Before the door slammed shut, its lower edge nicked Paul's foot by a fraction of an inch. At the same moment, Vincent had reached over to yank him back. They both remained plopped down, gasping as though taking their last breaths. Finally Vincent said, "It happened so fast! You okay?"

"I guess so, but Jesus! Cars, trucks … do they have motorcycles over here?"

The succeeding quiet lasted but a few more seconds before Paul said, "See what I mean?"

They left the car, Vincent with tightened shoulders, Paul with a slight limp. And there was no telling what either one was thinking.

Chapter 21

At the Wurzburg Residence, Paul was still upset over a truck nearly smashing into him; his foot hurt; and he was uncertain about continuing on.

> *Maybe we should make it this place only and forget the rest.*

They were handed a circular and Vincent's expression said it all: "Here we go again."

He helped Paul along as they were ushered to a row of chairs half-filled with tourists who were reading their copies. They did also:

> This former palace was designed by an unknown architect at the time—Balthasar Neumann. It took sixty years to complete. The shell was built from 1720 to 1744 and the interior

> was finished in 1780. Neumann's world-famous staircase, roofed by an unsupported vault, was decorated by the Venetian Giovanni Tiepolo with a ceiling fresco representing four continents. The painting, measuring 18 by 30 meters, is one of the largest frescos ever created. A magnificent sequence of rooms begins with the Vestibule and Garden Hall and continues via the staircase to the Imperial Hall, also with frescos by Tiepolo. There is a total of over 40 palace rooms for you to visit. Each has a rich array of furniture, tapestries, paintings and other 18th century treasures.
>
> Take your time and enjoy!

"At least it was short," Vincent said. If eyes lit up with excitement, his lit down. "Looks like we'll be doing more reading than seeing."

Meanwhile, anyone who happened to glance Paul's way, he regarded as suspicious.

"Your gun loaded?" he asked in a whisper.

"Sure is. Both of yours?"

"Sure are. Wish I had one in my hand when the truck was barreling toward us."

As suspected, Paul's mental and physical state influenced what he had to say next: "I'm all for calling it quits for today, Vin. It was a good idea but someone didn't agree. So let's rest until tomorrow. I do want to visit Bamberg though before we drop in on Emil Groner."

Vincent nodded.

In the morning, Paul felt well-rested and his foot no longer hurt. Most important of all, he had pushed the truck experience from his mind. He looked forward to a new day.

The city of Bamberg was among those in Germany that he had never seen. Called "The City of Beer", he had vowed to visit it and not for the intended purpose of sampling beer. He opened his briefcase and removed a card that was attached to an article about the city. He had never studied the card.

> Bamberg, Germany is a picturesque city in Upper Franconia (northern Bavaria) on the Regnitz River and the Main-Danube channel. It is built on seven hills, each crowned with a church or castle.

Paul looked back at Vincent and exclaimed, "Churches galore! I hope Emil can comment on their leaders and the people they serve."

"So should we visit any of the hills?" Vincent asked.

"We've got to … otherwise we could just have read the card … and not even bothered coming here. Let's at least go check on three or four."

Paul won out on what to see first: the Franconian Brewery Museum. There, after looking around, they learned that ten private breweries still operate in Bamberg, and that many of them have their own unique pub. So they strolled to one of them, the nearby *Schlenkerla*, and were told that nothing more than hop, malt and water were in a Bamberg beer and that producing it that way creates the smoked beer that's famous all over the world.

"I still don't want one," Paul said, partially covering his mouth and addressing Vincent. "I'll stick to white wine."

Then they went atop Cathedral Hill and gawked at a huge cathedral with four imposing spires. They never went in, but at its entrance was a plaque on a tripod. It indicated that if tourists viewed the structure from a distance, they would see four different architectural styles: Romanesque, Gothic, Renaissance and Baroque. It also indicated that inside was the only tomb of a pope outside France and Italy.

Paul wanted to continue on but this time Vincent won out, claiming fatigue.

"And boredom … right?" Paul asked.

"No, not that. Just tired."

But they settled on one final sight—one that wasn't on any of the seven hills. Paul had heard of it before: the Old Town Hall in the River. He recalled reading that years ago the bishop refused to allow a town hall to be built on any part of Bamberg land. Therefore, they rammed monstrous wooden beams into the Regnitz River and built their town hall there. Another plaque on a tripod indicated that the location of the building marked the border between the episcopal city on the hills and the island city of ordinary people. And that the beautiful frescoes covering it were in Baroque and Rococo styles.

Chapter 22

June 18

On the way to Chief Emil Groner's office, Paul said to Vincent: "The only problem with Emil is that he can't stick to one thing for very long … loves to talk, but skips around. Remember that?"

"Oh yes. I remember often repeating your questions to keep him on the straight and narrow. He would answer each one in three or four words, then change the subject."

"But on the other hand, he can go on and on about a subject. Or digress when you don't expect it. You never know. He's weird that way … in a lot of ways really … but he's a nice guy and knows his stuff. We'll soon see how it works out."

The chief's tiny third floor office was in the turret of an administrative building at the edge of the city. By the time Paul and Vincent arrived there, the sun had begun to pale in the eastern sky and it was turning humid. Both men hung their jackets over their arms as they climbed three flights to the end of a long and dimly-lit hallway. From that distance they were able to make out a male figure leaning against a door at the other end.

Halfway down he turned out to be the chief!

"Emil!" Paul shouted. "What on earth? How did you know we were here?"

"Don't you remember? I have hidden overhead cams. Even took your pictures."

The strength of their handshakes seemed to reflect the length of time that had passed since they were there last—just over three years.

"And that's why the hallway's kinda dark … so no one can see them?"

"No one yet. And no one's fallen yet either."

Paul guessed Emil to be about five years his junior. Of average height, he had a head of curly black hair that was a shade less shiny than his deep-set blue eyes, and his clothing was a shade less baggy than Paul's on a picnic day. Emil's badge was barely visible within a fold of his shirt, a fold that Vincent appeared to have an urge to pull apart.

Inside, there was no secretary, one curtained window, a small cluttered desk, and all the other necessities of a serviceable office squeezed into every available space. As the chief drew three chairs together and the sweet aroma of flowers sliced through the air, Paul said, "I smell flowers, but where are they?"

"I hid them, too … red and yellow roses. They're in vases behind the curtain over there. No need to tend to them much if they're hidden."

Vincent forced a wooden smile.

"So, Emil, what are you up to?" Paul asked and

immediately realized it was the wrong question to start with.

"Well, lots of things."

Paul had to follow up. "Like what? All about the law, right?"

"No, not really. About helping scientists get funding for gene editing techniques. Many new ones, you know. And promising."

"But what's that got to do with law enforcement?" Paul knew he was getting deeper and deeper into what he cared less and less about, in contrast to what he was there for.

"Nothing." It was the extent of his answer, and this time Paul smiled, but the others didn't. And Paul decided to take over.

"Hmm, interesting," he said. "We have a forensic science friend, Walter Sparks. He's starting to spend time on cyberwarfare and cyberterrorism, but only because he was asked to by the federal government. Now we have you … in law enforcement … spending time on gene editing techniques. Did the German government ask you to do it?"

"No, it's on my own. Then there's the …"

"Wait, Emil. Thanks for the information, but with regard to my call to you, we've been educated enough about Napoleon and crime, so let's not waste time on that. Do you have any ideas about religion as it now exists around the world? If I recall correctly, you were invited to be a member of the "Conclave of Faiths" years ago. You still a member?"

"That I am."

"Well then … when I recently removed some later recommendations to what I'm trying to assess, I was left with my initial search: the progress and legitimacy of religion."

"Of what you listed in your phone call, Paul, I figured **that** was at the heart of things, so I did some research and came up with an article on the Internet. It seems to jibe with what you're after and wait till you hear its title … 'The Legitimacy of Religion for the Progress of World Peace' Amazing! The only difference between this and what you're after is the business of world peace. It was written by a Kristen Sullivan, but I couldn't find the publisher's name. I made three copies of the article, one for each of us."

He handed copies to each man as he asked, "May I go over some key parts with you?"

"Go right ahead," Paul replied.

"To begin with, let me say that I think religion is legitimate, but there are some qualifications. And that the vast majority of my colleagues across Germany agree with me. That's what you're after, right? Not the feeling of what little-old-me is, but what the general feeling is **out there**."

"The general feeling … right."

"Okay then, men. As you can read, a Freudian, an atheist, a priest, and Ms. Sullivan are offering their opinions. I don't plan on attributing what I'm about to point out … you can check that for yourselves as we go along. But I'll just read the comments I underlined on my copy here. We can agree or disagree on their importance, but come to think of it, that's not why you're here, is it?"

Uh-uh. Here comes digression. But maybe not.

"Anyway, here's what I underlined:

> Religion is an enslaving art.
>
> Worshippers are captivated by various divinities.
>
> Religion is continually changing.
>
> Why do we need religion?
>
> Science is the answer to all our questions.
>
> Scientific theories have intellectual mobility.
>
> Religion is baseless … while science is pragmatic.
>
> Religion is not actual … it is a myth.
>
> How would that explain war, famine and disease?
>
> Religion is the implausible reason for the worst crimes the world has ever seen.

"I said I wouldn't attribute but now I will, because some statements a Roman Catholic priest makes involve … you guessed it … it's right there … Christianity. And to say he's biased is an understatement. He claims that:

Religion is the glue that unifies diverse groups.

Christianity forms the basis for a civilized society.

Religion has been cemented into our brains since our tender years.

Christianity is the religion that offers the most.

This religion promotes morality while others are unable to grasp reality.

Christianity has universal appeal while others only provide an ethnic zeal.

Judaism's allure is most limited to Jerusalem.

In Christianity, you can feast on cattle and swine.

In Hinduism and Islam, you are prohibited from … this.

"Then Ms. Sullivan writes: 'Don't Muslims, Christians and Jews believe in the same God? We are not as different as some people make it seem. Because in reality we have the same dream. Each faith seeks the greater good of humanity. Forcing people to follow one religion is purely impractical, and all beliefs have something worthwhile to share. We should exercise the peace-promoting values they carry … and coexist peacefully in a world full of differences'.

"So what do you think, my friends? Helpful or not? It's what I have to offer and may give you something to think about."

"Thank you, sir," Paul said, saluting. "We'll definitely do some thinking." On the whole, however, he was disappointed and silently concluded he wouldn't express the feeling in the book he had in mind. Nor—thinking of Emil's underlining—the reasons why.

And that was that. A short, sweet and to-the-point encounter to wind down their German visits.

Chapter 23

June 19

England was next. As often as Paul had been there, he never tired of browsing around in London's Cabinet War Room, and as soon as they landed at Heathrow Airport, he talked Vincent into agreeing that they should delay anything short of that, except for a series of taxi, bus, tube, van and leisure walking to observe as many sights as practical. And into not complaining about reading descriptive materials on display at some of them. Even the lifting of his shirt sleeve to see his watch was slower than usual.

"It's only ten in the morning, so what's the hurry?" he said.

But there was one thing that Paul **did** tire of doing and that was engaging in repeated conversations with key law enforcement people in key cities.

> *How many times can we ask the same kind of questions; engage in the same kind of chitchat; appear uniquely interested before the same kind of lawmen; receive closely predictable answers; and*

file them away for future scrutiny?

He hoped that the next few hours would be therapeutic, so he informed Vincent that while they were in London, he'd like to begin a new "order of business".

"It's not really 'business', Vin, but what am I to call it … 'order of sightseeing'? You get what I'm driving at, don't you? And it would comply with your plea of taking our time."

"Yes, I agree one-hundred per cent. We might even look forward to the next destination."

Neither man's look of satisfaction outweighed the other man's.

"Our meeting with Cliff Watt can keep," Paul said. "We'll just make it so."

They traveled by van to the elegant St. James Court Hotel, not far from Scotland Yard. Paul had stayed at the hotel twice before, considered it one of the finest examples of Edwardian architecture and so informed Vincent. And although Vincent had accompanied him on his last trip to London, Paul would continue to offer comments about succeeding sights.

They registered there, but since a room was not yet available they took a short walk past Buckingham Palace and St. James Park, then doubled back to learn that a room was available—small but comfortable and overlooking a courtyard that contained an assortment of water fountains. From their third story window, Paul spotted a man peering at him from behind one of the fountains. He wore no uniform, unlike security guards who milled around everywhere, responding to questions and opening doors for tourists. But he wore a patch over his left eye. Paul signaled Vincent. They searched each other's eyes but neither said anything until Paul gave the man a name … Mr. Nemesis.

After settling in, they left the hotel and began sightseeing in earnest. The sun grew brighter and the cry of circling birds became louder as they eventually came upon St. Paul's Cathedral. They didn't go inside but instead read a notice that was posted on one of its enormous doors:

> We welcome you to this historic Cathedral Church in the heart of London, a site which has been used for Christian worship since AD 604. Our congregation comes from all over the world and from different branches of the Christian Church. We invite you to join heartily in the singing of the hymns and to associate yourself with the Choir, as it makes an offering to God on our behalf through Psalms, Canticles and Anthems.

"Know what this just did for us?" Paul asked.

"No. What?"

"You read it all?"

"Yes. It wasn't long."

"The wording, 'Our congregation comes from all over the world' reminds me of what Sparky said about our visiting just seven countries."

"Which was? I forget."

"He said that those seven reflect the entire world, and this little notice right here fortifies it in my mind. And in a related vein, although I guess you'd call it a stretch, is the idea of so much back-and-forth travel. Thank God for only seven countries and maybe only a couple more depending on what we find out. I'll try hard not to become frustrated as has happened to me before, Vin."

They next strolled by the Towers of Parliament, the Prince Albert Memorial, Westminster Abbey and the famous Clock Tower as seen over the Westminster Bridge. Then to Trafalgar Square and a tube ride to Piccadilly Circus where they stopped for a quick pizza lunch. After that, they joined with others to feed some birds in St. James Park and then walked up Birdcage Drive to admire Big Ben and the well-known statue of Winston Churchill. There, they again spotted Mr. Nemesis off in the distance and Paul tried hard to wipe away the image.

The next two hours were spent in the British Museum where they studied its many wonders: the Beatle's lyrics, the Magna Carta, the Rosetta Stone, the Elgin Marbles, artifacts of early man, original Rembrandt sketches. And after returning to the Palace to witness the changing of the guard, Paul breathed more heavily, for they were ready for the Cabinet War Rooms. They were located on King Charles Street, deeply underground and protected by a six-foot pad of steel and concrete.

Near the bottom of its entrance was a tripod locked by chain to a metal beam. Paul looked three doors ahead and saw a smaller tripod similarly locked. Both contained typed articles protected by glass. During his last visit there, he hadn't bothered to read the articles but this time he did. The first one was written by Beverly Shaver and indicated that she was a freeance writer from California. With some minor extractions it read:

War Room: Step Back into World War ll

They are not faces featured on the standard tourist circuits. They must be sought out, often in unlikely settings. But when experienced, they convey an urgent sense of a drama played out in time. Their mementos and monuments can pierce the heart and alter a visitor's consciousness in some permanent way.

London's Cabinet War Room complex … is this kind of place. So that the world won't forget, the British government has painstakingly restored and opened to the public [these] underground headquarters where Winston Churchill, his War Cabinet and military chiefs worked. Here in the original settings, artifacts and exhibits tell the story of what happened [more than] 70 years ago at a nerve center of the Allied struggle against the Nazi juggernaut.

Within the complex, a continuous sound track chillingly recreates the ambience of London under blitz—the day and night sirens, "those banshee howlings", the thunder of exploding missiles and crashing structures as the British people, with their backs to the wall in 1940, endured a deadly rain of destruction and death. Heard too as one moves from room to room is the rich baritone clang of Big Ben tolling defiance and reassurance. Visitors stop in their tracks to listen to the unbearably poignant broadcast words of Churchill, the "bulldog" leader, rallying his people: "Fill the armies, rule the air, pour out the munitions, strangle the U-boats, sweep the mines, plough the land, build the wounded, uplift the downcast and honor the brave."

[This] self-guided tour, aided by a map with explanatory text, begins with the steel-beamed Cabinet Room where more than a hundred meetings were held between 1940 and 1945. The critical importance of decisions and strategies arrived at in this subterranean chamber is belied by its Spartan simplicity. There on the far side of the rectangular conference table is the prime minister's broad- backed chair, doughty and emblematic beneath the world map.

American visitors find themselves swallowing hard at the glass frontage of a cubicle, one of the most important facilities in the complex. The small bare room appears a shrine-like setting for a black cult object—a cradle telephone. Here was the ultimate in 1940s technology, a transatlantic hot line. From here, Churchill could speak directly by radio telephone to Franklin Roosevelt in Washington. On the wall to the right is a clock with black hands showing London time, red hands indicating Washington time.

Further down the corridor is the room where the typists worked round the clock, breathing lightly of the vent-delivered air, often sleeping after late shifts in dormitories in the sub-basement. The typewriters here resemble the dusty clackety machines stored in our parents' attics, and the duplicating machine on the center table, incredibly, is turned with a hand crank.

Like all truly important museums, [this] War Room complex is more than a memorial and authentic setting of great events. It works in sounds, images and small telling events—the grim gas mask lying next to a shabby string purse spilling ration coupons; the quill pens and primitive little adding machines with tin flak helmets hung on pegs above them; the door to the Transatlantic Telephone Room with the special lock marked "Vacant" and "Engaged" taken from a toilet door; the cloudy little hand mirror in the Mess Room hanging next to a poster advising "Better Pot-luck with Churchill today than Humble Pie under Hitler tomorrow. Don't waste food!"

With earphones turned on, Paul listened and read every word while Vincent followed behind, apparently doing the same thing. But then he passed Paul, arrived at the second tripod and read its article more quickly.

In the meantime, Paul paused at each and every cubicle, taking in Churchill's bedroom, the War Room with a fan for his cigar smoke, the colossal map with its scattered pushpins, and an array of colorful phones nicknamed "the beauty chorus."

At the second tripod, Paul again digested what was written in a much smaller article by David Knowles taken from *Travel & Leisure*:

> A 21-room time capsule beneath the former Office of Works building, [these] Cabinet War Rooms are a far better memorial to World War II than Europe's deserted battlefields. From here, Churchill directed the British campaign. You can almost hear his shoe leather slapping against the linoleum floor. Wherever you look in this bunker-turned-museum—at the thousands of pinholes on a world map marking torpedo strikes, at the BBC microphone that the prime minister used to address the nation—the place simply resonates with the past.

All in all, they had spent the first two hours of the afternoon there. And after walking back to the hotel, Paul's smile continued on through a final glimpse of Mr. Nemesis.

Chapter 24

Paul had always considered London a giant open-air museum with a chief law officer in charge of keeping it so. A law officer as unique as anyone he'd ever known. Their several discussions—whether by phone or in person—always left Paul guessing, for Cliff Watt had a habit of presenting two or more sides to every story, never giving in to a conclusion and leaving it up to listeners to form one … not unlike Germany's Chief Grumer. In a way, it brought everything into the loop but in another way, it distorted the loop and left inquirers hanging. Yet he was the best man to see in all of the United Kingdom despite some disillusion that Paul had chanced upon during their most recent conversation.

By the time Paul and Vincent's collective minds had struggled to maintain a slow-down mode and they had stopped worrying about Mr. Nemesis, they arrived at Watt's office. It was still the day of the War Rooms visit—around 3 p.m.—and Paul had again begun to run the usual topics through his mind: religion, crime, Napoleon. But he now added science. Science and all its discoveries, all its wonders, all its promises for the future. It was a double version of past thoughts.

> *First– can we somehow intertwine religion and science? Will God survive science or will science survive God? Chief Watt here has talked so often about science before and related it to health care ... and extended both of them into the setting of religion. He called it"humanizing health care". Will he do it again? And second—we have so many stops ahead. Can we vary the routine? I wish we could bundle them together.*

The office building stood out as a one-story dwelling, a short distance from their hotel and on the other side of Scotland Yard. Formalities were completed in one of Watt's three rooms––one obviously reserved for police work, one for study and the last, a small kitchen. They gathered around a tree stump table, on Scandinavian–style rattan chairs. Paul waved off anything to eat or drink and began to relate why they were there, but he was interrupted.

"Pardon me," Watt said. "I need to turn on my recorder, and yes, I still record all conversations. With good friends like I have here; with not-so-good friends; with sneaky friends. You name it—with everybody."

As he reached over to turn on a recording device atop the tree stump—hardly even looking at it—he said, "One of these usually lasts me less than a year. They run out before you know it. There've been times when I go to play it, and nothing was recorded. Or at best, just every other word. Then I have to buy a new one because I can't fix it. I probably keep manufacturers in business—at least some of them; maybe all of them. Who knows … or who wants to know?"

*See? An **entire** loop.*

Paul decided to have some fun. "Cliff," he began, "you've lost quite a bit of weight and even some hair. Must be all the work you've been doing, tinkering with your recorders."

"More than tinkering … I take them apart. And you're very observant, Paul, but you always were." He stood up to tighten his belt, then ran his hand over his jaw and scalp.

Paul remembered him as being obese with a full beard and a full head of hair. But now he looked trim and was totally bald. The beard remained but was nearly all white. He had never seen him completely bald, only now noticing an irregular port-wine stain like that of Mikhail Gorbachev.

"So let's get down to business," Cliff said. "The business of why you're here … which you told me about in your phone call. And incidentally, you've been a very busy man … that I know. So why do you go through all the trouble of so much traveling and so much investigating? Why not just take a rest for a few months … or years … or however much. You're still young and there'll be plenty of time left."

"Because I'm thinking of writing a book and I want it to be

about current religions as related to current criminal activities, and about the relation of the Napoleon years to both of them. But you know, I've got to add science to that now, and you're the one who can help me the most. You were talking about it before it became fashionable. And even health care. Are they all interrelated in some way? So do go on … the floor is yours."

Cliff looked painstakingly at Paul and said, "You asked for it. And I know you've thought of me as a 'double-sider'. You called me that to my face years ago and I wasn't upset because you were absolutely correct. Well, for what I have to say now, I'll try to be as direct a 'one-sider' as I can. Do you mind if I consult some notes? I put them together after you called."

"No, go ahead. I've consulted notes plenty of times myself."

"And shouldn't I first talk a little about criminal investigations?"

"If you wish."

"All right. Then after that, I'll go into my latest fad: learning more and more about science and medicine. I've even taken some courses over at the Bishopsgate Library."

"Must be the latest then."

"The latest. And I've got lots to say … hope you two can take it. No one around here listens to me, so you'll be bearing the brunt of my frustration."

"We can take it," Paul said. "At least I can. I have a wife, you know."

They shared a polite laugh.

"And let me say ahead of time that I'm sorry if what's to come isn't all that newsworthy to either one of you," Cliff added.

> *How on earth can this help what I'm after? But just listen to him, Paul. Maybe something valuable can be milked out of what he has to say.*

With that, the chief cleared his voice, removed a thick folder from beneath the recorder and referred to its contents as he began:

> I name this first part: "New Technologies in Criminal Investigations." As of the turn of the century, an average of forty percent of worldwide households had been touched by crime. Worse in some countries, less in others. And for eighty percent of crimes, the criminal was never caught. And why not? One reason is that solution technology lagged behind developments in other broad areas, such as business and industry … or government. But things have improved in the last twenty years or so. There's been great progress, for example, in chemistry, in molecular biology, in electronics, and in computer technology.

He had read it all from his notes, never once looking up. If he had, he would have seen both Paul and Vincent writing their own notes. The chief continued:

> Because of all the things I want to include, I'll touch on six specific areas only. Actually, I'll just list them for you because you know the details, I'm sure. They're DNA typing and databanks; casing and bullet databanks; new latent print technology; new instrumentation; image enhancement; and number six—artificial intelligence. For this last one, I'll add a tad. It consists of crime mapping, crime scene reasoning and logic, criminal profiling, getting into the mind of a killer. And that's sufficient for crime. I'm sick of it really. Dealt with it for over twenty-seven years. Even here and now with you, I can't escape it … because I'll be relating medicine to criminals and then science to criminals. I guess you might say that I've subconsciously arrived at medicine and science in order to suffocate crime. And there it happens again! It's everywhere in my life. Isn't suffocation a crime?"

Paul felt he had to rescue the chief from his own words, so he used *praise* as the vehicle. "All you're said so far, Cliff, is outstanding. I mean outstanding in your ability to condense, yet to be complete. And I'm sure Vincent agrees with me when I say I can't wait to hear more."

Cliff looked as relieved as a starving squirrel might look after stumbling onto an acorn. "Thank you for that," he said. "And now for medicine and criminals. The very latest is what you want, right?"

Both men nodded.

"I'll just plow ahead then. You've got the time, I hope?"

"We do."

"Here's what I'm prepared to talk about … mostly read. First off, I guess I'll just list the topics … like I have here … then go from onc to thc other. Six of them. And if some snoring occurs, I'll call it quits. Remember now, I've already covered criminal investigations."

Things had become so drawn out that Paul wondered if **any** listed topics would ever be addressed, but Cliff finally got his act together. "Here's the list," he said:

1—Tapping into computers

2—Drones and Smartphones

3—Digital Medicine. The Value of Apps

4—The Search to End the Scourge of Misdiagnoses

5—Gene Editing

6—Microscopy

Number one: Tapping into Computers. What I mean here is that regarding the business of

> medicine, I equate it to health care and hospitals … and in talking about health care, I'd like to stress something that may be different from what others may have told you. Here in England, criminals have learned how to tap into what prospective patients indicate on their computers when they answer routine hospital registration questions. I say 'routine' but not routine to a criminal … because the answers usually include very personal information about the patient and his or her family. Then the criminal can use the information to his advantage. To his 'criminal' advantage. Blackmail … identity fraud … protection … murder … you name it. And that's it for what I consider 'tapping'. Actually for what I consider 'tapping for zapping'. Heh, heh."

He made an imploring half-smile while a clear spasm crossed the faces of the other two as they put their pencils aside. But Paul thought it too soon to stop cooperating and said, "Like I brought out before, Cliff— your ability to condense. Good job."

"Good, but I suppose it could have been better," Cliff said. "Let's see how number two goes. It's 'Drones and Smartphones' and the first part concerns Switzerland. You were just there, correct?"

"Correct. Quite a country."

The chief fumbled around in his folder and withdrew a

three-inch cut-out from *Time Magazine*. It was about medical drones and he gave Julia Zorthian credit as the author. "Better for me to read this than to try condensing again. Besides, it's short to begin with … I'll do more condensing with the smartphone part."

> During a medical emergency, every second matters—including the ones spent driving samples to and from external labs for testing. But what if they could be flown instead? That's the idea behind a new fleet of delivery drones, developed by California-based Matternet for deployment in Switzerland. When lab technicians are done testing a sample, they simply deposit it at a nearby drone-docking station; then the drone takes off on a predetermined route back to a hospital, flying far above traffic. The initiative, developed in partnership with the national postal service, is set to launch in several Swiss cities by the end of the year. But Matternet has grander ambitions. If the tech works, it may well be deployed for e-commerce delivery and more.

"There you have it. Isn't it fantastic, fellas? One wave of the future."

"So many waves, they're overlapping," Vincent said, his first comment of the late afternoon. He and Paul resumed their note-taking.

The chief's eyes registered agreement and he said, "Okay, we have momentum going so here's the second half of number two … smartphones. I tied some passages together from a *Wall Street Journal* article written by Charles Wallace, a writer in New York. You see, I too read some of your U.S. publications. I won't include everything I've written with this one. It'll be pick and choose to give you a flavor of how these phones have opened up a whole new world for medical researchers. Remember that smartphones are mobile and that's key. Here goes:

> Doctors say abundant health data gathered by phones produce better, more timely results. It's the idea of 'immediacy'. Doctors believe that patients can receive feedback much more quickly than they can with information printed in the usual scientific journals … often printed years after the studies are conducted. A **big** time-saver. As an example then, the beneficial effects of exercise or diet or specific lab tests are speedily obtained and patients can adjust their behavior accordingly.
>
> I must mention a smartphone platform called ResearchKit. Doctors and scientists are now using it to create iPhone apps that collect data such as weight and blood pressure readings. Our British drug maker, **GlaxoSmithKline**, had become the first pharmaceutical company to carry out a

> medical study using ResearchKit. The study tracked three-hundred rheumatoid arthritis patients' fatigue, mood and joint pain over three months with data from iPhones. The last I heard, though … results haven't been released yet.

"And the last point I'll say about this topic is that while all phone-based studies were initially limited to your country, a number have reached Europe, such as a cardiovascular study which, I'm proud to say, was started here in the U.K. So how's that so far, folks? Learning anything?"

"Plenty," Paul said. "Learning and enjoying. Can't you tell? No snoring."

"I'm actually enjoying it, too," Cliff said. "But we've got to take a break and have some coffee or tea. Easy to prepare nowadays, what with modern coffeemakers and tea bags. How about it? Raise your hand if it's tea."

Two hands went up and Paul said, "I feel like a student doing this."

"We're all students, really," the chief responded as he turned off his recorder and left for the kitchen.

After tea, sweet-scented crackers and some light conversation, Cliff said, "Digital Medicine. The Value of Apps" is next, and I'll be referring to smartphones again. Shows how important they are in the scientific scheme of things. And speaking of the word 'again' I once more have to give credit to the *Journal*. I'll be reading parts of an article written by a former managing editor, Laura Landro.

He turned on the recorder, flipped to another of his pages and read some individual sections, pretty much word-for-word:

> Hospitals and doctors have identified digital tools that can assist patients in dealing with ailments such as diabetes, heart disease and lung disease. The early results are promising. New studies … show that the emerging field of digital medicine—a combination of remote monitoring (there's the smartphone reference), behavior modification and personalized intervention—can improve outcomes … . As a result, a growing number of hospitals and health systems are adopting digital programs that …can be delivered on a broad scale at low cost with the use of smartphones, wireless devices and sensors.
>
> Digital medicine allows examination in a personal way, delivering interventions when necessary, such as when patients aren't following their regimens or are having a flare-up in their disease.
>
> And speaking of sensors, listen to this. Certain medical centers are utilizing a system that encapsulates medications in a single pill with an ingestible sensor the size of a grain of sand. Once swallowed, the sensor communicates with a patch worn on the patient's torso, a patch that records

> the time the medication was taken as well as data such as heart rate, heart rhythm and body rest.
>
> The patch transmits the information wirelessly to an app in a mobile device, such as a smartphone or iPad, for the patient to monitor and share with a health-care provider, and sends an alert if a dose is missed. If a patient forgets to take a pill, he or she can be alerted by notification to their mobile device.

"Can't get any better than that, can it? Ms. Landro authored another article whose title you see on your list—number four: *The Search to End the Scourge of Misdiagnosis.* And here we go word-for-word again:

> Doctors are developing novel solutions to make sure they come up with the right diagnoses.
>
> A flood of new initiatives by researchers, physicians, health-care systems, nonprofits and malpractice insurers is yielding new insights and approaches. These include sophisticated computer programs, some that use artificial intelligence to help analyze and diagnose tough cases, and others that scan records for errors such as missed test results and appointments. Advanced technologies aren't just bringing the processing power of big data and machine learning to bear. They are also

> allowing more doctors to share their knowledge—including lessons they've learned from their own diagnostic mistakes.
>
> Many online tools have been developed to analyze symptoms and help doctors arrive at a diagnosis—with mixed results. But now a system that uses artificial intelligence can synthesize opinions from many doctors into a single cohesive perspective.
>
> The Human Diagnostic Project has developed an electronic consulting system that lets participating doctors enter a patient's background, symptoms, test results and other findings, then invites expert doctors to review the case, suggest a diagnosis and recommend next steps. Users can include specific questions, such as, "Does this patient need an MRI?"
>
> As doctors post their responses, the artificial intelligence-enhanced software combines and analyzes all the input, weighed by each doctor's relative expertise.

"Remarkable, eh?" Cliff asked. "That was what? Number four? Two left. Want another break or should we go on?"

"Go on," Paul said, apparently without giving it much thought.

"Gene editing then … holds tremendous promise. I've done extensive research on it and found that the best summary-article is one in your *Harvard Health Letter*. I'll use some of the words of its editor-in-chief, Dr. Anthony Komaroff:

> Regarding new discoveries in basic biology, one such one is a new technique for "editing" genes and it's called CRISPR. Many diseases are caused by defective genes or by defects in signals that turn genes on and off, and this brand new technique can correct these defects with remarkable precision and simplicity.
>
> Finding a specific part of a specific gene amid all of a human cell's DNA is like finding a needle in a haystack, but being able to snip out a precise part of the gene and to insert a "corrected" version of that part, is even more a challenge. However, that's what the CRISPR technique can do.
>
> Scientists can compare the function of cells before and after a gene has been edited. That allows scientists to answer many questions that previously were difficult or impossible to answer.
>
> Editing genes in cells in a laboratory dish is one thing. It's quite another matter to edit genes in the cells of a living animal or human. Diseases typically affect certain cells in certain organs. So, to correct those diseases requires targeting just those genes, in just those cells and organs within the body. As you can imagine, that is a real

> challenge.
>
> While scientists are excited about the potential of this new gene editing technique for the treatment of human disease, they are also cautious. A panel of distinguished scientists—including some from the U.K.—recently urged the world's scientific community to refrain from attempting to edit genes in human eggs or sperm until more is known about whether there may be potentially harmful results. That's because such edits would be passed on to all future descendants—amplifying the results, for both better or worse.
>
> While many scientists agree that it would be appropriate to use the technique to wipe out a disease gene from a child and its descendants, once it's clear that it could be done safely, they are concerned that some will try to use the technique to edit genes of an egg or sperm to achieve specific desirable traits—for example, to try to breed children who are taller or more intelligent.

"And that's what I have to say about this extraordinary process. Any comments?"

"Just that I'm at a loss for words," Paul answered. "Whoever would have 'thunk' it?"

"You're right … 'whoever'. And if we carry it to 'whenever', it's right now … as we speak.

"Well, with number six, I'll end with a few words about

another new microscopy technique. You mentioned Harvard before and now I'll mention Yale. There, I understand, structural biologists at its School of Medicine have received 'the mother of all microscopes'. Called the 'cryo-EM', it's a new device that allows investigators to see structures in ways they previously could not. Before, researchers could only **estimate** the structure and function of many systems under study. But now, for the first time, they actually can **see** them. And that's all I can relate about cryo-EM. It's just much too complicated for me to understand … and therefore to go on about it."

It was as if the three men had been part of a stage play and were about to start another of many rehearsals, for they all got up at the very same time.

"I'd guess you've had enough," Cliff said, "and I hope you now understand why I find all of this so much more interesting than routine matters involving the law. But before you leave, I want to bring up two more things. One is a new VISA system that's underway … I guess everywhere. It's referred to as a 'selfie' and deals with biometrics and credit cards, and in a single sentence, I can explain it. The payment processing giant, VISA, is launching a platform to allow banks to integrate various types of biometrics, such as your fingerprints, your voice, and even a photo of your face … to integrate them into approving credit card applications and payments. And the other concerns a mysterious phone call I received the morning after you called me. It was from a fellow I don't know, and still don't. He said he's from Belfast, Ireland and gave me his phone number but didn't identify himself. He then said he knew of a person by the name of Paul D'Arneau who was coming here to see me, and I nearly choked on the piece of toast I was eating. I let him carry on about some things I didn't understand except for the history of Catholics versus Protestants in Ireland. And that it was very important for you to meet him there tomorrow noon. He said it would be very financially worthwhile—five figures. Gave a specific location: at the dry dock where the *Titanic* was built. Have you been to Belfast before?"

"Once, but only for a short time. The treasure I was hired to find had already been found by the time I got there."

"Maybe you should take him up on it, Paul. It's only about three hundred miles from here—an hour by plane. I can arrange a flight. It's around dinner time there now, but after you leave here, I can call him for you, if you wish."

Paul had listened intently but neither by mouth nor expression did he immediately reveal any intention. He signaled Vincent for an off-to-the-side huddle that took five or six minutes and no doubt left the chief confounded. And so too was Paul. In the huddle, he did most of the whispering and apparently most of the thinking:

It's like the whole world knows our every move. Look at the places where we've been threatened or intimidated. I know them like the back of my hand:

At Bonfiore's with Guy Martin

At Fabio's

In Buenos Aires

In Switzerland

In the auditorium—the woman

In Paris

In Nuremberg

Here in London—Mr. Nemesis

At least eight times! Who's behind it all? A single person or a group?

If we go to Belfast, will it continue there?

When they returned to Cliff's side, Paul said to him, "We'll go. Peculiar place to meet though. I wonder why. As for arranging a flight? Thanks, but you needn't. We have a travel steward. Name's Ansel. He flies us everywhere … long distance … short distance."

After good wishes and mutual thanks, they left the office and headed for their hotel where they ate well and slept well. Just prior to that, however, they both agreed that the most intriguing aspect of their visit with Cliff was his informing them of the phone call from Belfast. And it was Paul who had concluded—with slight temerity— that he'd like to see what it was all about; that he'd like to satisfy a mounting curiosity; and, especially, that he'd like to learn how the mystery men knew their itinerary.

Chapter 25

June 20

Bright and early the next morning, they landed at the Belfast International Airport, just east of the village of Aldergrove and within walking distance of the *Titanic Dry Dock.* They could have stopped off at the Titanic Museum but decided not to because it was approaching the noon hour.

At the airport, Paul saw a lighted poster on a wall, as did Vincent. Paul didn't mask a thin smile.

"You may be wondering why I'm smiling," Paul said.

"That I am. Of course it's just another welcoming message."

"Ah, but this is different. I don't know about you, but I'm in no mood to sightsee around here. Too uptight about mystery men. So the next best thing is to **read** about Belfast. We've got a few minutes."

With that, they approached the poster and made room beside one another as they read:

Welcome to Belfast

Belfast is the capital of Northern Ireland—part of the United Kingdom. Belfast has experienced a renaissance since the 1994 ceasefire promised an end to the decades-old "Troubles" between Catholics and Protestants. Stretching along both sides of the River Lagan, the graceful city of Victorian and Edwardian buildings has become a cosmopolitan tourist destination. Belfast was a big industrial city in the 19th century, famous for its linens and shipyards—a city of great pride that was transformed by the Industrial Revolution.

The heart of modern Belfast centers around Donegall Square and the imposing City Hall. Be sure to see Yorkshire House and the Linen Hall Library, as well as the memorial to those lost with the *Titanic*. St. Anne's Cathedral is a calm and dignified refuge from the busyness of the street. The Ulster Museum is one of the highlights of any visit to Belfast, especially because of its setting near the Botanic Gardens. Queen's University represents the intellectual nucleus of Belfast. The Victorian and Edwardian flavor of the city is one of the most delightful surprises for any visitor.

Another side of Belfast evokes the memory of the 19th century, as Charles Dickens might have seen it. The Sinclair Seamen's Church (1857) draws upon the town's maritime heritage. The fine

> Custom House was designed and built by Charles Lanyon in the same year. Don't miss the ostentatious flavor of the Crown Liquor Saloon (1885) with all its rich detail. Clifton House was originally designed as a poorhouse in 1774. The Oval Church (1773) is the oldest house of worship in the city, and a very pretty one at that.

It didn't take long to reach the empty dry dock. They found the area frightfully somber with no person in sight, no sounds to hcar, no swampy smell from the nearby waterway. Overhead, a cloudy gray sky completed the picture. But the dock itself was imposing. Paul had never seen anything like it. There were ladders that began a foot or two from the cement base and ran the length of each side. Attached to the bottom end of each ladder was a strap that was the width of every ladder. They appeared to be made of rubber and stretched across the width of the dock to its counterpart on the opposite side. Some even ran diagonally across to other ladders. Paul couldn't fathom the exact reason for the rubber bottom but figured it had something to do with shock absorption during the liner's construction … kind of a cushion.

"I don't see him," Paul said. "I'll wait here while you go down to the other end and check."

Vincent left and Paul walked nervously back and forth, twice feeling for his guns and wondering how long to remain there. But there was more to read. Around the corner from where he was pacing, he noticed a large wooden placard. He walked over and read three side-by-side messages. Each had a title: Imagine. Think. Relive. He perused them all:

Imagine …

It's 1911. You're here at the Thompson Graving Dock … boots on cobbles and bicycle bells filling the air above you … the enormous steel walls of Titanic's hull seem to go on forever. You gaze upwards … toward the top decks … and the four majestic funnels filling the sky … the world's largest, most luxurious liner … at this moment in time.

Think …

About the sheer size of the dock … an impressive 259m long … an entrance of 29m wide … and a depth of 13m! Moreover … by floating the gate into the outside position … the length could be extended by another 11m … just as well, with Olympic Class Liners 269m long!

Fact: Over 12 White Star buildings can fit into this dock.

Relive …

The magnitude of … behind you … The White Star Building – reflecting the Arrol Gantry built over the Titanic and the Olympic Slipways – the

> same height above ground that the Titanic sat above water.
>
> Not forgetting a titanic landmark in Belfast's skyline today … the yellow Harland and Wolff Cranes – Golieth at 96m tall, and Samson even taller at 106m.

Paul didn't understand some of the script but didn't reread any of its parts. Instead, he thought of the movie with Leonardo DiCaprio and Kate Winslet. Then he walked back to the rear of the dry dock, leaned over and peered down to its deep bottom—a distance of 13m, but one he calculated to be more than forty-five feet.

Suddenly without warning, he felt a powerful push into his back and he went flying headfirst. But with a combination of backward bending and forward somersaulting, he landed doubled over on his feet … just barely. Thankful for the rubber cushion, he came through unscathed and unfazed except for anger and some back spasms. He straightened, dusted himself off, twisted around and looked up. He saw no one or anything out of the ordinary; but he did hear Vincent screaming and running to a position just above him.

"I saw the guy! I saw the guy!" Vincent said, guns drawn. "And guess what he was wearing."

"You mean his clothes?"

"No. Around his head."

"What?"

"An eye patch."

"Mr. Nemesis!"

So many questions. Why didn't he just shoot me? Does he or someone want me dead or just scared? Did he notice the cushioned bottom before he pushed? Is it a single person or a whole bunch in cahoots? Could one of them be passing on our next destination to another one of the bunch?

Paul made it up one of the ladders and felt it necessary to shake Vincent's hand. "I'm still here," Paul said, "and that does it. We either stick to our schedule or blow it apart and go wherever we feel like going. I, for one, say we should completely change the schedule." He didn't stop there, rattling off sentence after sentence as if they were gnawing at his innards. "We're our own boss. There's nobody telling us what to do. We made up the schedule ourselves. To hell with it now. Let's decide once and for all. Go to places we might find interesting. No need to call upon lawmen. They're not what they used to be anyway."

"I totally agree with what you're saying, Paul."

"Good. That's that. I vote for Scotland, then south to Portugal and Spain. When I went to South Queensberry, Lisbon and Seville before, there was more to like than dislike. I missed **so** much. It would be nice if we read the information bulletins in every airport … and enjoyed doing it for a change, damn it! But you know, I've been doing a lot of thinking, Vin—about something that's been pestering me, so hear me out. It's about those bulletins. I'm tired of looking for them, and even more tired of reading them. I don't know how **you** feel but we can read them or not, depending on …

"Depending on what?"

"On whether we want to learn about the place or not. If we're familiar with a city, don't waste time reading. Otherwise … well, you know what I'm driving at. But I refuse to be obsessed over circulars or bulletins or whatever you want to call them.

"Also one other thing—by not making our new plans known, maybe we might shake away our followers. Notice I'm not indicating that they're killers."

"I notice. Let's hope you're right. And I agree with your bulletin thoughts, Paul. But let me switch the subject and play devil's advocate. What about the primary goal … you know … religion, criminal investigation and all the rest?"

"We're not abandoning them. We'll still carry on in Hungary and Greece, but if any other country sounds appealing––like Iceland for example—we'll do the same as we've just done—go there. Think of it as primary and secondary. Primary are Hungary and Greece. Secondary could be places like Austria and Bulgaria. Primary we probe. Secondary we enjoy."

"Iceland? Where'd that come from?"

"I just thought of it. Never been there. See how spontaneous we can be from now on?"

"And you'll still write the book?"

"I don't really know."

"Then more devil's advocate. If you don't write it, the primary countries go out the window, I would imagine."

"Good points, Vinny Boy … good points. Let's see what comes to pass."

Paul forcibly extended his midsection forward and said, "Christ … the old back really hurts but … oh, well … there's one last thing. The only person I'm telling about this change in our travels is Sylvie. Ansel will know, but I trust him completely."

"Won't he tell Leon though?"

"I trust him too."

PART FOUR

Chapter 26

They walked back to the airport. Ansel was finishing a late breakfast and when he saw them, he leaped up and said, "That was quick. Everything go alright?"

"Don't we look smug?" Paul replied. "And I'm almost begging you, old buddy. We have some new destinations, but please don't mention them to anyone … even Leon. If he asks where you're taking us … that's a different story. But otherwise let's keep it a secret. Okay?"

"Okay."

At Scotland's Edinburgh Airport, they disembarked and taxied to St. Queensferry—a fifteen-minute ride. There, they had their own late breakfast of apple juice, coffee and grits.

Paul had never expected to miss an airport bulletin, but he had. He noticed one, however, to the side of the restaurant's exit door, and while Vincent was having his second order of grits, he wandered over to it and read its few words:

> South Queensferry is a port on the Firth of Forth, an arm of the North Sea, and a point of access to Edinburgh and the unique Celtic culture of Scotland. Although the Scots do not always get along with their Irish cousins, the two groups represent the best surviving elements of ancient culture of the Celts, which once flourished in most parts of Europe. Today the only surviving Celtic languages are Highland Scottish, Irish, Gaelic, Welsh, Manx, and Breton in north-western France. Another Celtic language, Cornish, survived in southwestern Britain until the last century.
>
> The ancient Celts (also called Gaels or Gauls) have been called the "founders of Europe." As early as the 8th century B.C., the Greeks, Etruscans, and Iberians were nibbling at the southern fringes of Europe—but the Celts dominated the northern and central areas with their large numbers and powerful tribal culture.
>
> Though badly neglected by historians, Gaelic people founded the first civilization north of the Alps. Some elements of their way of life still linger on in Scotland's music, games, woolen tartans, bagpipes, martial spirit, and fierce family

> loyalties. Because of their intense individuality, Celtic tribes never formed a political empire but remained a loose confederation of nations. Nevertheless, they shared a common tongue, a distinctive material culture, and similar religious ideas.

The reading left Paul not only informed but, for the first time among bulletins, entertained. And he looked forward to the ones to come.

Vincent approached him just as he finished the reading. "Good?" he asked.

"Couldn't have been better. I'll go through some of the things with you later, but for now, let's just see what we can see."

They took a guided bus tour to St. Andrew's, on the way removing their sweaters– for what had begun as cool and cloudy had turned to warm and sunny. The ride took them through pastoral country as the guide—charming and obviously retired from a different career— narrated non-stop: "St. Andrews is old and very historic. It was the scene of a bloody war between the Catholics and Protestants during the Reformation. That Catholic cathedral over there? It was burnt in upheaval. As you can see, only some ends remain, but authorities want them to remain. They're as old as the graves we're now passing. And look—that's St. Andrews University. Some say it resembles Yale from the outside. I hope it does from the inside."

As they continued on, the guide provided the commentary. "Here's the *Royal & Ancient Golf Club of St. Andrews* and the incomparable *Old Course*. I played it once, but never again. Flat but too tough."

Forty-five minutes later, the tour ended and they were left off at the bottom of a steep hill. They walked up to a hotel the guide had recommended, *The Dunegan*, and went to its theater for an Irish Folkloric show where they hummed along with a crowded audience as a young performer sang "Danny Boy."

By then, it was time for dinner. They ate the hotel's advertised special: Shepherd's Pie topped with Irish Champ which, according to their waitress, was nothing more than lumpy mashed potatoes—but delicious.

On the tender, Paul couldn't match Vincent's broad smile because of fatigue. He did manage to ask, however, "See? You had a good time?"

"I had a good time."

Chapter 27

June 21

In Ansel's hands, Iceland's Reykjavik was only ninety minutes away by plane. Its main airport, Keflavik, was loaded with tourists, including an area before the terminal's bulletin board.

"Watch this," Vincent said.

He nudged his way forward and, just in front of the board, turned completely around, raised his arm and pointed to a spot above and beyond the tourists. They all dispersed backwards and laterally, and he then signaled Paul to join him as he was about to read the bulletin. None of the tourists returned.

"Works every time," he said, "and for some reason, no one ever gets mad. Maybe most don't like reading bulletins anyway."

"Quite a trick," Paul said, "but let's read. It looks long but no doubt will be worth it. This is one of those unfamiliar places I was talking about."

Don't be fooled by the name Iceland. Although set in the North Atlantic near the Arctic Circle, the country is actually quite green, and sometimes even warm. But then, Iceland has never followed any formal rules.

Some of the geological conditions that make Iceland so unique also make it so inhabitable. Deep below the ocean is the Mid-Atlantic Ridge, a juncture point between two tectonic plates, the European and the North American. Think of them as two heavy slabs of stone resting side by side on a pool of boiling mud. As they slowly move and grind against one another, they release vast quantities of geothermal energy and volcanic activity. Iceland owes its origin to volcanic eruptions, which continue to this day.

That union of the cold northern climate with the explosive fire from within the earth produced this singular land of fire and ice, glaciers alongside volcanoes. It is wonderful that such violent forces of nature, traditionally feared and fled by humans, work more gently here.

Volcanic soil is fertile and productive. The clever Icelanders have tapped the geothermal energy to heat swimming pools and generate electricity. Energy production here is clean, efficient and cheap. And even the volcanic eruptions seem to be gradual and predictable, enabling residents to move to safety until danger has passed.

With the introduction of Christianity, bishoprics and monasteries were established and schools were not far behind. It was during this early period that the Sagas were written. Out of all contributions to world literature, the Islandic Sagas are the most characteristic of the Nordic countries. These adventure tales were written in the Old Norse language, which is the basis of modern Islandic. The education system is still excellent, and literacy is almost universal. More books are written, printed and read here, per capita, than any place on earth.

The northern most capitol in the world, Reykjavik is an international center of commerce and home to one of the most technologically sophisticated societies anywhere.

"And there you have it," Paul said. "Worth reading?"

"Worth it."

"So—before we tour around, I'll phone Sylvie and I decided to contact Leon, too." He glanced at his watch. "She should just about be getting up, and he should have been up for a couple of hours by now."

They walked to the nearest quiet place. Paul first phoned Leon and outlined the reasons for their new schedule. Leon indicated complete understanding and ended his part of the conversation with, “I’m not surprised, Paul. Foray after foray to learn more about religion and such can get monotonous. Your mixing it up is the best solution.”

Sylvie’s response was a different story. When each of the secondary destinations was detailed, she asked why the choice. In addition, she became emotional when explaining that the extra visits meant more valuable time away from Falmouth.

That was when Paul tried a comment that backfired. “From Falmouth or from you?”

She raised her voice, practically screaming. “From **me**. You don’t understand? I miss you.”

“I miss you too, Syl. I’m sorry I sounded so matter-of-fact. Presented it wrong.”

Both conversations ended on a positive note, with Leon saying, “Good luck”, and Sylvie apologizing and reaffirming an undying love.

Paul felt they were now free to check out the city. And instead of walking around—it was cloudy, cold and blustery—they piled into a tour bus and headed for a nearby peninsula. Whatever the guide didn’t point out, they detected themselves and before long, so much of what they had just read was verified. Volcanic land. Lava rocks covered by moss, lichen and small plants. Scarcely any trees. Buildings heated by thermal dynamics. No minerals such as oil.

Their first stop was an area much like Yellowstone without geysers. But there were mud flats and a pervading sulfur smell. Then onto Blue Lagoon where they exited the bus and walked down a cement path that was surrounded on both sides by tall, irregular rock formations. It ended at a small restaurant where they had snacks and, while chewing, exchanged stories with other bus passengers and watched people swimming. The most interesting stop was at a new Viking museum. There, Vincent agreed to pose for a photo with an Icelander dressed as a Viking. The man, in turn, described many past Viking raids from Greenland to the Black Sea. He then led them to a large cabinet and suggested they read what he called an admission that was inside its glass front. But not until he distanced himself from what it conveyed.

"This was years and years ago, my friends," he said, "and we have all changed dramatically since then."

Headlined PLUNDERING, they read:

> The earliest Viking assaults hit England late in the 8th century. Soon, longships were setting loose "stinging horns" and "fearful wolves" and "purely pagan people" every summer throughout western Europe. The raiders sacked monasteries and undefended villages, hauled away booty, and took captives for ransom or sale as slaves. Raiding parties grew from a few farmers following a local chieftain to armies led by kings. The invaders began to establish winter bases, so they could strike farther inland along major rivers. In some regions, Viking armies encamped, demanding tribute or taking territory.

Night seemed to have arrived sooner than elsewhere and they had dinner at the Crown Grill Restaurant, devouring the same type meal—Live Maine Lobster and Brazilian Lobster Tail as well as traditional steakhouse fare. Just before finishing, their waiter came by, sang a few lines of a strange melody and then followed with, “This showplace eatery will entertain you with an open, theater-style kitchen where chefs custom-prepare steamed shellfish—such as scallops, clams, mussels, countless other seafood platters and combinations—and cooked-to-order prime center Sterling cut steaks and chops.” Paul believed the waiter said it all as one hired not only to serve but also to advertise.

Chapter 28

June 22

Having been to Lisbon, the capital of Portugal several times, they considered it the best kept secret among all large cities anywhere. And although they were sleep-deprived, they looked forward to roaming around again.

In the airport terminal late the next morning, they saw a bulletin board and walked right past it. But they couldn't help noticing a tripod in their path, for they nearly knocked it over. It contained a map of the city and a message of four or five sentences. They scanned it in less than a minute:

> Our city lies on seven low hills at the estuary of the river Tagus, six miles from the Atlantic Ocean. We are on the west coast—with the Algarve to the south and the little town of Sintra to the north. Today, we thrive as a lively international city of one and a half million citizens. We offer a fascinating combination of old character and a

beauty all its own. Please visit what you can. Welcome and obrigada!

"Ah, the Algarve and Sintra," Paul said. "Remember how much we've seen before—with all the notices on display? Let's read some again if we feel like it, Vin. And not feel guilty. After all, we **did** ignore the stupid bulletin board."

They taxied to Hotel Mundial in the Baixa district, but their double room wasn't ready. So they walked around on cobbled walkways within expansive Rossio Square and stopped for coffee at a tiny pasteleria. They sauntered back to the hotel and found their seventh floor room ready. From that level, they spent almost an eternity at a window, looking out at an ever changing view of the old city. It was common to see such changes during Lisbon's morning hours, especially when a chilly dark day turned to sunshine, then back again to dark. Which they explained to each other. Then, after tending to the usual arrival necessities and still sleepy, they set out for the Tagus riverfront and on to Cais de Sodre where they purchased four-day public transit passes. They immediately put them to work on a # 44 bus, which they rode to the end of the line. There, they had an outside lunch at a quiet café and, on the bus again, dozed their way back to Rossio.

In the hotel lobby, they bought a bottle of wine and some cheese crackers and once upstairs, enjoyed a miniature "happy hour" before freshening up and leaving for an authentic Portuguese restaurant. The eating awakened them some, but by seven p.m., they were fast asleep in their room.

While shaving the next morning, it dawned on Paul that the boredom that eventually reared its ugly head during the "primary" visits was doing the same thing during the "secondary" ones. And they were only halfway through them. "Besides finishing here in Portugal," he mumbled to himself, "we have Spain, Serbia and Austria before we get to the last two primary ones—Hungary and Greece. **Redicalus!**" It was a word that his brother often used to emphasize the proper word: "ridiculous". He would talk Vincent into agreeing with the assessment and to support his newly made decision to abort the current schedule and return to the old. He thought of the past and then of the future, and it didn't take long for him to forge through the old direction into the new: going back to religion and criminal activities and forgetting about "pure enjoyment". He deemed it to be an absolute pledge and believed that it would take an awfully important reason for him to break it.

He left the sink before the remnants of cream were washed away; told Vincent about the change of heart; and was so astounded by what he heard that he thought some cream had slid from his cheeks to his ears and distorted his hearing.

"It interfered with my sleep, Paul, and I was about to say the same thing this morning, but you beat me to the punch."

Paul fashioned a triumphant grin as he slouched into a chair..

"We're in agreement then," he said. "Very helpful. And it may sound irrational, but I'd like to read all we can in both Budapest and Athens. And why? To make up for whatever we elected not to read before. Trying to learn, not only enjoy. We went to both cities before, but remember we didn't stay long. So as I said … let's make up for it and read whatever they have to offer, no matter how long it takes—although we should wrap things up rather quickly."

Vincent nodded and said, "Whatever. You be the judge."

"Good. Let's have breakfast, cancel the rest of the day here, and head to Budapest. I'll contact Ansel, but no other phone calls. Sylvie will be surprised when I appear sooner than expected, and as for Leon, he'd completely understand anyway."

Paul got up, walked in a circle, slouched back in the chair and said, "But there are a couple of other things jammed up in my head, Vin. For days now."

"Oh?"

"One—about histarians. I'd just as soon not consult with them unless something comes up where we'd need their help. Might get too complicated, and besides, we know what we're after and we can handle it all ourselves. And the other is about talking to those two prostitutes who board cruise ships. We can put that all off, too. It's lost its … its what?"

"Its luster?"

"Yeah, its luster. I don't know why we didn't realize it."

"Like I said: you're the judge."

While waiting for breakfast in a restaurant one floor above them, they spoke little and Paul thought little—with one exception. It was a confession of sorts:

If people were reading about our past few days,

would they look upon them as a travelogue? That's what they turned out to be, and it's not what I intended. The ones we planned on visiting are travelogue enough, but adding the others compounded it all. So screw travelogues. They're repetitive and shallow.

Breakfast still hadn't arrived and Paul took the opportunity to take stock of things and, in his mind, to lay out their resurrected plans more clearly. The plans had a definite pattern, led by an assurance that under no circumstance would they visit cities other than Budapest and Athens. He took into account that the number of characters they had dealt with in the past three weeks numbered at least fifteen, and that there were only two more to go before returning home. They were Commander Mark Ferenc and Chief George Frangos, both the leading law enforcers in Hungary and Greece.

And, what with trips to Ireland, Scotland, Iceland and Portugal under his belt, Paul envisioned those four countries as interesting … but diversionary. Enjoyable but not at all necessary in an overall agenda that stressed learning about worldwide religion and criminal activity. Plus, taking into account the discussions held in Germany and England, he now included matters of a scientific nature.

Paul then opened his briefcase to be sure it still contained printouts concerning the three- point topics: original reasons for visits; five things that make a church healthy; and five questions that must be asked from a criminalistics and forensic science standpoint. He found the printouts lodged among some thick folders.

Chapter 29

June 23

They were flying over the Danube River in the direction of Ferihegy Airport and Paul stared admiringly at the three well-known Budapest bridges: *Chain, Margaret* and *Elizabeth.* He couldn't resist modifying his mind some about taking in key sights and decided it wouldn't hurt to spend a few hours looking around. He so informed Vincent and would later phone Commander Ferenc about meeting the next morning. Two days before, Paul had called him and Chief Frangos about their upcoming visits and about the essentials he'd like to cover. In both instances, the timing was well received and both lawmen harked back to previous exchanges and to how helpful Paul had been.

He and Vincent were sitting side-by-side on the plane and Paul could almost taste the prolonged silence. It worried him. Finally Vincent said, "You know me, Paul. I was **hoping** we could handle matters more slowly than usual, and I guess we will be."

In the airport, it wasn't as though they deliberately avoided coming across a bulletin board. They searched for one, found it and after Paul said, “Here we go, Vin. Remember our new outlook.” He read the enclosed statement, not skipping a single word, but he couldn’t tell if Vincent did or didn’t.

In December 1992, Budapest celebrated its 120th birthday—the anniversary of Buda and Pest. But the metropolis on the Danube River can actually look back on two thousand years of history. And it’s fast regaining its splendor. Once the center of culture in the Austro-Hungarian Empire, the city and its buildings and treasures were neglected or damaged by a succession of invaders and occupiers. But with a democratic government in place since 1990 and a lengthy series of renovations, it is rebuilding many of its historic landmarks.

The capital of Hungary, Budapest, is the heartbeat of the country. In hilly Buda—on the Danube’s west bank—there is evidence of its political and imperial past, with the Royal Palace and the National Gallery—the embodiment of the history of the Hungarian people. Though Buda is marked by defeats and victories, its national pride has never diminished. On the east bank, there is Pest, the city’s contemporary face, a thriving center of commerce and art, filled with cafes, restaurants, boutiques, and theaters.

> The city-splitting Danube is an integral part of life of the city, not only in terms of its beauty, but also its vital use as a waterway for commerce and tourism. Three impressive bridges link the two sides: the Chain Bridge, Margret Bridge, and, at its narrowest point, the Elizabeth Bridge.
>
> Worthy of note in its communist past was the year 1956 when the people of Budapest rebelled, demanding freedom of speech and social reform. Soviet troops quickly responded and crushed the rebellion in a matter of days.

Below the statement was a short paragraph taken from the 1903 writing of Arthur Synons in *Cities.* Only Paul read it:

> In Budapest there is nothing but what the people and a natural brightness in the air make of it. Here things are what they seem; atmosphere is everything, and the atmosphere is almost one of illusion. Budapest lives with a speed that thrusts itself, not unattractively, upon one at every moment … The people with their somber, fiery, and irregular faces have the look of sleepy animals about to spring.

Since Paul felt the last statement captured the flavor of the region so well—as he recalled it in his previous trip there—there was some discussion about whether to visit some landmarks or to not wait till the following day and simply go meet with Commander Ferenc. They opted to sightsee and to limit it to the Pest side.

They rented a small limo, but before crossing over Paul drove to the well-remembered area of Castle Hill where they circled to its highest elevation and enjoyed a panoramic view of the city. The air looked and felt and smelled pure, more like that of a Connecticut village in early fall than on the rim of a European metropolis in early summer.

Soon they crossed the Elizabeth Bridge and registered at the nine-story Marriott on the left. It was the only hotel Paul had ever stayed at whose registration area was less of a lobby than a grand ballroom. Attached to a centered column was an announcement typed in red.

> Note our large Victorian ottoman that is embroidered with a Veronese shield and above it, coffered glass octagons by Murano. From where you stand, you can notice our many marble columns, our sisal carpentry and our many stained-glass windows.

> *What* **is** *this? Reading, reading everywhere and not a word to dodge!*

Paul didn't think a hotel lobby needed to be described, but there was even more reading after they inspected their luxurious room, disposed of their gear, and whatnot. They were heading to the limo when an employee handed each of them a slip of paper.

"Do read this, gentlemen. Compliments of our owners," he said.

They did:

The Tourist Prayer

Heavenly Father, look down at us, your humble, obedient tourist servants who are doomed to travel this earth, taking photographs, mailing postcards, buying souvenirs and walking around in drip-dry underwear.

We beseech you, oh Lord, to see that our plane is not hijacked, our luggage is not lost and our overweight baggage goes unnoticed.

Protect us from surly and unscrupulous taxi drivers, avaricious porters and unlicensed English-speaking guides.

Give us this day divine guidance in the selection of our hotels that we may find our reservations honored, our rooms made up and hot water running from the faucets.

Let us remember the Marriotts.

We pray that the telephones work and that the operators speak our tongue and that there is no mail waiting from our children that would force us to cancel the rest of our trip.

> Lead us, dear Lord, to good, inexpensive restaurants where the food is superb, the waiters friendly and the wine included in the price of the meal.
>
> Give us the wisdom to tip correctly in currencies we do not understand. Forgive us for undertipping out of ignorance and overtipping out of fear.
>
> Make the natives love us for what we are and not for what we can contribute to their worldly goods.
>
> Grant us the strength to visit the museums, the cathedrals, the palaces and the castles listed as **musts** in the guidebooks.
>
> And if, perchance, we skip a historic monument to take a nap after lunch, have mercy on us, for our flesh is weak.

"Not bad," Paul said. He hoped that its good-natured humor matched the spirit of what might loom ahead and reflected the success he anticipated. He expressed the sentiment to Vincent who, amazingly to Paul, selected three of his words: humor, spirit and success.

"They're what count, Paul—in this and any undertaking."

"Glad to hear you say that. And I hope you'll be glad to hear me out one more time. I'm not pressing for us to hurry through the next two days, but I really have enough material to write the book and I'm anxious to call it quits and head home.

What say you?"

"Amen."

"Okay. So let's do a little with the sights today and, starting tomorrow, go through the usual … learn whatever we can … then hightail it back to our own country. But we won't rush Mark or George. They're kind enough to meet with us, so we've got to hear them out. And I'll bet that both guys will concentrate on science, not on the law."

It was early afternoon and they were in the limo once more. Paul again did the driving and, at his suggestion, they pulled up near some of the famous buildings to observe their structural grandeur—like Fisherman's Bastion, Matthias Church and the Parliament House. In some cases, though, they entered a building and wandered around, or they stepped away from the limo to pose for photographs in Hero's Square.

Even more than an hour was spent on a horse farm just outside central city. There they exited the limo and were taken on a wagon ride through fields and woods and eventually ended up at a fenced-in field that pigs, geese, rabbits, goats and Hungarian oxen shared. Next, they sat on padded benches to watch a horse show: single riders, carts, and one rider standing on two horses while guiding six others in front of him. Then an announced bottle event: upright log with bottle on top. One of the horsemen demonstrated with a long bullwhip that he used to swat off the bottle from twelve feet away. He picked out Vincent from the crowd as a volunteer, handing him the whip. Vincent hit the neck of the bottle in one try, everyone applauded, and he was handed the whip as a prize.

They did it all slowly as the hours passed slowly, and soon it was time for dinner. So they entered a series of "dark forests" and eventually came upon a large restaurant that they had frequented two years ago, and Paul said it hadn't changed. Inside its revolving doors they were handed pots of brandy and near their table they observed rafter after rafter of corn, and once seated, enjoyed gypsy music, violins, singers and dancers as they hummed along with those at surrounding tables. During their meals, they took small bites to extend the time before finally reversing course for the Marriott and a night's sleep.

Chapter 30

June 24

Perhaps it was the overcast sky and drizzling rain that effected a slow pace during breakfast, but it was late morning before they arrived at Commander Mark Ferenc's office. It was in a three-story walk-up between twin churches whose spires gave off shadows that nearly obliterated its presence. It was called the *Law House* and was home to more attorneys than police officials. But the commander's office occupied nearly a third of one floor—the second.

Just as was the case with the previous night's restaurant as not having changed, so too had this office's arrangement and personnel not changed. The head office manager, Bridget, even gave both men a light kiss on their foreheads before ushering them toward the door to Mark's three-room suite.

"So how are you? He's been expecting you. How was your trip here?" she asked.

"Good to all three," Paul said as she gave the door a light tap, then left.

Inside, the suite looked more like an American

condominium complex than anything related to a police department. And Mark always looked more like a Philadelphia attorney than a Hungarian lawman.

The first thing anyone would notice in the suite's receiving room was an African mask hanging behind an 18th century wing chair. Not far from it was a collection of resting tables, two floor lamps and four swivel chairs. On two side walls, bookcases were stacked from floor to ceiling, except for one linear space. There, engravings of the Bonaparte family were displayed. And the third side, the far one, the one with a door to Frank's working room, was adorned with paintings, sculptures and photographs arrayed against pristine white walls.

Bridget must have alerted him, for the door on the far wall opened wide and Mark bounded out as if being chased by a Hungarian Kuvascz dog. The commander was a good six-feet tall and had dark hair brushed back with no parting. At the temples, streaks of gray approximated the color of his eyes. He possessed a richness to his smile that was slow to develop, but whenever it did, it seemed to make others smile more broadly. As did Paul and Vincent. Two scars on Mark's forehead dwarfed his other features, giving him a somber look as if he were worried about what to say next in addressing a jury.

He was outfitted in a buttoned dark jacket, a matching vest, and a striped tie. A light blue handkerchief fluffed from his left breast pocket. There was no sign of a bulge, but Paul wondered if a gun was present at the waist.

Formalities were meager especially from Paul's end as he handed Mark one of the printouts concerning the reasons for the meeting, the printout that Paul had read to him over the phone. They sat in three of the swivel chairs that Mark had brought together.

"Thanks for having us," Paul said. "You're no doubt busier than ever, so let's begin. Please … we'll listen as you talk."

"Yes, I've been waiting to do that. What you read to me and what I now have before me are important … obviously … but I must add science. And speaking of adding … most of my friends in law enforcement are adding science to their list of challenges."

Paul and Vincent just stared at him, or slightly above him.

"We are adding science because the ins and outs of religion and crime haven't changed much, at least around here, but science seems to be forever changing. And all for the good in most cases. As a blanket statement, I can say this about science and law enforcement. I'm often called upon by scientists to protect their laboratories, their experimental stations, and even the scientists themselves, from those who would do them harm. The offenders are made up from among their competition. Usually from other countries, but not always. And in one way or another, top notch mobsters get involved. So—getting down to the meat of the matter, I made notes about three subjects: artificial intelligence, neurotechnology, and the future of robotics. May I give my thoughts about them?"

"By all means. We're listening," Paul replied.

"All three sound complicated, and they are just that. But if I stick to the rudiments, I might make everything come out clear.

And … ah … is 'rudiments' a good word for what I'm trying to get across?"

"Excellent. 'The essentials'. 'The nucleus'."

"Good then: Artificial intelligence or AI. First of all, what is it? It's intelligence displayed by machines, not by humans. It's quickly becoming part of our information infrastructure. For example, certain recruitment companies analyze video interviews of job applicants so the employers can compare an applicant's facial movements and body language with that of their already existing employees. But it can get out of hand, and here's how I can relate it to people like me—in the job I'm in. There's a recent AI study that was supposed to identify suspected individuals involved in violent crime, police harassment and who gets out of jail. However, it failed miserably. It's because, I assume, the whole machine idea is still in its infancy. And I would say that's enough about that. You get the idea though, right?"

Vincent did the answering. "Sure do," he said.

"Now the next … ah … rudiment is neurotechnology. And again I ask, 'What's that'? As I wrote here in my notes, it's 'any technology that has a fundamental influence on how people understand the brain and various aspects of consciousness, thought and higher activities within the brain. It also includes technologies designed to improve and repair brain function'. Another way of expressing it is to say that neurotech is like a physical marriage of our brains and computers. And, to be sure, I've researched this till my own brain started to fall apart, but what I found regarding any tie-in with law enforcement is that some so-called experts insist that the precise location of criminality in this world can be found by using computers—no matter the seriousness of a crime."

Paul wished his chair had arm rests so he could squeeze one of them, but instead, he tried to control himself by running a thumb across his upper lip. And he could feel his collar and the back of his shirt turning damp.

> *This is stupid! Why go through all of it? We're really not learning anything more than we want to. And science isn't really part of what we're investigating.*

"The last is robotics. The simplest example of this involves a truck that now has a mechanical arm to pick up trash cans. Robotics is an engineer's way to do a complicated task or a repeated job after developing a system and a program to run it. And how does it help in law enforcement—if it does at all? It plays a role in modernizing mechanical devices in police squad cars—the devices used to take pictures of crime scenes and of criminals on the run."

A series of phone calls suddenly ensued and after the last one, Mark said he had to leave to help direct officers coping with a man threatening suicide at one of the bridges. Paul considered the call fortunate, not in terms of its nature but its timing, for he deeply wanted the meeting to come to an end.

As it turned out, Mark left in a hurry and it was Bridget

who offered best wishes before they too left in a hurry.

In the limo, Vincent asked, “So what did you think?”

“I think I didn’t think much. And I don’t know if I’m more disappointed or more completely thought out. But let’s wait till we get back to the hotel before we go over things. Or better than that, since there’s not much to go over, maybe save it until lunch time.”

“Good thinking.”

“At least it’s something positive.”

During lunch, the essence of what they covered was that the meeting was a waste of time.

“Plus effort,” Vincent said.

“Effort for what?” Paul asked.

“To stay awake. I’m really, really tired. Mind if I take a nap after we finish here?”

“Not at all. You do that and I’ll write the last Discovery Notes. I need them for writing the conclusion to the book.”

“Okay, but be careful. A mechanical arm might come out of the wall to help you write.”

Their laughter almost caused Paul to knock over a bowl of soup. “Hey, why not?” he said. “I could use the help.”

Once in their room, Vincent asked to be wakened in an hour and, falling back on his twin bed, he shut his eyes. Paul then changed into a dry shirt and began writing the Discovery Notes. As he wrote, his mind was divided between what had occurred since he last wrote them and what might be in store for them.

Checked out of hotel. Lunch at restaurant Sylvie recommended. Taxi drives us through glamorous areas. I'm not at all relaxed. I consult list of top law enforcers in 4 countries: Germany, England, Hungary and Greece. I call to announce our upcoming visits. Fly to Nice, then drive to Gordes and its monastery to meet with Friar Dominic. Now looks very old. Many historical books on shelves. Acts and sounds like a schizo. Talks about Napoleon and gives same info as last time re history. A long, long list. Says Napoleon's behavior became erratic. Says he—the Friar—is an histarian and coined the word. Says Napoleon might have been murdered and that body could have been stolen. Mentions Nap's lovers. Says Nap. had great respect for criminals. I determined we spend too much time on Napoleon and not enough on religion. Fly to Nurenberg, Germany. I complain to myself re repetitions—like reading so many circulars, so much sightseeing, same questions for lawmen. Read 2 circulars re the city. I change mind and say to Vin we should visit landmarks but do it slowly as he had recommended. Panel truck nearly runs me over, but only my foot was nicked. At Wurzburg Residence and we read another circular. Next a.m., go to Bamberg. Read about its 7 hills. Saw some famous places. To Emil Groner's office. He talks of scientists. Then turns to religion with long list of comments about it. England next. To hotel near Buckingham Palace. Spot man peering at me. Wore eye patch and I gave him a name: Mr. Nemesis. We visit famous spots. Again see Mr. Nemesis. To Cabinet War Room for self-guided tour. Had seen all on previous visit, but just as amazing. Another Mr. Nemesis sighting. Arrive Cliff Watt's office. He uses recorder. Talks of criminal investigations but also, science. Gives 6 topics and elaborates. Tells of strange call from Belfast. Man wants to see me near Titanic dry dock. Though his talking is endless, we learn much. I think about all the threats and intimidations aimed at me. Arrive Belfast. Another circular. At empty dock with "cushion" bottom. Read some posters then I look down at bottom. Man pushes me over but I land on feet. Rubber cushion helped. Vincent spots man running off. Says had eye patch. Mr. Nemesis again! I wonder why he didn't shoot me instead of pushing me over the side. We revamp schedule in favor of sightseeing in other countries. Primary and secondary cities. Now feel bulletins and circulars important. To Scotland, then Iceland—consider them secondary cities. Read many bulletins. Call to Leon and Sylvie. Leon favors new schedule.

> Sylvie not so sure. Next was Lisbon. Left there early when agreement reached to go to primary cities only. Also agreed not to consult with histarians or the two prostitutes who frequent cruise ships. Talk of recent past as one of travelogues. Not good. Consider secondary cities as diversionary. Must now concentrate on religion, criminality and science. Latter because lawmen beginning to do so. To Budapest. Read bulletins. Crossed Elizabeth Bridge to Pest side. "Tourist Prayer" in hotel lobby. Sightseeing. Next morning to Mark Ferenc's office. He talks of 3 science issues that relate to law enforcement. He leaves to respond to emergency. We leave. Meeting there a waste of time. In room, Vin takes nap and I do this. The last one!

Paul looked over at Vincent and found that he was sound asleep.

> *Next is the decision I've made. How will he feel about it? I'll soon find out.*

Thirty minutes later, Paul had no trouble waking Vincent but waited for him to become fully alert. Paul then asked, "Good nap?"

"Good nap."

"Then are you ready for this?"

"For what?"

"For something that might lead to your killing me."

"What? What are you talking about?"

"I think we should forget about Greece. As it now stands, I have plenty of material for the book; there's just so much sightseeing I can take; and we'll no doubt receive the same kind of information we received here."

Vincent didn't hesitate in responding, "Same wavelength, Paul, same wavelength. And I thank you, I thank you."

It was the kind of double talk that pleased the hell out of Paul.

They approached each other for an embrace and pats on the back. Paul then stepped aside and said, "So I call Chief Frangos to cancel. Finally, we end this three-week-long chapter in our lives and its home we go!"

EPILOGUE

Several issues are worthy of mention:

First—The villain in this story was Guy Martin! He was calling all the shots, from threatening Paul to arranging for various individuals to participate in scarc tactics against him. And to indicate Paul's location, wherever he went.

His real last name was Martinelli, once lived in Ireland, worked as a news reporter there and later at the *Herald Tribune* in Boston. In Ireland, his reporting was initially confined to politics but it was switched to religion in Boston. No one ever knew if he made the switch voluntarily or if the *Tribune*'s hierarchy demanded it. Years ago, he and Paul became good friends because of a mutual interest in the political side of religious beliefs.

How did Guy know where Paul would be located next? An historian "leak". Such leaks were not allowed among the membership, but Guy managed to take advantage of some on a regular basis. Ironically, it was one particular leak that eventually led to his downfall, even before Paul and Vincent returned to the States. In essence, Guy was betrayed over mentioning that leak to a fellow historian he should not have trusted, and he was double-crossed.

Was there a relationship between him and the Mob? Yes indeed, but it, too, went sour. Initially, he cooperated with Mob members but then he became a turncoat. It was why he convinced Paul to broaden his worldwide assessment of religion by adding an evaluation of "fronts". But as time went on, a large segment of the Mob turned against Guy, forcing him into gaining an upper hand. That segment instructed him to kill Paul, but because of friendship he could not do it. So he resorted to scare tactics instead, hoping it would fool Mob members.

Second—What about Paul's desire to study "the progress and legitimacy of religion" and any relationship to Napoleonic lore? Mission accomplished.

Third—Regarding the *Titanic* dry dock incident. Mr. Nemesis knew that its bottom was softened by a rubber cushion and that Paul's fall would not lead to his death. Paul had no idea why the eye-patched stalker wanted to meet with him there but regardless, he was never seen or heard from again.

Fourth—As for Eva Peron, the two prostitutes or the Synchronous Action Device, each faded from consideration in no time at all. As did Eva's cache of diamonds.

Fifth—Over the long haul, Paul cemented the value of religion for he had demonstrated that only a tiny percentage of pastors was involved in "front" activity. Prior to that though, combining religion with criminality and then adding science to the combination irritated him no end. And further on, when he realized that flying to countries other than to those in his initial plans constituted a travelogue, he became even more irritated. All of this was intensified by fatigue that he had let progress.

Yet through the maze, he understood that religion was more philosophical than criminality, that science was more technical than either, and that he was mistaken when he hadn't allowed religion to stand alone. But he finally reached an epiphany when he became rested and was able to sort it all out.

And sixth—Paul enjoyed writing the book. With help from Sylvie and Vincent, he completed it in a year.

www.ingramcontent.com/pod-product-compliance
Lightning Source LLC
Chambersburg PA
CBHW030820310726
48980CB00006B/567/J

* 9 7 8 1 9 2 8 7 8 2 9 8 8 *